Untamed Heart

ELDA MINGER

Harlequin Books

TORONTO • NEW YORK • LOS ANGELES • LONDON
AMSTERDAM • PARIS • SYDNEY • HAMBURG
STOCKHOLM • ATHENS • TOKYO • MILAN

To my brother Rudy,
whose love and encouragement
over the years
has meant so much to me

———————◆◆———————

Published June 1983

First printing April 1983

ISBN 0-373-16012-7

Printed in Canada

AUTHOR'S NOTE

In writing the sequences involving animal work for this book, I have stayed as close as possible to actual procedure. I would like to emphasize, however, that in any procedure with large exotics (i.e. cats, elephants), whether it is simple daily care or a complex stunt, the function of backup personnel is all-important. These people would be present at all times, ready to step in if trouble should occur. I have tried to imply their existence but could not write them all in as minor characters without hopelessly cluttering the story. I hope this one deference to dramatic license may be forgiven by keepers, handlers, and trainers, for whom I have the greatest respect and admiration.

E.M.

Chapter One

The lion's stare held the woman like an invisible net, golden eyes locked with green. The woman moved first, anticipating the instant when the big cat crouched—head low, ears flattened—and charged toward her over the stretch of dusty ground. She ran, pushing her body to its limit. A quick glance over her shoulder showed the lion gathering for a final spring. He was almost upon her when she turned, arms lifted and crossed to protect her throat. She leaped to meet him. Then she was airborne, carried beneath the big cat for almost twenty feet. Long, tawny hair flowed into heavy mane and was lost. They landed as one. The lion's heavy body pressed the girl to the earth. Closing her eyes against the dense fur above her face, she stayed perfectly still as the lion rumbled deep in his throat.

"Wonderful, Sam!" Jake Weston stood. The reporter beside him did the same, dusting bits of dry leaves and grass from his pants. He was busily changing the film in his camera as Jake continued to talk.

"She's one of my finest trainers. The best with the big cats."

The reporter watched as the slender woman raised her body slightly, pushing against the hairy animal. "Stanley, up!" Her voice was low and melodious, but she sounded firm. The lion moved with a sluggish rhythm. The weather was unbearably hot, and the woman wiped her hand against her damp forehead, then stood and grasped the lion by its mane. Walking with the big cat to a patch of shade under a cluster of palm trees, she picked up a length of heavy chain and snapped it around the beast's neck. She walked the lion as if she were out for a stroll with the family dog, leading him over to the two men. The reporter played with the strap of his camera and involuntarily began to back up.

The woman was smiling. It looked as if she were used to Jake's fatherly pride in her accomplishments. She turned to the reporter. "Did you have any other questions, Mr. Drysdale?"

The photojournalist shook his head. "Please call me Rob." He laughed nervously. "I'd never have believed it if I hadn't seen it myself. You're only my son's age, and I can't imagine any lion jumping on top of him!" At this close range she seemed somehow larger than life. He watched as she flicked back her tawny blond hair and eyed him with what seemed to be a tiny bit of impatience.

He placed a restraining hand on her arm, then immediately wished he hadn't. The green eyes had widened, then turned cold. "Wait, let me take a picture of you with the lion. I'll use it on the cover of my next issue." He watched as the green eyes seemed to warm slightly.

"All right."

Rob positioned Sam by a cluster of salmon-colored hibiscus, being very careful to stay clear of the lion.

"How do you want us to pose?" Sam asked as she casually unsnapped Stanley's chain.

"However you like. Take your time; it will give me awhile to set up my camera."

She looked glad that he had positioned them in the shade. The temperatures in Palm Springs were often overwhelming. She looked at Jake. "What do you think?"

Jake laughed. "Honey, you'll look good no matter where the cat is."

He's right, thought Rob. He was watching the slender

woman and the big cat through his lens. He noticed how
her hair was a tawny gold, almost the exact shade of the
lion's mane. Even in plain work clothes she had a lovely
figure. She was slender but her hips had definite feminine curves, and her breasts were full. As she turned
toward the camera he noticed the fine features—high
cheekbones and slightly slanted green eyes. *She even
looks like one of those goddamn cats,* he thought. He
swallowed and concentrated on setting up the shot.

Sam had positioned Stanley so he was lying down and
she was nestled behind his body, her head resting
against his mane. "Do you like this?" she called.

"Yeah, it looks fine." Rob shifted his feet nervously
as he scrutinized her through his lens. *Perhaps I could
ask her to go out with me for a few drinks after the
shooting,* he thought, momentarily forgetting his wife
waiting at home. Glancing up from his camera, he noticed Jake Weston watching him. Rob had the most un-
canny sensation that Weston sensed his thoughts. But
then, the old man had insisted on being present at the
photo session, almost as if he were protecting her. As if
she needed protection with that lion beside her. Rob
glanced back through his lens. "Okay, Sam, I'm almost
ready."

She licked her dry lips and ran a hand through her
hair. Patting Stanley reassuringly, she crooned, "I'll
take you home soon." The lion butted his head against
her hand playfully.

"Okay, Sam. Smile."

When Samantha smiled, Rob noticed, it changed her
face. White, even teeth flashed in an exuberant smile,
without any self-consciousness whatsoever. Rob
groaned under his breath as he snapped a few more
shots. *She has no idea what she's doing to me,* he
thought. Out loud he called, "Let's try a few standing."

"All right. Up, Stanley!" The lion raised himself to

his feet and yawned, showing a row of dense white teeth. Sam scratched his nose. She walked behind him, holding his mane, and threw a shapely leg over the lion as if riding a horse. "Is this okay?"

"Yeah. Fine." Rob snapped away while he thought about ways to get Sam away from Jake Weston. He marveled at her ease in posing. She changed positions quickly and didn't seem to possess the terrible inhibitions so many people had in front of the camera.

He snapped picture after picture as Sam sat astride Stanley, then she crouched in front of him and let the lion lick her face. She shook paws with him, playfully pulled his tail, and did everything she could think of to inject life into the pictures. When his roll of film was almost finished, Rob signaled he was done and began to take down his tripod.

Sam breathed a sigh as if glad the whole experience was finished. She snapped the chain back around Stanley's neck and began to walk toward the compound.

"Hey, Miss Collins, wait!" Rob scrambled after her, his equipment making his movements awkward and ungainly. When he caught up to her, she was scratching the back of Stanley's head absently.

"Can't Jake take care of the rest?" Her question was polite, but he sensed something he couldn't quite define under her natural reserve. Fear, perhaps? But that was ridiculous, she worked with wild animals. He backed away from the lion as he began to speak.

"There are a few more questions I'd like to ask you—"

"Are you tired, Sam?" Jake's voice cut in quietly, and Rob sensed a subtle warning.

"No, Jake. I can finish the interview."

The three of them walked slowly back to the compound as Rob plied Sam with questions.

"How old did you say you were again?"

"I just turned twenty-eight a few weeks ago."

"And you enjoy your work?"

She smiled. "Yes, I do."

"Don't you ever wish you had a husband and family? You know, a more normal life?" He was quick enough to observe that her green eyes clouded slightly, but when she answered the question, her voice betrayed nothing.

"It will take a very special man to understand my love of animals and the way of life I've chosen for myself."

Rob continued, undaunted. "Is there anyone special in your life right now, Miss Collins?" He knew the second he voiced the question that he had overstepped into her private life. She turned her face away from him, and he couldn't see her expression.

"I don't see what this has to do with animal training," Jake cut in.

"Well, perhaps you're right," Rob replied hastily. He changed tactics. "How did you fall into exotic animal training as a profession? It's rather unusual for a woman, isn't it?"

"My father trained animals, so I grew up around them. There was never any question of what I wanted to do."

"Wait a minute . . . your father was John Collins? But wasn't he killed in a freak accident? Wasn't he filming in India and—"

"Yes. Are we just about through?"

"Of course, Miss Collins. Sorry about bringing up bad memories, but— What do you see for yourself in the future? What's your next assignment?"

"I'm working on a documentary about people who buy exotic animals and try to make them into pets. It's going to be shown on television later this season."

"Do you know what you'll be doing next—"

"I don't know what my next job will be." She smiled

politely, but Rob noticed that it didn't reach her eyes. He had done something, he wasn't sure what, but she had frozen him out. That was very clear. "I think Stanley is getting overheated. I'm going to take him back to his cage."

"Yes, of course," Rob muttered. "How thoughtless of me." He watched as Sam picked up speed, the lion matching her stride. They moved beautifully together, both creatures at home in the wild. Rob would remember Sam for a long time afterward, the slender woman with her hand resting gently on the lion's tawny back. As they crested a gentle hill framed by tall, waving grass and the golden late-afternoon sunlight, Rob stepped back and lifted his camera to his eyes. He snapped the picture effortlessly, and it was this one, with both woman and lion completely unaware they were being watched, that would grace the cover of a national magazine a few months later.

He watched as she walked away. The pictures would have to be enough. She certainly wasn't going to allow him to come any closer.

RYAN FITZGERALD set down his razor and strode to his desk. Punching down the button on the intercom, he said tersely, "Connie, no more incoming calls tonight. At all." His secretary answered in the affirmative and Ryan hung up. He swore softly under his breath, then walked back to the bathroom that was part of his office. Picking up the razor, he stared at his reflection. The man looking back at him was haggard. He was glad when the steam from the hot water clouded the mirror.

So what the hell are you going to do? he thought. He finished shaving and wiped his face with a hot towel. Peeling off the towel wrapped around his waist, he turned to the shower and began to adjust the warmth of the spray. He wanted it hot. The hasty overnight flight from Puerto Rico had not left him in the best mood.

Satisfied with the temperature, he stepped into the shower, letting the needles of water bring feeling into his numb, tired body. His mind drifted back to the mess in which he had left the movie company, and he groaned.

He tried to clear his mind, tried to still the turbulent thoughts. He needed a solution. And he needed one fast.

Ryan reached for the soap and massaged the lather across his forearms and chest, enjoying the feel of the hot water as it slowly loosened the kinks in his shoulders. Reaching lower, he soaped his thighs and lower legs, then straightened, ducking under the full force of the shower to rinse his entire body quickly.

He turned on the cold water and stood underneath it, hoping the temperature might revive him and provide the one last rush of energy needed before this long night was over.

He turned off the water and stepped out of the shower stall. Knotting a towel around his stomach, he jerked his head up when the intercom buzzed.

"Damn it!" He stalked to the desk and picked up the receiver. "Yes!"

"Ryan, it's Michael. I didn't think you would want me to take a message. He needed to talk to you."

"Okay, Connie. You did the right thing. Put him on." Ryan relaxed back into the soft leather chair behind the large oak desk. He reached for a cigarette.

"Hello, Ryan." Michael's voice was faintly amused.

"How did you know I was in Los Angeles?" Ryan had known Michael Stone for years. They had attended USC together.

"I have my ways. But seriously, I called you in Puerto Rico, and Helen gave me the whole sad story."

Helen! Ryan narrowed his eyes. He lit his cigarette and took a deep drag. Helen was the least of his problems at the moment.

"So you know all about it?" He closed his eyes, feeling the beginning of a headache in his temples.

"Most of it. What are you going to do?"

"Spend the next few days tracking down another animal trainer."

"Do you know where you're going to start?"

"I haven't the slightest. But I *do* know I'm not going to leave it up to those casting people! This time I want someone tough who'll get those animals to do the right things."

"Are you much behind schedule?"

"Three weeks." He took another drag from his cigarette, then stubbed it out. "Just about every other scene has an animal in it."

"At least you had the sense to fire the trainer when you saw things weren't working out."

"Thanks, Michael. Listen, I've got to cut you short. I have to begin stalking my next victim."

"That's what I called about. As soon as I heard the nature of your problem I did some calling around and found out a few—"

"Tell me!" Ryan cut in impatiently.

"Do you remember Jake Weston and John Collins?"

Ryan frowned, deep in concentration. "I remember them. Wasn't Collins. . .killed by a tiger?"

"Yes. But Weston still runs an exotic animal compound out in Palm Springs," Michael offered. "He has several trainers there at any given time, and they're the best. It couldn't hurt to give him a call."

"You've made my evening!" Ryan reached for a pencil and began to jot down a few notes. "Weston did a few jungle pictures in his day. I'm sure he'll be able to recommend someone. If all else fails, I'll pay *him* to come down."

Michael laughed. "If you're still stuck in the morning, call me at my office, and I'll see what I can do. I'll let you go now. Good luck.''

"Thanks." Ryan hung up the phone and stared at it. Then he lit another cigarette, picked up the receiver, and began to dial.

"Am I late for dinner, Jake?" Sam smoothed her pale gold hair back with a hand that trembled slightly, and as she watched Jake she knew that he had noticed.

"You're fine, honey. Come in and have a drink with me." Jake put a reassuring hand under Sam's elbow and walked her from the front porch of his ranch-style home into the large living room.

Sam glanced around the room. It was a comforting place, a second home to her for as long as she could remember. Evidence of Jake's personal style was everywhere: the blue-and-white dhurrie rug, the rugged dark beams, the clean lines of the bold red overstuffed couches and chairs. Large, terra-cotta urns filled with fragrant sagebrush flanked the couches on either side. A wooden Texas chest that Jake had refinished sat in front of one of the couches, and a Wyeth painting hung above the massive stone fireplace. It was a man's house, and Sam felt at home in the familiar surroundings.

"What will it be, Sam?"

"Do you have any ginger ale?"

"Coming right up." Jake walked over to the bar in the corner of the living room. It was carved from pine, and Sam knew that he had rescued it, piece by piece, from an Old West saloon in Nevada. It was obviously Jake's pride and joy, and he delighted in using it whenever he could. Opening a small refrigerator he had installed, he filled two glasses with ice.

"I was proud of you today, Samantha."

"Thank you." Sam accepted the glass of ginger ale Jake handed to her. The two of them sat on the comfortable sofa.

"You'll stay for dinner, of course," Jake teased her gently.

"I'm not that hungry." Sam watched as Jake's expression changed slightly. He was worried about her, she could tell. She was comforted by the fact that this man, who had been a second father to her after the death of her own, cared so much. Sam had always come to Jake before with anything bothering her, but the feelings she had today were still too raw. The reporter had upset her. She had sensed intuitively that he had been interested in her, but it was her reaction that upset her. Though she had been able to freeze him out of her life, she had been scared inside. At twenty-eight, she had felt she had reached a certain point in her life where events in her past no longer had the power to haunt her. But she was wrong. And that was what scared her the most.

"Maria made your favorite chili. Are you sure?"

Sam forced herself to concentrate on the conversation at hand. "Maybe just a little."

He stood up and took Sam's glass. After setting both glasses down on the bar, he headed toward the kitchen. Sam followed.

The room was huge. The brick floor and glazed tiles on the walls gave it a cozy, intimate feeling. Glass-front cupboards surrounded the kitchen working area, along with a large gas restaurant range. Cheery blue calico curtains hung in the windows, and split oak baskets completed the country look. A work island in the center contained drawers, storage bins, open shelves, and a sink. There was a cozy seating area on the other side of the room, with a huge oak table and hand-carved chairs. Ferns, Swedish ivy, and miniature geraniums filled the airy space with color and scent. A small stone fireplace was on one side of the dining area, with mugs and other knickknacks on its mantel. Several pictures of Sam with various animals hung on the French-blue walls.

But the biggest appeal in the friendly room was the smell of cooking that wafted into every corner. No one could resist Maria's cooking, least of all Sam.

"Sit down, honey." Jake motioned her into one of the chairs. He sat down to her right and called out his wife's name.

The slender Mexican woman who entered the kitchen was the closest to a mother Sam had ever had. Maria had a timeless quality about her. She had always been there, never seeming to age. She had taught Sam to garden, cook, and sew, and had also helped her through the difficult transition from girl to woman.

Now Maria stood with her back to the two of them, dishing up the fragrant chili from a huge pot on the stove. She carried it to the table, along with a small basket of homemade tortillas and a crock of soft butter. A salad of avocados, hearts of palm, tomatoes, romaine, and garlic came next, along with a pitcher of fresh lemonade. After making sure everything was on the table, Maria sat down at the other side of Jake.

The three of them ate in silence. Sam was aware of Jake's eyes on her, and she knew he wasn't fooled by the fact that she was pushing her food around her plate. She took another spoon of chili and began to chew automatically.

"You look very pretty tonight, Sam. Are you going out with Matt?" Jake asked.

Sam smiled. Jake had made his opinion of Matthew Simmons perfectly clear. One thing Jake wasn't was subtle. She shook her head. "No, I thought I'd just dress up a little." She smoothed her hands over the soft denim of her jeans. A plaid Western shirt, a denim vest, and cowboy boots completed her outfit. She had dressed up hoping the simple action would put her in a better mood, but her feelings of unease persisted.

"Jake is right," Maria said. "The green in your shirt goes with your eyes."

"Thank you." Sam was suddenly aware of their mutual attempt to cheer her up, and she decided to shake off whatever was bothering her. "Do you think Mr. Drysdale got the story he wanted?" She directed her question to Jake.

"I think what he wanted—" Jake began, but the shrill ring of the phone interrupted him.

"Let it go," Maria said.

"I'll be just a minute," Jake replied. He left the kitchen and headed for the den.

"That man! If it isn't one thing, it's another." Maria began to clear the table, and Sam got up to help her.

"Sit down. Jake told me all about your interview today. You must be tired." Maria motioned for her to sit, her delicate hands expressive. Sam knew better than to fight. Though she was small in stature, Maria ruled her kitchen with an iron hand. Sam sat down. She strained to hear something of the conversation in the other room but couldn't make out a word. Pouring herself another glass of lemonade, she leaned back, propping her boots up on the seat of the chair across from her.

She was deep in conversation with Maria when Jake rushed in from the den. "You'll never believe who just called me."

"Who?" Maria and Sam spoke almost in unison.

"Ryan Fitzgerald, the director of that jungle picture being filmed in Puerto Rico. You remember that article I read in that cinema magazine, about the jungle picture starring Helen McNair?" As Sam and Maria glanced at each other in amazement, Jake raked his fingers through his thick gray hair. "It seems that he ran into some trouble with the last trainer and had to fire him. A friend of his suggested us, and he wants me to send someone to his office in Los Angeles tonight!''

"But it's almost six!" Maria protested.

"Who are you going to send, Jake?" Sam questioned.

"I'd go myself, except that those maned wolf pups are due any day." He thought for a few seconds, his brow wrinkled in concentration. His eyes widened in curious speculation as he looked at Samantha. She slowly shook her head.

"Count me out, Jake." Her stomach turned over at the thought of working with movie people again, especially the type that ran with a crowd like Ryan Fitzgerald's. She had seen his picture plastered on too many tabloids, and though she knew that half the sensational stories couldn't possibly be true, it seemed that every time the media mentioned him it was to talk about his latest conquest. She'd had enough of that particular type of man in her marriage.

"You've got to go. You're the best with the big cats. And you've had experience with chimps and elephants. Go see what this man wants and convince him you can do it!"

"But, Jake," Sam protested, feeling an uneasy knot beginning to form in the pit of her stomach.

"Honey, this is the chance of a lifetime. Work on one film can lead to another, then another. You can't afford to pass this up." Sam heard his sigh of frustration, and she remembered the times they had argued over the direction her career as a trainer was headed. She had insisted that she was happy working on the compound and occasionally driving to Los Angeles to take part in a film, but only after she had done some research as to who was working on the particular project. Jake insisted that she was throwing away a natural talent and tremendous opportunities for advancement. And now it was as if this particular job brought the entire argument to a head. She knew an instant before he spoke that he wasn't going to let her get out of it this time.

"I want you to go." He raised his hand in a warning gesture before Sam could speak. "Sam, please. Just do the interview for the compound. Matt isn't qualified, Susan is only a beginner, Colleen is in Africa, and Joe is still working on that zoo project."

"Susan could handle it, she's far from a beginner. If you sent her with someone else, the two of them..." Her voice trailed off as she saw Jake lower his eyes to the table. He seemed to be intently interested in the floral arrangement in the center.

A horrible suspicion raced through Sam's mind. "But you already told him that you were sending me, right?"

Jake nodded his head. "You're as ready as you'll ever be. Call me the minute you get back, and good luck!" He gave her a quick hug and was out the door before Sam could think of anything else to say.

As SAMANTHA drove along the desert highway toward Los Angeles she finally admitted to herself what had been depressing her earlier. The journalist's questions about home and family had brought on an all-too-familiar sense of desperation concerning her life.

Sam had been married once, with disastrous results. Only eighteen and still suffering the aftereffects of her father's sudden and violent death, she had gone to Los Angeles as the assistant animal trainer for a TV series about a family with a live-in tiger. Paul Hartnell had been the co-star of *Tiger by the Tail,* and he had asked her out the first day they met. They had dated quietly, and after a few months Paul asked her to marry him. Sam had been overjoyed. Since she was an up-and-coming animal trainer and Paul's professional star was on the rise, their marriage was publicized in all the

Hollywood gossip papers. They had been romanticized as the ideal, innocent young couple in an industry in which marriage rarely held up.

Sam had never questioned Paul's love for her. Looking back, it was painful to believe she had ever been ignorant of what was really going on. She had worked, supporting them both, while Paul lounged around their small apartment, complaining about the parts not being offered him.

The marriage had barely lasted a year. Paul was selfish and abrupt with her, even in their physical relationship. Sam had never really enjoyed his embraces, and in time came to believe that in some perverse way it was her fault. Their futile attempts at lovemaking all but ceased. Having grown up in a world of men, Sam hadn't had a girl friend in whom to confide. She had remained silent.

It was all coming back to her now. She swallowed painfully as vivid images flashed before her. The night that had ended their marriage, she had arrived home with a bag of groceries and a small bottle of his favorite Scotch. They had argued earlier in the day, before she had left for work. Sam had thought that perhaps after a quiet dinner they could talk and mend the rift growing between them. She had walked into their bedroom only to find Paul making love to a well-known starlet in their bed....

Shaking these recollections from her mind, Sam tried to concentrate on her driving, but she had to follow the memory through to its conclusion. She had left the same night, after throwing the bottle of liquor against the wall above the bed. Paul hadn't even moved out of bed, hadn't said a word to her. Sam had gone back to the compound, to the only home she had ever known after her father's death. Jake had taken her in without any questions, and the next day she had started repairing and refurbishing the house her father had left her. After the divorce, she never heard from Paul again.

The experience had hardened her. Unable to talk to anyone about what had happened, she had immersed herself in the few relationships she had trusted since childhood. She dated sporadically, but with both eyes open and a slight feeling of distrust. The innocence, her secret childhood belief in a happy ending, had been shattered in one intense evening.

She stayed away from the world of movies, and for a time believed that all people in the entertainment industry were the same—they were either superficial and obsessed with themselves, or had serious trouble distinguishing fantasy from reality. Nothing was really what it seemed in the world of movies. Paul had certainly turned in a convincing performance.

But as she grew older she realized how different people were, and that blanket statements could not be made with any degree of intelligence. She had begun dating again, more seriously this time, because she had finally admitted to herself that she was lonely. Unfortunately, none of the men she encountered were what she was looking for.

She had fallen into a relationship with Matthew Simmons simply because he had a sense of humor and was kind to her. Though he was not as good a trainer as she was, he never made an issue of it, and their relationship drifted along on a very easy level. Most of the time Sam was content, but there were evenings when she lay awake in bed, wondering where her dreams of passion and romance, fidelity and trust, had all gone. She had once believed that there was someone waiting for her, that she would know him when she saw him, that they would live happily ever after. Well, she had thought Paul was that special person, and the pain after their separation had almost killed her.

The blare of a horn brought her back to reality, and she realized that she had been only half watching the road. Her fingers were gripping the steering wheel with such intensity that her knuckles were white.

She loosened her grip, breathing deeply in order to calm her racing heart. The noise of the horn had startled her, but it was the onslaught of painful memories that had upset her. And she still had an interview to endure before she could return to the safety of the compound.

She glanced up and saw a sign that announced she was entering Los Angeles county. The traffic was already becoming more intense. Sam stepped on the accelerator, and her small green Volkswagen skimmed over the highway. The sooner she got this farce of an interview over with, the better. She wasn't looking forward to meeting Ryan Fitzgerald.

Chapter Two

"*You're* Sam Collins?"

Samantha smiled at the secretary. She was used to people being surprised when they found out she was a woman.

"Yes, I'm Sam. I have an appointment with Mr. Fitzgerald."

"But you're not the person who trains wild animals?" The secretary still sounded as if she couldn't believe her eyes.

"Yes." Sam knew she didn't look imposing. She was barely five feet seven inches tall, and her build was slender. People more often took her for a dancer than an animal trainer. She prompted the secretary gently. "I was told Mr. Fitzgerald wanted to see me right away."

"Oh, yes. He's been waiting for you all evening since he called." The woman hesitated. "You work with *tigers*?" Her brown eyes were huge.

Sam laughed. "It's not as frightening as it sounds. At least animals are a little more predictable than people."

The phone rang, and the secretary jumped. Picking up the receiver, she answered the call in a soft, cultured tone. She was cut off abruptly. The caller was so angry that Sam, sitting on the small office sofa in front of the desk, could hear the loud voice. She rose, rubbing her hands nervously over her jeans.

When the secretary finally hung up, Sam spoke. "I'd really better see Mr. Fitzgerald. I was told he wanted to talk with me immediately."

"That was him," the secretary replied grimly. "I'll show you to his office."

"Thank you." Sam tucked her plaid blouse more firmly into the waistband of her jeans as she followed the secretary down the long hall.

"I don't know a lot about animals, but you must have a very exciting life." The secretary sounded wistful, as if she would have given up her job in a minute if something more appealing came along.

Sam felt her stomach begin to tighten at the prospect of this meeting. She clenched her hands into fists, forcing herself to calm down. *It's only an interview,* she thought. *I don't have to do anything I don't want to do.*

Her train of thought was interrupted as she was shown inside a large office. It seemed different from the extremely modern and impersonal reception area. This room was stamped with a presence. Someone lived and worked here. The furniture was large and imposing, all heavy dark wood except for a lighter-colored oak desk. There were papers that looked like pieces of a script thrown all over one end of the large room. An ashtray on the massive desk was filled to overflowing with cigarette butts, and several used glasses rested on the blotter. Sam wrinkled her nose at the smell of stale cigarette smoke.

"Where's Mr. Fitzgerald?" she asked.

"He'll be here in a minute. Do you want any coffee?"

"Yes, please." Sam rubbed her temples with her fingers. She'd been up and working since six that morning and was beginning to feel the strain. Fighting Los Angeles traffic hadn't put her in a better mood.

"I'll get it right away. Cream and sugar?"

Sam nodded.

The secretary left noiselessly, and Sam stretched her cramped muscles, then walked to the desk. She noticed several pieces of the script with red penciling all over the pages lying in a haphazard fashion on top of the desk. Curiosity overcame her. She picked up a piece of it and began to read. Her mouth turned down at the corners—it was awful. She was about to reach for a second page when a deep male voice jolted her back into the present.

"What the hell are you doing in here?"

Sam's head snapped up. The man who had entered the room filled the large office alarmingly with his presence. All of her senses were heightened instantly.

Tall and bronzed, he had dark brown hair and blazing deep blue eyes. Sam looked over his body before she could help herself. She sensed that underneath the well-cut business suit was a body of iron. He moved with an easy masculine grace as he approached the desk, his eyes never leaving her face. Sam felt herself wanting to shrink back. But she remembered one of the first things she had learned when training animals: Never show fear, or you are finished. Straightening her spine, she set the script on the desk and extended her hand.

"Hello, Mr. Fitzgerald. I'm Samantha Collins."

His deep blue eyes blazed with an icy fire. Then, to Sam's astonishment, he threw back his head and laughed.

"Tell me another one, little girl. Where's Mr. Collins?"

Sam forgot her fear as her quick temper came to the fore. "*I'm* Mr. Collins. And if you don't believe me, you can call Jake Weston." Her eyes never left his. He was certainly a potent specimen of the male animal. The look he had given her had nearly started her trembling. He reminded her of certain animals at the compound. The trick was to train them to obedience without breaking their incredible spirit. This man would never be broken, and she doubted he'd met the woman who could tame him.

There was a knock on the door, and Ryan called, "Come in!" The secretary hurried inside, gave Sam a quick, nervous smile, and left the coffee on the low table in front of the leather couch.

My God, thought Sam. *Everyone on the premises is afraid of this man.* She squared her shoulders defiantly and picked up her coffee. Holding it to her mouth with steady hands, she sipped it slowly as she took in Ryan Fitzgerald.

He was a good deal taller than she was, easily taller than six feet. His face looked as if he spent a lot of time outdoors. Small lines radiated like star bursts from the corners of his eyes. Sam imagined he could be quite handsome... if he ever smiled. But the blue gaze that studied her was cold. He picked up the phone and began to dial.

She turned her back on him and walked to one of the large windows, sipping her coffee as he began to speak.

"Hello, I'd like to speak to Jake Weston. Yes, I'll wait."

Sam sensed his eyes on her, she could almost feel his intense gaze burning through her thin cotton shirt. She couldn't even taste her coffee, she was so aware of Ryan Fitzgerald. She stared out the window, unseeing.

"Hello, Mr. Weston. This is Ryan." There was a pause, and Sam could imagine Jake's concern on the other end of the line. "No, nothing's wrong. What do you mean by sending me a girl to do a man's job?" His tone was amused, condescending. "You said you were sending me a Sam Collins, but when I got back to my office this evening, I found a very attractive young woman who claims to be—" There was a pause, and Sam smiled to herself. He was arrogant enough, and she was glad to puncture his ego a bit.

"She is? But I asked you for the *best* trainer, and I

cannot believe— She is?'' Ryan sounded incredulous. Sam bit her lip to keep from laughing, but her laugh stuck in her throat as she heard his next words.

"All right. That's fine. Send him along. I'll interview him in the morning. Tomorrow at eight.''

Ryan hung up the phone. Sam put her coffee down at the same time and turned to face him. She knew Jake had suggested Matthew.

"You're going to interview Matthew Simmons tomorrow.'' She threw the challenge at him directly, without flinching from the delicate subject.

"Yes, I am.'' Ryan's eyes were hard as he raked his arrogant gaze over her slender form. "Miss Collins, it's nothing against you personally. But I can't believe a woman could handle all she'd be up against if she joined us on location.''

"It's your loss, not mine,'' she replied tightly, forgetting that in the beginning she hadn't even wanted to go out on this interview. She picked up her bag and started for the door. Just as she reached it, she felt large warm hands settle on her tense shoulders.

"Miss Collins, I—''

His touch coursed through her body like a flame. She jerked away from his hands and whirled on him, all her anger and frustration exploding at once.

"Don't you touch me!'' Sam faced him, her emerald eyes snapping, her color high. "You wouldn't touch Matthew, would you?'' She saw his face begin to darken ominously but rushed on, the heat of her temper adding emotion to her words. "Mr. Fitzgerald, you may not believe women are as capable as men, but some day you're going to have to catch up to the twentieth century! Jake told you I'm the best with the big cats, *and I am!* If you prefer to work another way, it's your business, but I think you're arrogant and insufferable.'' She took a deep breath. Her body was beginning to tremble with reaction. "And you're so wrapped up in your own prejudices, you can barely see what's as plain as the nose on your face!"

She paused to take another deep breath and heard the sharp intake of his. But she was so angry and unsettled, she went on, uncaring of his reaction.

"It's common knowledge in the industry that you're having trouble with the animals on this picture! I could help you salvage it, or at least put some of those animals out of their misery by calling the proper authorities! It's just damn frustrating when ignorance comes in the way of—"

She stopped talking as he took her by the shoulders, his fingers digging into her upper arms. "Perhaps it's a good thing I *don't* want to work with you," Ryan growled. "The last thing I need on the set is an over-emotional woman! Save it for your boyfriends!" With an exclamation of disgust, he let her go and walked over to his desk.

Sam watched him as he reached out and turned on the desk lamp. He sat down heavily in the chair behind the desk. She noticed how his strong features were emphasized by the light. Something in his face, perhaps a sense of weariness or strain, seemed to reach out to her emotions. She felt feelings that she couldn't quite define welling up inside of her. Sam stood rooted to the spot until Ryan looked up and noticed she was still there.

"What do you want?" She didn't answer—she couldn't. Her throat constricted painfully. Her emotions were running wild with her and she didn't know why.

He looked at her, his eyes narrowed. "I'll reimburse you for your time and the gas you used getting here." He reached into a desk drawer for his checkbook.

She left quietly before he could look up again.

SAM DROVE BACK TO THE COMPOUND at top speed, venting her frustration on the empty freeways. It was already after midnight when she pulled into the driveway of her house.

The stars in the sky were brilliant in the desert night. Sam thought they could almost be plucked from the heavens. Usually she delighted in the soul-stirring qualities of the area, but tonight her restless thoughts were far away from her physical surroundings.

She opened the screen door and put the key into the lock. Pausing for just an instant, she looked around the riotous beds of flowers that surrounded the small walk up to her front door. She loved to garden, and her small stucco house was always engulfed in bright splashes of color. The sweet, seductive scent of night-blooming jasmine teased her senses.

She let herself in and switched on the light. No matter what kind of mood she was in her home never failed to comfort her. She had decorated it on a small scale, as it had two small bedrooms and a den, a living room and a kitchen. The walls were painted a pale, soothing blue, and the windows were draped with small country prints. There were green plants everywhere, and several pieces of good oak furniture that she had refinished herself added grace and beauty to her surroundings.

A large orange cat jumped off the small blue sofa and wound his way around her legs, purring loudly.

"Hello, Rusty." She knelt down and scratched his back, then moved her hand to scratch under his chin. She had found the old cat out in the fields behind her house one morning while she was gardening, and he'd never left. He ruled the house with dignity, letting the other animals know that they could stay as long as they realized it really was his house.

Sam went into the kitchen and poured him some food, then refilled his water dish. As Rusty began to crunch on his food Sam headed toward the bathroom. She undressed as she walked, letting the clothes fall where they landed.

Once she was inside a hot shower the water began to relax her tense muscles, and she leaned up against the cool tiles.

What is the matter with me? she thought. Samantha had been an exotic animal trainer long enough to realize that she was taking part in what was essentially a man's world. During Sam's training Jake had warned her about the pressures a woman would face, and she had run head-on into prejudice many times before this particular evening. Why had she lashed out at Ryan?

If only he hadn't touched me. Lathering her hair with both hands, Sam shut her eyes and tried to blot out the mental picture she had of Ryan, but his brilliant blue eyes and sardonic smile kept creeping into her mind.

Rinsing herself off, she climbed out of the shower and wrapped a towel around her body. Tomorrow was Sunday, and she could sleep in. The thought gave her little comfort as she combed her hair and prepared herself for bed. She set her alarm automatically, then grimaced and shut it off. After unwinding the towel from around her body, she climbed in between the sheets of her brass bed and lay down. As she turned over she gazed at the ceiling.

I wonder what it would have been like working with him? Her thoughts surprised her and she turned over on her stomach, punching her pillow into shape. She was angry with herself for thinking such thoughts—she was opening herself up to be hurt again. The man had been insufferable, after all!

Except, of course, that she would never see Ryan again.

Sam closed her eyes and tried to sleep. She listened to the wind playing through the branches of the trees outside, then smiled as she caught the sounds of the lions roaring in their cages over at the east end of the compound.

She felt Rusty jump on the bed, circle around for a bit, then knead the old patchwork quilt with his claws before he settled in for a good night's sleep. She heard him begin to purr as she finally gave in to sleep. Her last conscious thought was that she'd work with the littlest lion cub in the morning, but her dreams were filled with visions of a dark-haired man with blazing blue eyes.

A WEEK LATER Sam was out on the open desert, exercising her favorite horse, Ali. The gray Arabian stallion was high spirited and quick to respond, and somehow his restless temperament matched Sam's mood.

"Easy, boy." She slowed the fiery horse to a trot, placing a hand along its silken neck. As the animal proceeded at a more leisurely pace Sam had a chance to enjoy her surroundings.

The desert never failed to excite her. Sam couldn't understand some people's disdain for the area. Perhaps they thought all they would see would be pale, washed-out hills and drab tumbleweed. But the vista of color in front of her was as vivid as an artist's palette. Silver sage and bright purple verbena undulated gently in the early-morning breeze. The flowers were astounding: wild white daisies, rich yellow buttercups, scarlet-blossomed hummingbird bushes, orange poppies, and apricot-tinted mallows. Dark, umbrella-shaped carob trees were visible in the distance, as were the roseate mountains. Sam was always able to draw strength from her surroundings, and she had decided on an early-morning ride for precisely this reason.

Ali shook his head, and the bridle jangled. In a moment of whimsy she had attached small bells to his headgear. Their sweet notes pierced the still air. Sam looked down and saw a ground squirrel behind a bush. Its quick movements were making Ali nervous.

"Steady, that's a good boy." She turned Ali and slowed him to a walk. Chiding herself gently, she determined to keep her mind on the present. After all, she couldn't keep thinking about a job that had never been hers in the first place. But was it the job or the man? She sat up in the saddle for a moment, stretching her legs. The leather creaked beneath her. The clear desert air was cool and spicy with the smell of herbs.

She didn't want to keep thinking about Ryan, but he was never far away from the back of her mind. She couldn't remember when a man had ever affected her this strongly. Matthew had been accepted for the job, and he had left with a minimum of fanfare. Jake had never said another word about the interview. He must have figured out what happened from Ryan's phone call.

Sam's attention was caught by a small fleck on the horizon. Soon she recognized it as a horse and rider moving toward them. Urging Ali forward with her knees, she let the stallion have his head, and he began to gallop toward the rider. It wasn't long before she recognized Jake on his palomino, King.

"What are you doing out this early?" he asked her as their horses fell in beside each other.

She patted Ali's neck. "I thought this one might need a little exercise."

Jake smiled. "Anything else?"

He was just too perceptive, she thought. Sam frowned, then looked out toward the horizon and the hills. The sun was coming up over them, washing the area with golden tints. She looked back at Jake. "I was thinking about the interview."

"I knew it was bothering you." Jake seemed to be studying her face carefully as he spoke. "I almost called you late last night. Matthew flew back."

"From Puerto Rico?"

Jake nodded.

"Then who's taking care of Ryan's animals?" As she mentioned his name her heart began to race crazily. Damn the man!

"No one at the moment," Jake replied. "I'm glad you didn't fly down there. From what Matt told me, the whole operation is in utter chaos."

"What's going to happen to the animals?" Sam persisted. "Are these people planning on finishing the picture or not?"

"They're trying to rewrite the script so there's as little animal involvement as possible. The writer flew down the day before Matt left. They're still trying to salvage things." He let the palomino have its head, and the large horse began to investigate the ground, looking for something to eat.

"And the animals?"

"It's worse than we thought." Jake's blue eyes were clouded with worry. "The last trainer before Matt took most of his animals with him, but a few of them are independently leased. They're still there, and no one knows how to take care of them properly. Matt did his best while he was there, but he told me most of them looked miserable. There's a white lion, a baby elephant, a few chimps and birds, and a tiger."

Jake pulled gently at the reins, and the palomino's big head came up. He turned the horse in the direction of the compound, and Sam followed. Ali had had enough exercise. Besides, Sam wanted to find out more about Ryan's film.

"Is there anyone there who can do anything? Call the authorities?"

Jake smiled ruefully. "Not really. The actress who has the leading role hates animals and has been putting the entire crew through hell. Everyone is tired of being on location, and the only thought is to get home as quickly as possible. I'm afraid the animals are last on the list.''

"What can we do, Jake?"

"I'm not sure. I'm not sending another trainer down. Actually, if it weren't for the animals, I'd say to hell with the entire project."

"They must be suffering in the heat. Where are they filming?"

"Somewhere in the middle of Puerto Rico. The jungle there is as dense as any you'll ever find, but it's near enough to San Juan to drive in for supplies."

"I can't believe that anyone would put any living thing through that much agony just for a motion picture."

"You'd be surprised what people do to animals in the name of making the almighty dollar."

They were almost at the compound now. Ali and King were trotting briskly, and the sun felt hot on Sam's back. The jogging movements of the Arabian beneath her helped dissipate some of her anger. And most of it was directed at Ryan. After all, he was in charge of this entire mess, and she assumed that he could put a stop to it at any time. Thinking of him made her clench the reins tighter. She couldn't remember feeling this strongly in a long time.

Jake seemed to sense her mood. "Don't worry about it, Sam. I'll get on the phone and make a few calls. Perhaps the film can be shut down on the grounds of cruelty to animals."

The rest of the morning went badly for Sam. She couldn't stop thinking about the animals no matter how busy she kept herself. And thinking of the animals naturally led to thinking about Ryan. The man upset her, there was no doubt about it.

After a quick shower and breakfast, she went into

town to pick up some groceries, but got a flat tire on the way back. Though she fixed it quickly, she was frustrated and grimy by the time she pushed the screen door open and stumbled into her home.

As she was putting her groceries away the phone rang. It was probably Matthew, calling to tell her he was back. She waited before picking up the receiver.

"Miss Collins?" She recognized Ryan's voice instantly and felt hot color surge into her cheeks. What colossal nerve he had!

"Yes?" She deliberately made her voice sound cool and disinterested.

"This is Ryan Fitzgerald. I'm calling from Puerto Rico." His voice was rich and masculine, and something in its sound made her shiver.

"Oh, how nice." Sam bit her lip. She had a sudden urge to hang up on him. She knew what he was going to ask her to do.

"Miss Collins, I need your help." He wasn't pleading, just stating a fact.

She said nothing, waiting for him to continue. A part of her enjoyed the fact that he had to ask.

"Matthew flew back last night," he continued. "But I'm sure you know all about it."

"Jake told me this morning." With some effort she kept her tone of voice cool. Her hand was trembling on the receiver.

"The animals are in bad shape. I need someone who really knows what he's doing."

"Or she," she added softly.

She heard Ryan's breath come out in an exasperated sigh. "Yes, damn it, or she!"

"Mr. Fitzgerald, after what you put me through in your office, what makes you think I'd ever want anything to do with you or any of your projects?"

There was a long pause. *He's probably not used to a*

woman shooting straight from the hip, Sam thought.

Finally Ryan spoke. "I don't really expect you to do anything for me, but I know as a trainer, your first concern is the animal you are working with. These animals are suffering, I don't know what to do with them, and I need you to help me."

"Why did Matthew leave?" The words were out of her mouth before she could stop herself.

Ryan bit out the words in response. "It seems you were right. He wasn't qualified."

Sam said nothing, shocked by his sudden admission. All of her petty dreams for a revenge on Ryan were coming true, but somehow the victory was bittersweet. Suddenly she wished she had met Ryan outside the narrow confines of an employer-employee situation. The thought surprised her. But there were still the animals to consider, and she plunged ahead.

"Couldn't you shut down production? Why not stop the whole thing and send the animals back to the States?" She was sincere in her request, no longer wishing to humiliate him.

Ryan seemed to sense this, even over the phone. "I can't. My reasons are personal." He paused, and Sam could sense the strain he was under. "I'm only going to ask you one more time."

She closed her eyes.

"Will you please fly to Puerto Rico and help me finish this picture?"

Before she had time to consider the consequences the words came rushing out of her mouth.

"Yes, I will." Sam opened her eyes. How would she ever explain this to Jake? Even over the phone, Ryan managed to exude a powerful influence over her. She couldn't think rationally when he was involved.

"How soon can you get down here?" Ryan sounded relieved, but now he was all business.

"I can fly out tonight if you want me to."

"There's a flight leaving Los Angeles at six this evening. It stops over in Miami, but you'd be in San Juan in the morning. Can you be on it? I'll arrange to have a ticket waiting for you at the airport."

"Yes. Is there anything I can bring?"

"Just yourself. I'll pick you up when you get here."

"Good-bye, Mr. Fitzgerald."

"Good-bye, Miss Collins. And thank you."

She hung up the phone and stared out the screen door. Suddenly, separated from Ryan's voice, with its seductive and persuasive qualities, she confronted her snap decision head-on. *Why am I walking back into the business after so many years—and why with a man like Ryan?* But before she could consider her actions further her glance rested on the clock above the fireplace. It was ten minutes to one. She'd have to hurry to make it to Los Angeles International before six.

THE SMALL PICKUP jolted down the freeway. Sam kept her eyes straight ahead. She knew that Jake was displeased with her decision. But she could be as stubborn as he was, and if it meant not talking all the way to LAX, then it was all right with her.

They were about fifteen miles from their destination before Jake broke the uncomfortable silence.

"Sam, I wish you'd reconsider."

She squared her slim shoulders. "I'm a trainer before all else. Matt told you the animals were in bad shape— I've got to try to ease their suffering, or shut down production. You must understand what this means to me." When Jake remained silent, she continued. "I'm sorry if you're displeased, but you're not going to change my mind."

"As if I could!" He shook his head.

Sam partially turned in her seat and placed a hand on

the older man's arm. "If anything goes seriously wrong, I know you're only a phone call away."

"I'll catch the first plane out if you need me."

They continued the drive in silence. Sam sensed that the important things had been said.

Los Angeles International was in its usual state of frenzy as Jake maneuvered the truck into a parking space. It was not until Samantha was in line to board the plane that Jake voiced his unspoken worries.

"I don't like it, Sam. I'm not going to stop you from doing what you think is right, but I'm not pleased about you working for Ryan." He lowered his voice. "After he turned you down, I did a little reading on the man. Watch yourself; he's got quite a reputation."

Sam felt her face flush slightly. She wished that Jake had thought of all this before he'd ever sent her on the interview. "Jake," she said, speaking with more confidence than she felt inside, "I'm capable of handling myself around any man!"

He grimaced. His voice was louder than usual in an attempt to be heard above the noise of the crowds. "Your father would have told you the same thing. I've worked on a lot of pictures, and it's easy to mistake the camaraderie that develops between the members of a film crew for something else... something more permanent."

"I know, Jake."

"I just don't want to see you get hurt."

Sam thought quickly back to her first marriage, to the months of emotional pain and humiliation with Paul. She wasn't going to get hurt again; she'd watch herself. She squeezed Jake's hand.

"I'll be careful this time. I don't even really like the man." Her stomach fluttered traitorously as she said the words. "I'll do the best job I can and then get out."

"Well, it's too late now." They were almost up to the

boarding gate. "I'll tell you the truth. When I sent you on the interview, I was hoping like hell you'd get this job. Now I'm not so sure."

There were only a few passengers ahead of her in line. Sam turned swiftly to Jake and threw her arms around him. The last vestiges of the quiet, isolated life she had chosen were slipping away at an alarming rate.

"Hey, Samantha." As she stepped back she noticed a suspicious brightness in his blue eyes. Her own were stinging, and she blinked. "You'll knock 'em dead," Jake said gruffly. "Go on now, we're blocking traffic."

She walked backward, watching him, until she turned to give the attendant her ticket. Before she entered the boarding ramp she heard Jake call out, a bit reluctantly, "Give 'em hell, Samantha!"

Chapter Three

"Wake up, miss." The flight attendant shook Sam's shoulder gently. "You'll have to fasten your seat belt. We're preparing for our descent into San Juan."

Sam sat up and stretched her cramped body. When she had boarded her flight yesterday evening, no one would have been able to convince her that she would be able to sleep. She had read several magazines and managed to write out a rough list concerning the animals—their care and health requirements. But exhaustion had overtaken her. After the stopover in Miami, she had fallen asleep and slept straight through until now.

She peered out the window, glad Ryan Fitzgerald had had the foresight to ask for a window seat. The changing hues of the Caribbean were jewellike in intensity: sapphire changed to aquamarine, then emerald to deep amethyst. Sam glanced at her watch; ten in the morning eastern time, right on schedule. She fastened the seat belt snugly around her waist and settled back into her seat.

It was a smooth landing, the plane touching down gently. Sam remained in her seat, letting the others crowd into the narrow aisles. She disliked hordes of people. There was plenty of time anyway. Ryan couldn't possibly be shooting on a Sunday.

Ryan. At the thought of his name, Sam remembered the fierce, penetrating blue eyes and the incredible animal energy the man seemed to possess. She shivered involuntarily, then straightened her shoulders. He needed her. More importantly, the animals needed her. She would finish this job and go back home.

Then why did the mention of his name give her vague feelings of apprehension on the one hand, and tinglings of anticipation on the other? Sam remembered when he had touched her in his office. Since Paul, in any situation with a man, she had been determined to be the one to keep things under control. Her cool, blond exterior matched the finesse with which she evaded any sort of messy, passionate interlude. Matthew was certainly easy enough to handle.

But Ryan affected her differently. She seemed to lose all sense of reason around the man. And the most infuriating thing about him was that she sensed he was aware of this.

Just do your job, she thought, and then jumped as she felt a hand on her shoulder.

"Do you need some help with anything?" It was the flight attendant again. His gray eyes were full of concern. Sam noticed the plane was almost empty.

"No, I'm fine." She got up and reached for her shoulder bag. "Just a little groggy."

"A flight this length can be hard on the body. Take it easy the first few days. And enjoy Puerto Rico."

"Thanks." Sam made her way out of the plane on shaky legs. What was the matter with her? She smoothed the skirt of her pale blue shirtwaist over her legs. Thank God for silk blends; it hadn't wrinkled too much. She hoped she looked more professional than she felt. Perhaps she'd have time to freshen up before Ryan arrived.

She walked rapidly down the boarding ramp, her heels tapping a staccato rhythm. As she rounded a bend and came out into the small lobby in San Juan International Airport, she saw him.

Ryan looked more disreputable than ever, in faded

jeans and a yellow T-shirt that set off the darkness of his tan. Sam couldn't help but notice how the bright material stretched tightly over his smoothly muscled chest. She smiled her hello as she walked up to greet him.

"Where the hell have you been?" he growled.

The smile faded from her face. How had she ever thought this man attractive? She answered him carefully.

"I decided to wait until the rush died down."

"The first person got off over fifteen minutes ago!" he accused. "I wish you'd told me over the phone how enthusiastic you usually are over any new job!" His voice had a biting, sarcastic quality to it.

Sam counted to ten in her head, trying to control her temper. When she spoke, her voice was calm and devoid of emotion, completely at odds with the way she felt inside. "If you're in such a hurry, then I suggest we go and collect my luggage so we can leave."

"An excellent idea," he replied, and turned and walked brusquely away.

Sam followed him as quickly as she could. What was the matter with the man? Even a bad day of filming gave him no right to take his aggressions out on her. She had been hired as an animal trainer, not the resident whipping boy. She'd have to set him straight.

Barely seeing the tropical fountains and palm trees that were incorporated into the architecture of the airport, she caught up with Ryan at baggage. Sam watched as suitcase after suitcase slid down the ramp and circled in front of them on a conveyor belt.

"What do yours look like?" Ryan asked abruptly.

Why, so you can criticize my taste in luggage? she thought silently. Out loud, she replied, "A green suitcase and a large box." She brushed a stray wisp of hair away from her face, and silently blessed herself for having had the foresight to wear it up off her neck.

The main passageways of the airport were open-air rather than air-conditioned. Though a roof sheltered them, walls were nonexistent. The building was open to vivid blue skies. The clear tropical colors and the scents of flowers in the hot air assaulted Sam's senses. Puerto Rico was beautiful in the same shimmering way as an impressionistic painting. The colors almost hurt her eyes, yet she was compelled to look.

She glanced away from the vivid beauty outside to the man standing next to her. Sam covertly watched Ryan's face as he scanned the conveyor belt with his piercing blue eyes. He was darker than when she'd seen him last—the Caribbean sun, no doubt. His hair had red-blond highlights woven in among the dark brown. She sensed more than ever that undercurrent of primitive energy. It made for a fascinating specimen of a man.

She could feel his blue eyes boring into her. "You *did* get your luggage on the plane, didn't you, Miss Collins?" He was sarcastic again, this time insinuating by his tone that she was somewhat less intelligent than a small child.

Her temper flared slightly, but Sam fought to control herself. "Yes. I'm sure that it will be down at any moment." She wiped her forehead surreptitiously.

Ryan glanced at her in annoyance. "There's an air-conditioned tourist office. You can rest there, get a few brochures, and a free rum drink."

Sam glared at him. "No, thank you." He was treating her as if she were merely a tourist! She'd pick up her brochures privately.

They waited and watched as piece after piece of baggage was claimed. Sam tried to remember the circumstances of her departure. She and Jake *had* arrived at the airport at the last minute. Perhaps there was a slight chance...

"Well, it's not on this plane." Ryan turned and

walked over to a small glassed-in office next to the baggage claim area. He opened the door and stepped inside.

Sam watched him out of the corner of her eye, her attention still on the conveyor belt. She saw him approach a young man behind the counter. Her dress was sticking to her back in a most uncomfortable manner, and she reached behind her to pull it away. Where was her luggage?

A slightly built man tapped her on the shoulder. "That's all, miss. Go check in the office if your bag was not on the belt." He pointed in the direction of the room Ryan had entered.

Sam walked over and let herself in through the glass door. The air conditioning felt wonderful as it hit her face. There was no use postponing the inevitable confrontation with Ryan. He was upset about something and determined to make things as miserable as possible for her.

"What does your luggage look like?" Ryan attacked her as soon as she closed the door.

She looked up at him, wishing the floor would suddenly open up and take him far away from her, but she kept her voice under control. "A green suitcase—American Tourister. And a large cardboard box, reinforced with black electrical tape and string."

Ryan turned back to the young clerk and continued to converse in Spanish. Sam couldn't make out much of the conversation, because words were exchanged too rapidly. She'd have to learn more Spanish quickly. Feeling helpless and very uncomfortable, she sat down in one of the nearby chairs. There was nothing she could do.

She closed her eyes. Everything was so different from what she had imagined. She had known working with Ryan was not going to be easy, but she had had no idea he was going to turn out to be such a brute. Breathing deeply, she calmed her jangled nerves. *Save your strength for the other animals,* she thought. *They're what really counts.*

She sensed something change in the air and opened her eyes. Ryan was standing over her, looking down. And he was furious.

"The next flight from Los Angeles arrives at ten tonight. There's a good chance your luggage is on it." He paused, as if waiting for her reaction. When she remained cool, he continued. "I'm taking you back to location, and then I'll drive in tonight and pick up your things. Let's go." He turned and walked away.

Sam picked up her shoulder bag and began to run to keep up with him. After her long flight, she didn't feel up to racing after this madman all day.

"Ryan!" she shouted at the top of her lungs. Several people turned and stared, and she felt her face flame. But she stopped running and stood her ground. He turned to face her.

"I'm not going anywhere with you until I get my luggage."

His blue eyes narrowed into slits and he opened his mouth to speak, but Sam kept talking. "I have important medications and vitamins for the animals in the box. It does me no good to go back to your film location and see the poor things suffer. I came out here to do a job and I'm going to do it!" Her voice was very soft, but there was a silken strand of steel woven in under the surface.

He studied her face for several seconds, and the close scrutiny nearly did Sam in. "Ah, yes," he drawled as he walked back to join her. "Miss Champion Animal Trainer." Sam felt her pulse flutter wildly, but she kept a firm grip on her composure. "I did a little reading up on you after our interview. You just may be as good as Jake says you are." He smiled suddenly, and Sam was amazed at the transformation in his face. "Okay, Supergirl, you win. What do you suggest we do with ourselves until ten this evening?" The blatantly appraising look he gave her figure left Sam with no doubts as to what he thought they might do.

"Is there someplace I can get something to eat?" At his look of amazement, she almost laughed. "The food on the plane was terrible."

"Like I said before, you win." Sam caught her breath at the intensity of Ryan's gaze. "We can go into San Juan; it's only six miles east."

They walked out to his car, side by side this time. Sam noticed with satisfaction that he slowed his steps for her. He unlocked the passenger door of his silver Jaguar and she climbed inside. Ryan slid in behind the wheel, and soon they were headed for downtown San Juan.

"It doesn't seem much different from Los Angeles," Sam remarked almost to herself. She was dismayed to find that the island had its share of high rises and billboards.

"You'll get a taste of the jungle once we're out on location." He eyed her speculatively. "Think you're up to it?"

Sam tilted her chin defiantly. "I used to go camping with my father all the time. I can handle myself." She leaned her face out the window and closed her eyes. "I can smell the ocean."

"The whole island is less than four thousand square miles," Ryan remarked. "No part is farther than twenty miles from the coast."

Sam settled back in her seat and began to enjoy the drive. Even with Ryan's initial burst of temper, nothing could take away the excitement of her first trip to the Caribbean.

High rises began to give way to small restaurants and

boutiques. Brown-skinned children in bright clothing, and small mongrel dogs played on the sidewalks and in the alleys. Sam's senses were bombarded by color everywhere: Magenta and scarlet bougainvillaea spilled over fences and rooftops; pots of deep pink and pristine white geraniums, and lush green ferns lined the front walls and doorways of small whitewashed houses and old-fashioned stucco apartment buildings.

"This is lovely," she breathed.

"You haven't seen anything yet. Since we have so much time to kill, I thought I'd take you to Old San Juan."

"What's that?"

"An area of the city where they've preserved the old forts and mansions. It's like stepping back in time."

Sam noticed that the atmosphere of the city had changed subtly. Ryan pulled the sports car over to the curb, parking it on a shady side street.

"This is where we get out. The streets are too narrow for cars in the older part of the city." He walked around and opened the door for her, offering her his hand. "Come on."

Sam stared at his outstretched palm. *Dr. Jekyll and Mr. Fitzgerald.* What incredible changes this man went through. She started to protest, then caught herself. If Ryan was going to make an effort to atone for his abominable behavior at the airport, she couldn't be nasty. Anything was better than the frigid atmosphere that had existed between them.

She gave him her hand and stepped out of the car. His fingers closed around hers as if the action were the most natural thing in the world. She felt the warmth of his palm tantalize her hand. She gripped his smooth flesh gently, afraid to exert any pressure. He might get the wrong idea. She was here to work.

He guided her into the city, and Sam was enchanted

by what she saw. Narrow streets, paved with bluish cobblestones, wound past balconies of wrought iron that exploded with floral color. As they walked past impressive cool stone buildings Sam caught quick glimpses through arched doorways of colorful courtyards and private patios. Brightly woven hammocks hung from windows, and exotic smells teased her senses. Ryan was right, it *was* like stepping back in time.

Before she could take in all but the fleetest impressions, he was steering her into a dark restaurant, his hand firm on the small of her back. The floors were marble, and the high ceilings were carved in an intricate pattern. A fountain splashed in a courtyard nearby, and the thick ancient stone walls offered respite from the hot tropical sun.

The waiter led them to a small table set with snowy linen and lovely antique silver. Sam certainly hadn't expected this! She had imagined the Puerto Rican equivalent of McDonald's for lunch, certainly not something this elaborate. She looked at Ryan and knew that her puzzlement was clear in her expression.

He shrugged his broad shoulders. "What are expense accounts for? And anyway"—his stern, forbidding mouth quirked up at the corners—"I expect to be well paid in return." His eyes glinted humorously.

Sam wasn't sure whether he meant the lunch, her work, or perhaps something else. It was the "something else" that unnerved her. She chose to ignore her uneasy speculations and picked up a menu.

It was completely in Spanish. She made out a few familiar words, then looked across the table at Ryan.

"I'll order for you," he said.

Their waiter came over, and once again there was a rapid exchange in Spanish. When he left, Sam spoke up.

"Does everybody speak that quickly here?"

Ryan considered her question. "Yes, they do. Much

faster than Cubans or Mexicans.'' He smiled. She noticed the way the blue gaze softened when his smile reached his eyes. As his visual inspection of her became more admiring Sam felt her legs start to tremble. She glanced down at the white linen. He was devastating.

She almost wished that Ryan had continued to be nasty. He was easier to dismiss. This side of him was much more attractive, and she wasn't sure she knew how to deal with it. He seemed too self-assured, too certain of getting what he wanted. He was the great lover and hunter, and she sensed she was his prey. But then, just as she thought she had another side of Ryan figured out, he surprised her again.

''I'd like to apologize for the way I treated you in the airport this morning.'' Sam stared at him and, for just an instant, she thought that she was hearing things. She watched as Ryan ran his fingers through his hair in a gesture of frustration. When he spoke again, she knew that the words were more difficult. He was a proud man, and apologizing didn't come easily. But explaining his vulnerabilities was another thing altogether.

''Shooting has been going very badly. I was hoping to get in a good morning's work before leaving to pick you up, but nothing seemed to go right.'' He glanced at her as if studying how all this was affecting her. Sam stayed perfectly still; she didn't want to do anything to jeopardize this moment in time. She had a feeling that it was a huge step in the right direction for their relationship.

Ryan cleared his throat. ''I wanted to have things a little more under control before you came out,'' he admitted. ''It was just one of those days when nothing works.''

Sam nodded. ''I've had those.'' Why did she have the strangest sensation that what they were talking about had nothing to do with what they were feeling? Ryan's apology was sincere, of that she was certain. And the fact that he was vulnerable and honest enough to let her know why he was so frustrated made her like him even more. But this feeling was something else. It was as if both of them had a heightened awareness of the other, as if there were some connection between them.

She forced herself to meet his eyes and found her answer in them. She saw desire in the blue depths, but also something else. It was almost as if Ryan were as confused as she was by these feelings. Sam wasn't afraid; she returned his gaze with unwavering steadiness, feeling the dark blue eyes warm her. A funny sensation started to bloom in the pit of her stomach, and she felt her lips curve into a soft smile as she recognized the unfamiliar stirrings of desire. Her heart raced crazily and she felt like her blood was rushing through her body with an accelerated rhythm.

She felt her eyes widen slightly and saw the answering response in his gaze. *So he knows,* she thought to herself. She licked her lips nervously and saw his gaze move to her mouth, the look as potent as if he had suddenly kissed her. Her fingertips moved to her lips to make sure, and she saw him smile softly, almost wickedly.

She couldn't look away from him; all of her energy was focused on the man in front of her. Sam felt as if the years of emotional coldness were slowly being stripped away by this warm, vital man. She felt her stomach tighten as she saw his hand reach across the table to capture hers.

But before he did, their waiter arrived with their drinks. The moment was broken, and Sam looked away.

"Is this a piña colada?" she asked, trying to keep her voice steady. What had come over her? Had she imagined the entire thing? She focused her attention on the drink in front of her. It was huge and garnished with a spear of pineapple.

"Yes. Puerto Rican rum is the smoothest in the world. It's also considerably stronger. Try it." Ryan lifted what looked like a Coke to his lips. He looked as cool and composed as he had before the apology.

"What are you drinking?" Sam asked, hoping that her voice didn't sound suspicious. She had the unnerving impression that he was trying to seduce her. What was worse, she didn't think she would mind.

He laughed softly, and she had the impression that he knew what she was thinking. "Rum and Coke with a twist of lime." He raised his glass to hers. "Here's to a successful relationship." The double entendre was unmistakable as he caressed her with a look from his deep blue eyes.

Sam felt her heart beating a rapid tattoo against her rib cage. Ryan Fitzgerald was certainly unlike any man she had ever met. Picking up her glass with amazingly steady hands, she clinked it gently against his. "To the picture."

She sipped the thick drink. It was delicious, smooth and creamy, with hardly a trace of alcoholic taste.

"It's the fresh coconut." Ryan answered her question almost as if it had formed in her mind. "Probably every other piña colada you've ever had was made with the canned stuff, but here it's the real thing."

She took another sip. The cool drink felt good after walking through the heat of the afternoon. It tasted like a milkshake.

"I hope you like fish," Ryan said as he saw the waiter approach the table with their meals. "I ordered the red snapper; it's the specialty today."

Sam nodded her head. "I love it." The dish placed in front of her looked magnificent. The fish had been cooked in a sauce that contained olives, onions, capers, tomato, vinegar, garlic, and pimiento. "What is this called?" she asked as she began to cut the fillet with her fork.

"*Chillo con mojo isleño.* I've had it here before. It's superb."

As Sam tasted the flaky fish she had to agree with Ryan. The snapper was obviously very fresh, and the delicate sauce only served to enhance the flavor. She had thought she might be nervous eating with Ryan, but he was proving to be relaxing company.

For dessert he ordered papaya cubes cooked in sugar and cinnamon, with white cheese, and strong black coffee for himself. Sam leaned back from the table after her last mouthful.

"Not still hungry, are you?" he asked.

"No." With her stomach comfortably full and the postflight tension easing out of her body, she was enjoying her accidental holiday with Ryan.

The waiter appeared to clear their table and presented Ryan with the check. Ryan picked it up, studied it for just a second, then put it back down with his American Express card. He glanced at his watch.

"Still only two in the afternoon. What do you suggest we do from here?"

Sam avoided his gaze. "We could walk around Old San Juan. The little I saw was fascinating." She felt a blush come into her cheeks and hoped Ryan couldn't see it in the dim light of the shaded restaurant. Suddenly she felt very vulnerable at the thought of going anywhere with him. The attraction between them had been intense enough even in a crowded restaurant.

She stood up and followed him outside. The tropical sun was brilliant and hot. The narrow cobblestoned streets were almost vacant. They walked in silence for a short time until Ryan spoke.

"The people who live here have the right idea. They get out of the sun and take a nap during the hottest part of the day. How does that sound?"

Sam thought quickly. Actually, she *was* tired. A nap

sounded like heaven. But did Ryan mean separate rooms, or was he implying a certain degree of intimacy? Snatches of her conversation with Jake last night at the airport flooded her memory.

"I'm fine. Let's just walk."

To her surprise Ryan took her hand in his, and they continued their exploration of the old city. But Sam didn't really see much of the local charm and color. Her senses were too attuned to the man beside her.

She could feel his fingers linked through hers. His hands were warm and slightly callused. Though he held her hand firmly, he made no move to deepen the pressure or make the gesture more intimate. Sam found herself liking him for that.

They walked down the shady side of the street. The stores lining the side were small and dark, but Sam had the impression that inside they were larger. Glass windows held displays of intricate lacework, carvings, and pottery. There were also the standard picture postcards, cheap souvenirs, and booklets on the sights to be seen. Bright yellow signs proclaimed that Kodak film was available in every store.

But it was the island's appeal to the senses that was much more seductive. Sam was beginning to adapt to the humidity, and she found it was relieved by cool breezes off the ocean. Flowers bloomed riotously everywhere she looked, and fragrances teased her nose.

Ryan walked easily with her, stopping when she wanted to look at something, then matching his pace to hers as they continued down the street.

They were almost around the corner when Sam saw a wooden sign swinging in the breeze.

"The Gentle Swing. What's that?"

Ryan looked down at her, a humorous glint in his deep blue eyes. "I have a feeling you'll enjoy this shop.'' Squeezing her hand, he ducked through the small doorway, pulling her after him.

The inside walls were cream stucco, but hammocks of every size and color seemed to burst from the walls much the same way flowers bloomed on the iron balconies. The door was open, and each time a breeze entered, all the hammocks were set swaying as if in their own private dance. Sam was enchanted.

''Look at this one! It's so tiny!''

Ryan laughed. ''That's a baby hammock. But cats love them, too.''

Sam opened the fastening of her purse. ''I've got to buy one for Rusty. His old bed is coming apart.''

Ryan frowned. ''Do you have children?'' he asked.

Sam smiled. ''No, Rusty's my cat. I think he'd like one of these, if he doesn't tear it to bits first.''

A woman approached them, and Ryan began to converse with her in Spanish. Though the language still moved quickly, Sam was beginning to pick up a word here and there. She listened, fascinated, at the rising and falling inflections in both voices. Spanish was certainly beautiful the way it was spoken here.

Ryan turned toward her. ''Sam, this is Carmen. She asked me if you'd like to try out a hammock.''

She was about to refuse politely when she saw the shy expression on the girl's face. Carman couldn't have been more than eighteen, and Sam had the distinct impression she hadn't worked at The Gentle Swing for too long a time.

''Sounds good to me. But please let her know I definitely want a small hammock for my cat.''

Ryan relayed this information to Carmen, and the girl smiled. She answered Ryan and motioned for Sam to follow her.

''She has something she thinks you'll like,'' Ryan said.

Sam followed the young girl past several hammocks toward the back of the store. Behind a large desk, inside a small hammock, a fluffy black-and-white mutt slept peacefully.

Sam knelt down and smoothed the soft fur back from the small face. The little dog stirred, then sighed and settled back to sleep.

She stood up and smiled at Carmen. The language felt stiff on her lips, but she attempted to put together a sentence.

"Su perro es muy gracioso. Your dog is very cute."

Carmen smiled again, and this time her brown eyes sparkled. *"Gracias, señora. Su esposo es muy guapo."* She looked up at Ryan. He grinned.

"What does *esposo* mean?" Sam glanced up at him. She'd have to pick up a book of Spanish phrases on the way back to the airport.

Ryan's facial expression was amused, the lines around his eyes and mouth deepening. "She just told you that you have a very handsome husband."

"Oh!" Sam turned back to Carmen and tried to think of the right words to convey the truth. The thought of that intimate a relationship with Ryan disturbed her. But she couldn't think of the right Spanish expression. She glanced back at him.

"Tell her the truth."

Ryan laughed. "And spoil her romantic dreams? I don't think so." He took her arm and led her back toward the large hammocks. "So, my little *esposa,* which hammock would you like to try out?"

"Very funny. How about that red one?" As Ryan put his arm around her waist she added, "Alone."

"What's this? *Mi querida!* How could you do this to me?" He affected such a woebegone expression that she had to bite her lip to keep from laughing.

"My darling nothing. It's alone or not at all."

"You drive a hard bargain."

Carmen had followed them back toward the red hammock and now she spoke to Ryan.

"She wants you to take off your belt and shoes. Anything sharp might tear the material."

Sam studied his face for a minute, then decided he was telling her the truth. She removed her belt and handed it to Ryan, then stepped out of her shoes. Carmen began to arrange the mass of strings into something resembling a surface. Before Sam knew what had happened, Ryan picked her up and held her over the hammock.

The physical contact with his body was so intense that it took a minute before Sam got her breath back. When she did, she decided to put an end to this farce.

"Put me down. Right now." Her voice was low.

"Of course, *mi amorcita*." He set her down within the hammock. Sam almost forgot her anger as the folds of woven string enveloped and supported her body. The hammock was loosely woven so that the cool ocean breezes could be felt all around her body. She stretched and touched her hands against the smooth cotton.

"This is wonderful!" She glanced over at Carmen. *"Me gusta mucho."* She kept her gaze averted from Ryan's profile. *Mi amorcita.* My little love. Though she knew the words couldn't possibly have been sincere, that hadn't prevented a small thrill from racing through her body as he said them. She just had to keep remembering that Ryan was her employer, nothing more.

As she closed her eyes she felt a small sense of understanding toward all the other women in Ryan's life. He was an attractive man. But more than that, he had a vitality, an energy about him that seemed to make life exciting. And she was discovering that he was easy to be with. And fun. She had only landed in San Juan that morning, but it seemed she had known Ryan longer than that.

She relaxed back into the gently swaying cocoon the hammock provided. Tension eased out of her arms and shoulders, and she turned on her side. The sensation was something like being on a water bed. Each part of her body was supported; she could twist and turn any way she wanted to.

She could hear Carmen and Ryan talking softly in the background. Sam remembered she had to get up and pick out a hammock for Rusty. She'd get one for Jake and Maria, too. But she'd just rest a little bit more.

She felt something warm and hard against her and she moved closer to the warmth. Rolling over on her back, Sam buried her face against warm, slightly musky scented skin. She felt something tighten around her waist. The sensation was intensely pleasurable, and she moved closer still.

As she began to slowly wake up, sensations and bits of feeling began to take shape, assume their proper identities. Still curled up and very comfortable, she opened her eyes slowly.

She was lying next to a man. Ryan. In Puerto Rico. Consciousness returned. *Oh, my God.* She gingerly tried to ease her body away from his, but his arm tightened. She wasn't sure if he was teasing her. Perhaps he was asleep as well. His words put an end to that thought.

"Did you sleep well?" There was an unmistakable hint of laughter in his deep voice.

Sam struggled to sit up. The hammock gave her no support and she fell back against Ryan's body.

"Steady." He grasped both her upper arms in his and held her slightly away from him. She steadied herself against his chest, her palms pressed flat against hard muscles. She could feel the warmth of his body with her hands.

"You look embarrassed." It was a statement, not a question.

Sam nodded her head and recommenced her efforts to get out of his embrace. She finally eased her legs over the side and sat up. Her body was trembling. But not from anger. If she was truthful with herself, she had enjoyed those fleeting moments before she regained full consciousness. It had been a long time since she'd touched another human being that closely. Ryan seemed to be waking up all sorts of emotional cravings deep within her.

Sam tried to locate Carmen. She saw her at last, talking to an older woman and demonstrating how to get into a hammock. She was aware of Ryan's eyes on her as she felt a hot flush creep up her neck and into her face. At least he couldn't read her mind.

"You shouldn't feel embarrassed. You looked so comfortable sleeping that you helped her sell two other hammocks before I joined you."

She turned to face him. Sam didn't know what she could possibly say. She hadn't meant for things to progress this fast between them. She caught herself. She hadn't meant for anything to progress at all! If anything, she had hoped to keep her cool, aloof persona in full operation. Ryan was making it next to impossible.

"What time is it?"

He looked down at his watch. "Close to six thirty. You were really out."

She nodded, then pushed her hair back off her face. She sighed, realizing that her carefully upswept hairstyle had come undone. She began to twist her hair in her hands when she felt Ryan's touch.

"Leave it. I like it down."

She met his eyes for long seconds, then looked away. A part of her was tempted to twist up her hair and walk outside to find the first bus back to San Juan International. But she simply stood up and wriggled her feet into her shoes.

Ryan got up and called to Carmen in Spanish. Then he took Sam's elbow and guided her outside.

"What did you tell her?" she asked.

"I said we'd be back in a little while to buy your hammock, but that I was taking you out for something to drink." He wasn't looking at her, he was watching the street signs.

Sam walked quickly, trying to keep up with him. What had happened to the Ryan of this afternoon, who had been so willing to let her define the pace of their day?

He turned a corner, and they suddenly stepped into a plaza. The open area was paved with smooth bluish cobblestones. To the side, a small sidewalk café spilled soft golden light into the deep blue of twilight.

"Do you feel like eating anything?" Ryan asked.

Sam shook her head. "Just something to drink." Her stomach was jumpy. She wasn't at all sure she'd be able to keep anything down.

He left her at a table and walked over to the bar. Sam sat back in the wrought iron chair and watched him as he ordered. Though she was getting chilly, Ryan seemed perfectly at ease in his shirt and jeans. With his dark hair and skin, he blended in, until you looked at his eyes. She took in as much of him as she could, safe in the knowledge that he couldn't possibly know she was watching him. Sam admired the clean line of his body, the broad shoulders and trim hips. His stomach was flat, his thighs muscular. She remembered the way his body had felt against hers in the hammock and looked away. She didn't want to remember the way she had almost responded.

He returned to the table, a can of beer in one hand, a glass of juice in the other. Placing the juice in front of her, he raised the can to his lips.

She tasted the juice—fresh pineapple, with a spear of

the fruit as garnish. The tartness was exactly what she needed. She took several swallows and set the glass down.

He was watching her. She looked away.

"You intrigue me, Sam."

She met his eyes. "Why is that?"

"I have such different impressions of you. The first time I saw you in my office, I thought you were rather hard. Yet today, asleep in that hammock, you were soft as a kitten. Which one is really you?"

She picked up her glass and finished her juice, then set it down. "Both, I suppose." But she felt her hands tremble. In truth, she was closer to the woman in the hammock than she'd ever be to the woman he had met in his office. She could fight and spar with the best of them, but her heart wasn't in it.

As if reading her mind, he said, "I think I like the woman I held in my arms this afternoon."

"I wish you'd stop talking about it. We fell asleep together, that's all."

"I can enjoy myself, can't I?"

I'll just bet you do. Her green eyes sent him a silent message.

I really could with you. Desire was plain in his dark gaze.

She stood up. "We have to be at the airport by ten. Why don't we stop back and get the hammock, then drive out. I don't want to be late."

"Whatever you want."

As they walked back toward The Gentle Swing Sam marveled at the transformation that had come over Old San Juan. Lights from shop windows cast shadows across the cobblestones. There were people in the streets now, voices calling out to each other in the rhythmic, romantic language. She saw several couples strolling hand in hand, completely absorbed in each other. The windows by the balconies were open, and people sat up above, watching the procession in the street.

She found it more difficult to keep up with Ryan. He slowed his steps for her, even offered her assistance with a firm hand on the small of her back. They were buffeted by people. Sam was relieved when Ryan gently pulled her into a side doorway.

"I can't believe the crowd. It's Sunday night."

"It's also tourist season. Everyone comes out at night on the island." He guided her farther down the narrow entrance. "We can catch our breath here."

The building they had entered was old. The stone was smooth underneath her feet, and Sam wondered how many other people had walked this same path before her. She followed Ryan, confident that he must know where he was going.

Seconds later he led her into an enclosed courtyard. The thick stone walls muffled the noise outside on the street. The only sounds to be heard were the gentle splashing of a tiny fountain and the soft, indistinguishable noises from brightly lit windows above.

It was dark where they were walking. Sam had to concentrate on her footing. She didn't want to catch a heel on an uneven stretch of cobblestone.

When they reached the far corner, Ryan turned toward her and leaned up against the stone wall. They were almost enclosed by foliage. Something green and leafy that Sam couldn't identify in the dim light trailed up the side of one wall. The scents of night-blooming flowers were stronger now than they had been during the day. She recognized jasmine, but that was the only one she knew.

She rubbed her hands over her arms with a quick gesture. It didn't go unnoticed.

"Are you cold?"

Before she could answer his warm hands slid up her

arms. Sam closed her eyes. Was it his touch warming her flesh, or was it her own response? She bit her lip and willed herself to stay detached.

When his hands fell away, she thought she had won. Then she felt his hand on her chin, lifting her eyes to meet his. The back of her neck hurt from looking up at him. She couldn't see his expression in the dim light, could barely make out the hard planes of his face. But she sensed him looking at her and lowered her eyes to his mouth.

She wanted him to kiss her. The desire that had started as they lay side by side in the hammock erupted with such a gentle force that it left her unafraid of her own passion. His mouth was still; there wasn't a trace of the mocking smile she had seen so many times before.

She raised her head, met his gaze of her own volition. Someone opened a shutter just far enough to spill some light where they were standing, and she caught the expression in his eyes. Her heart began to pound heavily when she recognized desire. He wanted her.

Somewhere, in a distant part of her brain, she heard something shouted in Spanish, then the shutter slammed close. They were in darkness again. Sam's eyes were adjusting to the light. She could make out Ryan's form against the stone wall. She didn't move away when he reached for her.

His hands encircled her shoulders and he drew her against the entire length of his body. Sam leaned into him, then took a deep breath and relaxed against his hard frame. She loved the way his hands felt as they moved over her back, lightly, yet intimately, touching her skin through the thin silk material of her dress.

She wanted to hold him as well. Her arms slid slowly up his sides, over his hard shoulders, and around his neck. She turned her face into his chest and felt his heartbeat underneath her cheek.

His head lowered and she felt his lips, softly touching her temples, then her cheekbone, as she raised her face to his. His hands moved up to her face, cupping it, and he rubbed his thumbs over her jawline. Her mouth was eased open with gentle pressure, then his lips came down over hers.

The sensation was exactly what Sam had intuitively expected. A liquid fire of pure sensation licked its way through her body and made her strain tighter against him. She felt his hands move over her back, then lower still to cup her buttocks and pull her body tightly against his. She could feel the hard ridge of male flesh, and a sweet ache made her legs start to tremble.

She remembered other men, other kisses, remembered trying to anticipate their sexuality from the brief, sweet intimate encounter. But in Ryan's embrace there was no time for speculation. Her mind had already raced far ahead, picturing them entwined in each other's arms, picturing him taking her to the highest reaches of ecstasy as quickly and hotly as he was right now.

She opened her lips willingly, not caring what he thought, not caring that they were in an open-air courtyard. The man with her made the small stone enclosure as intimate as any bedroom. There was nothing but her senses, and they were filled with his hands, his mouth, his tongue. His movements were slow and assured. He didn't paw her, simply excited her, building that excitement slowly, step by step, until her body shook with longing, expressing its plea for release more eloquently than any words.

His tongue filled her mouth, moving over the sensitive interior and drawing out her response. The light, gentle caresses his hands had been giving her were slowly changing to heavy, deeper strokes. Her body was tight against his, yet she longed to touch him more deeply, to blend their bodies and become one.

His hands were in her hair, gently massaging her head, sending tiny shivers up her spine in response to their erotic ministrations. Sam felt his hands on her cheek, then her chin—soft fingertip touches, like a feather.

Then he broke the kiss and simply held her. She felt pliant and warm in his strong arms. Sam was heady with new sensation, made reckless by desire. When he angled their bodies so she was against the wall with his body close to hers, she didn't protest.

"Do you know what you do to me?" His voice was a caress, coming at her softly out of the semidarkness. She smiled, and suddenly felt all powerful. That she could do this to him surprised her. She pressed her hips tightly against his, molding the softness of her body against the hard arousal of his. Reaching up, she traced her fingertips against his lips in light, teasing circular movements. He captured her hand with his, taking her fingers and inserting them in his mouth one at a time. The soft, seductive motion of his lips made Sam close her eyes tightly and bite her tongue against groaning out loud.

His fingers were playing with her ears, stroking lightly over and around them, barely in them. Sam shivered, and Ryan pulled her closer. She could feel the intense warmth from his body; it was a palpable force. His mouth found her ear, nipping the lobe and moving to the outer ear.

Then he brought his face back to hers, his nose rubbing against her hair, then down until they touched noses. Sam inhaled sharply as he stepped back, and the cool evening air touched her overheated body.

His hand closed over hers, holding it tightly. This time it was an erotic embrace, tight and seductive. His thumb played with her soft palm, teasing the sensitive skin. She felt his lips brush her ear.

"Let's go to the airport. I'll take you into San Juan to buy a hammock before you leave." Sam knew what he meant. The sooner her packages were picked up at San Juan International, the sooner both of them could return to location and resume what had begun with such intensity in the deserted courtyard.

He led her back out into the crowds of people, but Samantha barely saw them. She was only conscious of the man beside her, the way her hand felt embraced in his.

Outside the courtyard among other people, sanity began to return, slowly, with an awful sense of finality. As Samantha followed Ryan, weaving her way through the throngs of tourists, her mind started working more logically.

She had thought her greatest challenge would be taking over care of the animals and making sure the picture came in on time and under budget. It was going to be a demanding job, she was sure of that. But it wasn't going to test her in the same way the events of just one day promised to.

Her greatest challenge was going to be Ryan Fitzgerald.

Chapter Four

Samantha leaned back against the soft leather seat of the sports car and closed her eyes. Their journey was almost finished. Soon she would be able to stop traveling and rest.

Her thoughts flew back to the dark courtyard in San Juan. A flicker of hot sensation began in her stomach, and she looked straight ahead, ignoring the man beside her.

Ryan had put an end to their embrace. If things had been left up to her, she wasn't sure if she would have stopped him or not. The thought was disconcerting. She didn't want to appear unprofessional in front of Ryan. She fidgeted slightly. If she was honest with herself, her fears were deeper than simple unprofessionalism. She didn't want to repeat the same mistake she had made with her ex-husband. Yet Ryan affected her senses powerfully. Even as he drove the Jaguar deeper into the night toward the dense jungle, she was acutely aware of his every move, every glance.

Their trip to the airport had been quick. Luckily her luggage was aboard the later plane, and once they picked up the suitcase and box, Ryan insisted they stop for coffee. They then started the trip to location, deep in the middle of the island.

She leaned toward the open window, welcoming the rush of cool night air. Strange exotic smells teased her senses and she recognized a few: jasmine, rose, and something that smelled like magnolia. She couldn't be sure and didn't trouble to identify all of them. There would be plenty of time later. She could barely smell the ocean, as there was more of a plant scent, cool and green and verdant. Palm trees whispered in the ceaseless breeze, and she heard a distant clicking that she assumed to be bamboo moving in the wind. The island seemed to assume a magical persona at night, with rustlings and scents and dark secrets in the undergrowth that turned silver under the moonlight.

She sat back, rolling up the window against the cool evening. She was glad she'd had the foresight to change clothes at the airport. Dressed in jeans, a pullover sweat shirt with a hood, and her cowboy boots, she felt ready to tackle anything. Well, she amended slightly to herself, anything but her relationship with Ryan.

Sitting in the front seat of the sports car with Ryan in very close proximity, Sam steered her thoughts to more practical matters. That she was physically attracted to Ryan was a certainty; she hadn't felt as alive with any man in a long time. She was also sure of his attraction to her. But was it enough? She wasn't sure if Ryan looked at her as a challenge or if he really felt something for her besides desire.

But how can I expect him to know how he feels when I don't even know about myself? Her thoughts were confusing. It seemed like an eternity since she had arrived in Puerto Rico, but less than a day had elapsed. Feelings and emotions were crowding in upon her at a terrifying speed, and she didn't know how to handle these strange new sensations.

Perhaps it's better if I just don't think too much. Sam glanced at Ryan from under her lashes, trying to seek reassurance in that simple movement. But it merely unsettled her more.

He was a relaxed driver, but there was a tension between them almost palpable in the soft tropical air. He had barely spoken to her on the way to the airport, and once inside San Juan International, they had had crowds of people to contend with. The drive itself had been quiet enough, though she had sensed his eyes on her a number of times. But now his full attention was on the road.

Sam's gaze flitted over him restlessly. His hands on the wheel were capable and firm, the fingers long and well shaped. His dark brown hair blew back from the almost sculpted look of his facial bones. His mouth was arrogant and firm, and he looked the part of a man who was used to getting what he wanted. *Not that he did tonight,* she thought, and smiled to herself at her nonverbal audacity.

"What's so amusing?" he asked, and Sam was aware once again of the compressed energy behind his words.

"Nothing, really." *Brilliant conversation, Sam! You'll have to give lessons sometime.* She groped for something neutral to talk about and seized upon the first thing she heard. "What's that noise?"

Ryan smiled, and something in his expression made her chest tighten. The harshness sometimes apparent in repose slipped away, to be replaced by a supremely masculine charm.

"It's the coquí." He began to elaborate. "It's a small variety of frog that lives in the trees and comes out after dark. The males love to sing, especially after it rains." He grinned. "Some of the evenings on location are noisy, but you get used to it."

The sports car's only noise was a low, purring sound, so Sam was able to hear the little tree frogs quite clearly. When she turned to face Ryan, she forgot her nervousness.

"I can hear it! I thought they were crickets, but they really are saying co-quí!"

Ryan reached over and took one of her hands in his. Raising it to his lips, he pressed a kiss into the soft center of her palm, then lowered it to his muscular thigh, his warm hand still covering hers.

Sam felt her blood begin to race wildly as a tingling flash of sensation began to rush up her arm and into her body. Her response was instantaneous, but Ryan didn't seem to notice. She thought quickly about pulling her hand away, but the action seemed too juvenile. Besides, the moment to do it had passed. If she really was honest with herself, she'd have to admit she did not dislike the feelings Ryan evoked in her.

He kept talking in his soft, resonant voice, and Sam felt herself calming down. The first tingling sensation was replaced by a warm, alive feeling. It was almost as if she had been walking in her sleep before meeting Ryan. Now her senses were fully awake.

"Its proper name is *Eleutheradcatylus portoricensis*. But I'm sure you know, animal trainer that you are." Sam was amazed by the quick rush of happiness she experienced at Ryan's words. He was teasing her! She liked this side of him far better than the hard, driven man she had met at the airport.

"No, I didn't, but I'm surprised you do."

He quirked an eyebrow at her. "I have many talents, some you have only now begun to explore." There was a flirtatious gleam in his eyes. Sam had the distinct feeling whatever talents he was referring to had nothing to do with tree frogs.

"I'm sure you do." She laughed softly. "I'm going to catch a coqui and take it home for a pet." She held her breath, hoping this light, teasing moment would go on forever.

"No, you couldn't. They can't survive anywhere off the island. Well, they survive, but they don't sing."

"There must be some logical explanation," Sam mused.

"Always the behavior specialist," Ryan teased. "The

natives say when placed in a strange land, it suffers from a broken heart and can't sing."

Sam stared at him, wondering where the hard, arrogant man of the earlier evening had disappeared to. If anyone at the airport had told her that later the same evening she and Ryan would be talking about tree frogs and romanticizing them, she never would have believed it, but here they were.

She cleared her throat. "Probably they stop singing because of differing vegetation and conditions of living..." Her voice trailed off. Ryan's dark glance met hers for an instant. She looked away. "But I'd like to think the poor little things might be homesick."

"What's this? Do I have a closet romantic here?"

If you only knew! she thought. Out loud she replied, "Why should it be incongruous? Just because I take part in a man's world? Why do you assume any woman who works for a living has to be as hard as a man?"

Ryan laughed. "Oh, is that what I was implying? I don't think you're hard at all!" Sam knew he was making a deliberate reference to their evening in the courtyard and she blushed to the roots of her hair.

"I'd rather we didn't discuss that." The minute she said the words she regretted them. Instinctively she knew she had shattered their earlier calm.

"When would you propose we discuss it, then?" he asked with enough sarcasm to make her wince. "Or are you one of those women who has to make herself ashamed of anything sexual in order to get any pleasure out of it?" Sam turned toward him angrily.

"I just don't like being treated like a plaything!" She felt herself putting distance between them.

"Was that what you thought I was doing?" Ryan let go of her hand and gripped the steering wheel until his knuckles were white. "I thought I was making love to a woman I desired very much!"

"Desired! That's right." Sam was amazed to find herself almost shouting at him. "Your reputation precedes you, Mr. Fitzgerald. But I can tell you this right now—I won't stoop to being just one more woman in a cast of thousands!"

"Do you believe everything you read?" There was an amused undertone in his voice. Somehow this infuriated Sam even more than if he had continued arguing.

"Oh, come on! Perhaps it isn't as bad as the papers say, but you certainly haven't been living the life of a monk!"

"No." He started to laugh. "I can't defend myself. I am totally at your mercy, Samantha."

To her complete surprise she started to laugh, too. In the space of a few seconds, with a deft touch of humor, Ryan had made everything all right.

He reached for her hand again, and this time she had no thoughts of pulling away. He kissed her fingers slowly, one by one, his eyes still on the road. She felt her stomach start to quiver, then desire flowed into her body, languorous and sweet.

The sky above was luminous with brilliant stars, and Sam felt as if the two of them were completely alone.

"I'd like to pull the car over and make love to you right here," Ryan said lazily as he continued his exploration of her palm. His lips moved to her wrist. "But," he continued, "I think that when I finally do make love to you, I'll want you somewhere we can be comfortable." His eyes were sparkling wickedly. Sam looked down at her arm. She was breaking out in goose bumps, and it wasn't from the cool breeze. She heard Ryan's voice again, as if from a great distance. "Someplace with no phones. No other people. Just the two of us." She realized that he was maneuvering the sports car to the shoulder of the road. And then he turned off the engine.

They were surrounded by silence. Ryan lifted Sam's chin gently so their eyes met. She felt as if she were drowning in the dark blue of his gaze and was surprised to find she needed to be closer to him. Blind instinct took over as her hands crept up and wound themselves around his neck. She felt his fingers around her waist, pulling her closer to him, almost into his lap. Though the cramped interior of the Jaguar was very uncomfortable, Sam was barely aware of her surroundings as she raised her face to his.

The instant his lips met hers it was as if hot fire licked up inside her body. She moved closer to him, feeling the tips of her breasts press against his chest through the thick material of her sweat shirt. He probed her lips apart gently and explored the inside of her mouth. It seemed as if he were drawing something unbearably sweet from her. She felt his hand move up her leg, massaging the denim-clad length of her thigh. His fingers had just reached her sensitive inner thigh when she broke off the kiss and covered his hand with one of hers. He kissed her again, and the silken pressure of his lips increased, but she held her hand firmly on top of his until he moved it up along her body to her breast. Sam gasped as she pulled her lips away again and leaned her face against the warmth of his shirtfront. Her palms moved to press flat against him. When he shifted to kiss her again, she pushed herself slightly away from him.

"No, Ryan. Wait...."

He clasped both her hands in one of his and kissed her quickly on the corner of her aching mouth. "Can't you see, Samantha," he said thickly, "or is it like this with any other man?"

She shook her head, then leaned against his chest again. All of her energy seemed to have left her, and if he had wanted to physically overpower her, she wouldn't have stopped him. But Ryan eased her back in her seat and smoothed the pale strands of hair back from her face.

"We'll be at camp within half an hour. I keep forgetting how tired you must be. Forgive me."

The words tore at her heart, because she knew the effort he was exerting. The same feelings were running riot through her own body. God, how she wanted him! She felt embarrassed and rather self-conscious by the way she had responded to this man, but also gloriously alive. She closed her eyes, hearing him start up the car and put it in to gear. He pulled out on to the road again and pressed down on the accelerator, picking up speed.

Sam tried to sit up, but her body felt soft and unsteady. She leaned back in her seat, and the truth hit her with astounding clarity. There *was* something special between them: It had to be more than simple physical attraction. She seemed to have the power to arouse Ryan to the same heights of ecstasy as he did to her. But there was something else as well. He could have taken her there, on the desolate road, and she wouldn't have been able to truthfully say it had been entirely against her will. But he seemed to be attuned to her emotional needs and had decided to wait until she expressed that she was ready. Perhaps he did care for her more than she suspected. Maybe there was a side to Ryan Fitzgerald the press hadn't examined.

After an indeterminate length of time, Ryan turned off the highway, but this time he didn't stop the car. He drove slowly, gently maneuvering the Jaguar over a dirt track that seemed fairly smooth. Away from the open expanse of road and night sky, and under tall palm trees and other thick foliage, darkness set in. It was as if they had been swallowed up whole by the night. Sam strained to see ahead but could only make out what the swath of headlights cut through. Large flying insects were attracted to the light, and she reached over to make sure her window was rolled up completely.

It wasn't long before Ryan pulled into a clearing and shut down the engine. When he turned off the headlights, they were in pitch darkness.

"We're here." He reached for her and gave her a swift kiss, more a promise of sensual things to come than a beginning. Sam watched as he turned on a flashlight and got out of the car. He walked around to her side and opened the door, reaching inside for her hand to help her up. She gave it to him willingly, and as she rose out of her seat she swayed slightly against him. His arm slipped around her waist and he held her gently.

They began to walk through the darkness, with only the beam of the flashlight to guide them. Sam could feel the warmth of his hand as it rested on her hip; could feel his fingers tucked underneath the ribbed band of her sweat shirt.

There were tiny rustlings in the underbrush as they walked toward their destination. Sam didn't stop to think what they might be. Her senses were entirely concentrated on the man beside her.

Ryan walked easily, with the grace of a natural athlete. Sam could almost believe they were alone on earth, a primeval pair, together in the jungle at night. She felt her lips curve into a smile; how Ryan would tease her about that! He'd certainly tell her she was a hopeless romantic. But what was he, then? Sam felt sure there was still much she didn't know about him.

He slowed his pace, and they entered a clearing. Bright moonlight illuminated everything, silvering the vegetation and giving it an unearthly quality. He stopped, his arm tightening around her.

"This is it." He was studying her closely.

"Right here?" Sam looked around quickly, but she still couldn't make out a lot. Then, suddenly, amorphous, silvery shapes began to take on more distinct meaning as she recognized them. Tents came into view, along with several Jeeps and a pickup.

"The animals?" Her voice was low. She didn't want to wake anyone up.

As if in answer to her question, she heard the thin, plaintive wail of an elephant trumpeting. "They're over on the far end of another clearing," Ryan said. "The entire area is fenced off."

"That must be the baby." She spoke her thoughts aloud.

Ryan grinned. "That little beast has been responsible for more mischief on the set! I hope you'll be able to handle him."

"Elephants are extremely smart," Sam said, but before she could continue she was aware of another person coming toward them in the clearing.

The moonlight seemed to emphasize the woman's voluptuous figure. She was dressed in something sheer and flowing that left very little to the imagination. Sam felt her stomach knot in sudden apprehension, and she swallowed the lump of fear in her throat as Ryan loosened his hold on her and walked forward to greet the woman.

"Ryan, it's you!" The woman threw her arms around his neck and pulled his face to hers for a long, sensuous kiss. Sam could see her press her body against his. Was it her imagination, or did Ryan seem to pull away slightly? Or was it just what she wanted to see? But then they were close again; there was no moonlight visible between the two figures as they stood together. Sam heard the woman's breath escape in a soft sigh, saw her coil herself even closer to Ryan. Worst of all, now it seemed that Ryan wasn't resisting.

But what had she expected? Sam glanced away from the two of them. Surely his display of affection in the courtyard and later in the car had meant very little to a man like Ryan. She could have kicked herself for her ardent response. How could she have made herself so vulnerable to him? Why should he have any interest in her when the most beautiful actresses and models worked with him every day? There was nothing she could offer him that would compare. Sam looked down at her worn jeans and scuffed cowboy boots. Favorite clothes, worn many times—functional and comfortable, but clearly not feminine enough for a man like Ryan.

She glanced up again at the romantic little tableau. The two of them were talking softly, or rather the woman was talking and Ryan was listening attentively. Were they going to be rude enough to leave her standing there all night? Sam's anger began to build as she thought of the short notice she had given Jake, the long hours of her plane flight, the strain of her missing equipment. Ryan had no right to ignore her like this! She was getting paid and was a working member of this production. The least he could do was tell her where her bed was.

She cleared her throat noisily, and the woman jumped. Shading her eyes from the bright moonlight, she peered toward the edge of the clearing where Sam stood in the shadows.

"Darling, is there someone with you?" she asked petulantly.

Darling. Sam's stomach turned over as she heard the woman use the intimate expression. No, these two were certainly more than friends. She remembered Ryan in the Jaguar, claiming they had something special between them. He obviously had something special going with the entire female population.

She decided to take the situation into her own hands. "Ryan, could you show me where I can sleep tonight? We can talk in the morning about the animals. Right now I'm extremely tired." She knew she sounded curt, but she was too upset to care.

"I'm sorry, Sam. Come over here." Ryan motioned for her to join them. Sam walked uncertainly toward the cozy pair. Ryan kept his arm around the woman and put the other around Sam's shoulders.

"Helen McNair, meet our new animal trainer, Samantha Collins." Sam watched as he eyed both of the women, and she had a sudden suspicion that he was enjoying the entire situation immensely.

"How do you do." The actress's tone of voice was frosty, but she held out her perfectly manicured hand in a show of friendship.

"Fine, thank you. It's a pleasure to meet you. I've seen several of your films." Sam had to force the words out, but to her surprise they sounded sincere. *She's not much of an actress if she can't disguise her feelings,* she thought cattily.

"I think we'd better turn in." Ryan suddenly took control. "Sam needs to see the animals early in the morning, and I need *you* for a script consultation." Still keeping an arm around each woman, he began to walk toward the group of tents.

As they got closer Sam made out a large, expensive trailer. Somehow she wasn't surprised when Helen walked up its small steps and opened the door.

"Come by for a drink later, all right?" Her invitation was clearly for him alone. Sam lowered her eyes, pretending fascination with a loose thread on her jeans. She disliked this woman intensely.

"Not tonight, Helen. We've got an early call. I'll see you at breakfast." He turned around and walked away, his arm still around Sam.

After the trailer door closed and they were some distance away, Ryan chuckled. "What do you think of her?" he asked.

Sam stared at him, incredulous. He was asking her opinion of a woman who obviously had some intimate connection with his past, and probably his present. But she would be working on the movie for at least the next six weeks. Much as she hated to, Sam decided to be diplomatic.

"She's extremely beautiful. Her eyes are really turquoise, aren't they?"

"Yes. But sometimes she uses contacts to heighten their color on film."

"Oh." Sam fell silent for a moment, then decided to try for another compliment. It couldn't hurt her to be a good sport.

"What color is her hair? It looked auburn. It's absolutely stunning on film."

Ryan laughed, a low, amused sound. "Lady Clairol." At Sam's look of indignation he responded, "Most of the women in my life have very few secrets from me."

He was teasing her again! But about this? She couldn't understand his attitude. Abruptly Sam decided she'd better get to bed or she wouldn't be able to cope with anything. Movie people were beyond her comprehension.

"I'd like to get some sleep," she informed him quietly. "Where should I put my sleeping bag?"

He stopped walking, and Sam noticed they were in front of a large tent. Her glance went from the structure to Ryan's face, then back to the tent again. As comprehension dawned on her she shook her head and backed away from him. "Oh, no. Ryan!"

His eyes were dancing with suppressed amusement. "I'm afraid so, Samantha. There wasn't much time to make accommodations for another woman on such short notice, so tonight you'll have to sleep in my tent."

Chapter Five

Samantha looked up at Ryan in horror. Regaining her composure, she crossed her arms and glared up at his amused expression. "That's totally impossible," she told him calmly. "And if this is your idea of a practical joke, I don't think it's a very funny one."

"It's no joke. I simply forgot about making arrangements."

Sam turned away from him. "I'm sure I can sleep with Helen in her trailer. She can't object to my using her floor for one evening."

Ryan laughed. "You obviously don't know Miss McNair very well. She's never been one to share with another woman."

Sam swallowed, trying to clear the tension in her throat. "Then give me my sleeping bag and I'll sleep outside."

All traces of amusement left his face. "I don't think you want to do that. The scorpions could make your evening very unpleasant."

Sam paled. She hadn't considered that she was in unfamiliar country, and that conditions were different than they would be in California. She also remembered reading about scorpions in a class on venomous snakes and other dangerous animals. They were nasty creatures, and their bites could range from the uncomfortable to the deadly.

"You win. But I'm going in there to sleep. That's all."

"You weren't so sure of that in the car this evening."

Damn the man! Was he going to liven up his days on location by making her bear the brunt of his humor? What angered Sam even more, he was right. Until she had seen him embrace Helen, she had thought per- haps— No, she *had* wanted him to make love to her.

"I changed my mind. Take it or leave it," she said through gritted teeth.

Ryan smiled at her. His easy masculine charm caught her off-balance once again. Why was the man so damn good-looking? Would she be able to resist him if she spent the night in his tent?

"I'll take it," he replied. "Come on, let's get your stuff."

It took only one trip to the car to transfer Sam's suit- case and box of animal supplies to the tent. Once inside, Ryan lit a lantern and sat back in a canvas director's chair.

"Make yourself at home," he said as he spread his arms in a gesture encompassing the entire space.

And there wasn't much to it. With barely enough room for Ryan to stand at the tallest point, the tent had obviously been designed for two people, but two people who wanted to spend their evenings in close contact.

Sam took off her boots, then stopped. She stared at him in amazement. Was he just going to sit there while she undressed? She found her voice.

"Would you mind going outside while I change?"

His brows shot up in amazement. "It's awfully cold outside. And besides, it's nothing I haven't seen be- fore."

Sam stifled the impulse to laugh. The man was im- possible. But her first emotion was quickly replaced by a second. She didn't want to think what might happen if Ryan began to make love to her while she was partially clothed. She had made herself vulnerable enough this evening.

''Then could you at least turn your back?'' She wasn't able to hide the slight tremor in her voice, and she was certain that Ryan noticed, because he stopped teasing her.

He stood up and turned away without a word.

Sam pulled off her jeans and sweat shirt, then shed her underwear. It felt strangely erotic to be undressed behind Ryan's back. Ignoring the images that flashed through her mind for just a split second, she reached for her suitcase. Digging around inside, she cursed herself for bringing only skimpy nightwear. Ryan's voice made her jump.

''It's too humid to sleep clothed most nights. There's a cotton blanket over to the left on top of my bag. You can wrap it around you.''

Sam found the pale blue blanket, and decided it offered more coverage than anything she had brought with her. She wrapped it around herself sarong-style, tucking the ends in carefully. Then she reached down in to her suitcase and pulled out her hairbrush. Passing it swiftly through her hair, she put it away.

''You can turn around now.''

He turned, and she noticed his eyes, dark with familiar passion. His glance swept her from her bare shoulders to her feet, the look as intimate as a caress. She looked away, once again unnerved. This was going to be harder than she thought.

''Where am I sleeping?'' There wasn't much room on the floor, with Ryan's sleeping bag unzipped and spread out.

''We'll have to rig up some sort of barrier between us.'' His eyes seemed to glint wickedly, or did she imagine their expression in the flickering lamplight? ''Even *I* can't promise what would happen if we were close together on the floor with you looking like that.''

''Like what?'' Something deep inside her wanted to push him a little and test his reaction.

He looked at her, and she was left with no doubts as to what he was referring to. Though he made no move to come near her, Sam felt as if he were visually undressing her, exploring every secret place on her body. She clutched the blanket tightly around her and turned back to the task at hand.

She watched as he unrolled a small army blanket, then retrieved a piece of string and stretched it across the top of the tent. Securing it at either end, he draped the blanket over it. Sam watched the play of his muscles under the thin cotton T-shirt. Her thoughts wandered back unbidden to the courtyard in San Juan, remembering how his warm skin had felt under her restless hands.

She came out of her reverie as he touched her bare shoulder.

"It's all set. You just have to lie down."

She hesitated for just a moment before she felt his hand, warm and firm against the small of her back. Their faces were very close; she could feel his breath against her cheek.

"I had no idea female animal trainers were as passionate as you are." He picked up a strand of her soft bright hair and twined it around his fingers. "If I had known"—he smiled wickedly—"I would have hired you months ago."

"Ryan, you're getting the wrong idea. What happened out in the courtyard—" She paused, searching for the right words. "I think I was just tired and overwrought. That's all." Even in the dim light of the lantern, now that she was getting used to it, she noticed his eyes were smoldering ominously. "What I wanted to say is—I don't want you to get the wrong idea about me. I'm here to work. That's all."

The silence stretched between them. Sam grew more uncomfortable by the minute. She shifted away from his hand uneasily.

"I think I'll go to bed now. What side do you want?"

"You little liar."

"What?" She could feel her pulse beating in her throat.

"You're a liar." He stepped away for just a second, his body as graceful as a panther's. Sam watched him as he peeled off his clothing and reached over to turn off the lantern. Then he was back, holding her against his chest. She felt the rough hair on his body teasing her bare shoulders.

"Damn it, Ryan! I'll scream."

"No, you won't." His head was close above hers. "I've never taken a woman against her will and I don't intend to start now!" He laced his fingers through her hair and brought her mouth up to his.

Oh, God, she thought, the instant before their lips met. *Jake was right.*

Ryan was clearly a master in the art of lovemaking. Sam had been prepared to fight him, but what happened took her completely by surprise. Though Ryan held her captive with a firm hand, she couldn't have asked for a more tender lover. His lips covered her cheeks, her eyelids, the curve of her neck. He kissed her brow gently, then lowered his lips to hers. She turned her face away, but he captured her mouth. She clenched her teeth, but the minute his lips touched hers, she shuddered in response and felt herself opening to the sweetness of his lovemaking.

Her blanket was beginning to fall away. She made a desperate attempt to pull it tighter, but Ryan took her hands in his and placed them around his neck. She grasped the muscles in his shoulders, the smooth hot feel of them her only reality in a spinning vortex where sensation was rapidly becoming her master.

The blanket fell away. Sam felt his hands on her body, teasing, tormenting, giving her small temptations of the ecstasy awaiting should she choose to give herself to him. Blindly, instinctively, she told him of her feelings with her body, accepting his caresses, moving her hips so her body was more accessible. One of his hands trailed down her bare spine, sending a wave of fire through her blood. She felt his large hand move up, then touch her own and release it from around his shoulders before he placed it intimately on his body.

She drew her mouth away from his and gasped softly, leaning against him.

"Can you feel how much I want you?" His words were a husky whisper.

In answer, she tightened her fingers on his shoulder. Shyly, with her other hand, she touched him gently, heard him groan. It excited her, this power she had over him. Paul had never made her feel this way. But Ryan found her desirable. Right now she didn't want to think of anything beyond what was happening in this darkened tent.

She felt his hands on her hips, then he was urging her down onto the sleeping bag. She knelt down, sighing with pleasure as he lay beside her. No other man had ever made her feel this way. She was unprepared for the feelings Ryan evoked in her and powerless to stop him. Locked away in a tiny corner of the tropics, alone in his darkened tent, Sam felt as if their lovemaking was the most natural and desirable thing on earth.

She could feel his sleeping bag on her back as the weight of his body pressed into hers. Then he was on his side, and his hands were making featherlike caresses across her breasts. He touched the sensitive skin around her nipples but avoided the areas of heightened sensation. She felt like taking his hand and guiding it, but she liked the way sensations were building inside her, slowly and inexorably. His fingers stroked her breasts and chest with light, soft movements, and she bit her lip to prevent herself from crying out with pleasure. She could feel her breasts becoming more and more tender, her nipples hardening with desire.

Yet he kept up the delicious love play until she was half out of her mind. Finally she reached for his hand and guided it to one sensitive peak.

His thumb and finger pinched it lightly, and Sam buried her face in his chest, groaning. Then his fingers lightly flicked over the sensitive tip, then his mouth. As she felt his warm, moist tongue lick her gently, then felt his lips tenderly close over her aroused flesh, she forgot her reserve and moaned softly.

The slight stubble of his beard scratched the delicate skin between her breasts as he moved his attention to the second breast. It seemed to swell even more at his insistent lips as he gently tugged the sensitive nipple to full arousal. He took his time, enjoying the ardent response she was giving him. This time, when he slid up to kiss her, she twined her arms tightly around his neck.

His sensual mouth explored hers fully with fierce delight, his tongue warm inside her mouth, his lips firm and insistent. Sam moved the palms of her hands over his thick hair, pulling him closer to her. He seemed hungry for what she could give him, and Sam was far beyond the point of reason. Her body pleaded for sensual fulfillment in a way she had never experienced before. She kissed him back and her full response blazed between them, passion completely out of control.

She felt his weight above her, felt the fullness of his desire pressing against her stomach. He bit her earlobe gently, bringing her out of her haze of passion.

"Tell me," he whispered.

"What?" she murmured, her palms against his lower back. She loved the feel of his muscles beneath his smooth, hot skin.

"That you want me," he answered, his voice thick with desire.

She turned her face away, suddenly shy. He cupped her face in his hands and turned her to meet his gaze.

"There's nothing wrong with a woman telling a man she wants him," he whispered. He kissed her again, teasing her sensitive lips. "Tell me. I want to hear it."

Sam felt the last vestiges of her icy wall of reserve begin to break. Tears of longing and fear came into her eyes.

He studied her, all the while caressing her feverish body. "Are you afraid?"

She looked down at his chest and nodded.

He cupped her chin and raised her head so their eyes met. His brilliant blue gaze narrowed as he studied her face. "Are you a virgin?"

She shook her head, trying to keep her innermost thoughts at bay. *In so many ways I am.* She closed her eyes and swallowed.

"Can you tell me?" he urged, his hands smoothing the tears from her face.

She nodded. "I want you, Ryan. I want you to make love to me."

He kissed her again, this time so gently and intimately that Sam felt fresh tears start in her eyes. She felt his hands slide over her stomach, then lower still. He eased her thighs apart, touching her gently, almost reverently. She felt his muscles tighten in response to her soft caresses, and he moved to cover her and join her in total sensation.

But then he stopped. Sam was immediately aware of the stillness of his body. She moved her hands over his back and thighs, trying to pull him closer to her. She could have sobbed in frustration; she was mindless for the moment, unable to stop herself or still her body's instinctual movements.

Ryan's hand caressed her hair as if she were a child, gently, so tenderly that she quivered. He bent his head and kissed her quickly on the lips.

And then Sam was aware of the noise outside.

First she heard undergrowth snapping, then uneven footsteps. And then an all-too-familiar voice.

"Ryan? Where are you, Ryan?" The words were slightly slurred. Helen wasn't drunk; just high enough to be happy.

Ryan covered Sam's mouth with his hand. Her heart leaped with relief. He wanted Helen to leave, he wanted to be with her! She lay still.

"Ryan! Come out and join me for a little drink." There was a pause. Sam could hear the wind sighing through the palm trees. She was amazed no one else was jolted out of sleep by the racket this woman was making. But perhaps none of the crew wanted to get involved.

"Ryan! Where are you? You promised— If I catch you with—" The rest of the sentence trailed off. There was more crashing. It came closer to the tent.

"Damn!" Ryan got to his feet noiselessly and pulled on his jeans, then his boots. Sam felt tears of frustration and anger fill her eyes.

He reached down quickly to give her another kiss and whispered, "I'm sorry." She clung to his hand, but then he was gone, and she could hear him catching up with Helen.

"Ryan! *There* you are...." Sam turned over on the sleeping bag and reached for the blanket. The tent was dark; Ryan had zipped the door shut behind him. She was alone in the darkness as she heard them walk away.

Her tears came quickly, born of frustration and something else. Without Ryan at her side, Sam began to view their physical relationship in an entirely different light. How different it was when he was there, when her instincts cried out and urged her to acknowledge what was beautiful and awe-inspiring in its intensity. But the aftermath left a taste bitter as ashes in her mouth.

The truth was, Ryan would never belong to one woman, and Sam could never consider giving her heart to a man who wasn't faithful. It had happened to her once and she had been unaware until the last day of her marriage. The pain had been overwhelming, but it had cleansed her. It had made her realize that if she couldn't live with certain standards, she had a right to aspire to others. She was a firm believer in fidelity.

And Ryan was an incredibly handsome man in the midst of beauty every day of his working life. At his age, with his habits, it would be hard for him to change.

I don't want to have an affair with him, she thought bitterly. *I want to be special.* She pulled the thin blanket tighter around her.

But perhaps he went outside merely to help Helen back to her trailer and get her settled for the night. At this new thought her spirits lifted. He had certainly seemed like he didn't want to leave her. Perhaps it was only a matter of time before he would come back.

She pushed her hair up and away from her face and neck. Though the tropical air was soft and fragrant, it was also humid. She touched her damp arm gently and remembered the way their bodies had come together, the light film of perspiration making them almost become one. Almost, but not quite. . .

She rolled over and punched the sleeping bag angrily. Where was he? Certainly it wouldn't take him that long to walk across the clearing to Helen's trailer and deposit her there! *I sound like a jealous wife,* she thought tiredly. But then she remembered what she was—a possible mistress, not a life partner.

Her restless mind flitted back to the moments before Helen's untimely interruption, then angrily pushed the images away. What was the matter with her that she could become so quickly involved with a man who clearly didn't share her feelings?

And she was sure that he didn't. He would have been back sooner. How could he leave her, alone and vulnerable in the dark, after all they had shared? Hadn't the entire experience been as intense for him? He couldn't possibly have faked his responses.

Her thoughts latched on to the one thought she had been unconsciously avoiding since Ryan's departure. Perhaps the truth of the matter was that Ryan was only capable of physical passion, and emotional love was something he wasn't able to handle. The media certainly gave credence to that thought.

She curled herself into a tight ball on top of his sleeping bag. Starting tomorrow, she would make him aware she was there to work, and not open to the idea of a casual affair. If he chose to fire her, it wouldn't be the first time she'd lost a job to sexual discrimination.

But what hurt the most was that she had trusted Ryan. And he had betrayed that trust by leaving her to go with Helen. If his love affairs were that casual, she wanted no part of them.

Unable to control her thoughts, she drifted into a troubled sleep, but visions of a dark-haired man with flashing eyes haunted her until well into the early morning when she woke.

Chapter Six

Sam peered out cautiously from the flaps in front of Ryan's tent. She certainly didn't want to run into him this morning. It had been bad enough that he'd never returned last night. Satisfied no one was up and about yet, she zipped the door behind her and stood up.

Now what? she thought uncomfortably. God forbid anyone should do anything to make her first few days at work easier. She cast a sleepy eye over to a clump of tents on the other side of the clearing and realized for the first time that Ryan seemed to have deliberately pitched his as far away from everyone else as possible. *The better to seduce you with, my dear,* she thought bitterly, and started to walk in the direction she thought Ryan had pointed out the other night.

"They're over on the far end of another clearing," she murmured to herself, remembering what Ryan had said. Her eyes moved restlessly, hoping to pick up some kind of visual clue.

Suddenly her natural sense of humor and basically optimistic outlook caught up with her. "You're doing great, kiddo," she said to herself, sighing. "The great animal trainer can't even find the darn animals." No sooner were the words out of her mouth when she heard a shrill squeal. Trust the baby elephant to wake up before anyone else. She broke into a run in the direction of the sound.

As she stepped into the dense jungle from the edge of the clearing, Sam had to marvel at the intense beauty of her surroundings. Foliage was so thick that, though the sun was rising quickly, it was still cool and shaded where she walked. She bent several small branches conspicuously so that she'd be able to find her way back.

It was exciting to walk through virgin territory, to feel as if she were the sole explorer on some fantastic tropical paradise. Looking up, she recognized gigantic rubber plants fighting for space with tall banana trees. Huge clusters of the yellow fruit grew high up, out of reach. Occasionally she spotted vivid hibiscus, and once or twice an orchid, or an entire bunch of the exotic flowers growing in profusion.

She stumbled onto a path and decided it had to lead to the animals. Breaking into a run, she wove her way in and out of the silent jungle.

When she emerged into another clearing, she saw huge cages on the far side. Sam slowed to a walk. She wanted to disturb the animals as little as possible, because this way she could observe and assess them individually. She wanted to know what she was up against.

The first cage contained the white lion Jake had told her about. He was asleep on a makeshift ledge that someone had built on one side of his cage. His coloring made him unusually beautiful, and Sam noticed he didn't seem to be too thin. As he heard her approach he opened one eye and grunted lazily. Sam smiled. He looked like he'd be no trouble. "Your holiday's over, boy," she called as she made her way to the next cage.

What she saw disturbed her. A large black-and-orange tiger paced nervously in his small area, and she watched as his restless movements caused him to knock over his water bucket. She stayed a fair distance from the cage and continued to observe. He snarled softly at nothing, and Sam frowned.

A bird sailed through the early-morning calm and called raucously. The tiger stiffened and flattened his ears. He crouched and snarled.

Sam felt an instant of unease. Jake had mentioned a tiger, but this one didn't seem to be in workable shape. She decided to walk up close to the cage.

As soon as the animal saw her, his eyes widened and fixed on her. With a roar that shattered the early morning, he threw himself against the steel bars of the cage, thrusting his forepaw through a gap in the enclosure and lashing at her, his claws extended.

Sam was shocked. Not only did the animal seem to have a mean temperament, but he wasn't declawed, which was standard practice for working cats. She stepped behind a large rubber tree and, once she was out of the big cat's sight, she peeked around and saw he had resumed his pacing.

She started out in the direction of the other cage, taking care to keep out of the tiger's field of vision. She'd have to speak to Ryan as soon as possible about having one of the tigers from Jake's compound shipped to location. There was no way she'd even attempt to work with this one.

She noticed the small chimpanzee immediately and approached the cage warily after her encounter with the tiger. Chimps were tricky anyway; she had heard of one of the girls at the compound being grabbed through the bars and held against the cage until someone heard her screams. They were stronger than they looked and almost too smart for their own good.

This one watched her as cautiously as she watched him, then began to make small hooting noises. *So far so good,* she thought. Some of them, if they disliked you, would throw things at you and scream. This one seemed even-tempered and just a little curious.

She sat outside the cage for some time until the small animal came up to the bars and stared back. She advanced toward him slowly, glad he didn't turn and run or try anything mischievous.

"Hi, sweetie." She spoke softly and almost laughed at the human expression in the soft brown eyes. She stood up slowly, not wanting to frighten the animal, and stretched her sore muscles. She hadn't slept on a dirt floor for a long time.

It looked like she and the chimp were going to be good friends. The little primate watched her as she walked away and it made mournful sounds. *It's probably starved for human company,* Sam thought. If she could find any notes from the previous trainers, she'd start working with him in the afternoon.

Her last stop was to see the elephants. They turned out to be her favorites. There were two of them, a large Indian female and her baby. The little one squealed when he saw her, and Sam couldn't help but laugh when she saw him, remembering Ryan's remarks about the trouble he'd caused. Elephants were extremely intelligent animals. Sam had always enjoyed working with them.

The mother was chained in the usual fashion, by the left front and the right hind leg. Both animals were surrounded by a makeshift wooden fence. The baby obviously wouldn't go anywhere without its mother. The small elephant's head came up to Sam's shoulder, and she judged him to be close to one and a half years old. Elephant calves nursed for two years, so this little one would still be dependent on his mother.

She approached them slowly. The older elephant added her rumbles to the baby's squeals. They both began to reach out with their trunks, and Sam felt tears burn behind her eyelids. She had felt so alone this morning. But these large animals welcomed her in their own way and dispelled her feelings of loneliness.

She noticed a clump of bananas that had fallen from a nearby tree and, walking over, pulled two pieces of fruit loose and peeled them. The larger elephant was silent, watching her and swaying gently. The baby squealed louder, and Sam laughed again. If anyone back at camp was still asleep when she returned, she'd be surprised.

"Here, you little monster!" She put the piece of peeled fruit in her palm, and the small elephant's trunk snaked out and snatched it from her hand, then he swiftly stuffed it into his small mouth. The large dark eyes gleamed. Sam felt a swift rush of joy. No matter how troubled she was, animals had always been a source of comfort and solace to her. She could never understand how anyone could dislike them.

She peeled another piece of fruit and was feeding it to the mother elephant when the little one reached out with his trunk and began to pat her back.

"Stop it!" She turned around and backed away, watching as the small trunk slowly descended. "I'm on to you." She continued to talk to the baby. "Ryan tells me you're always into something, so you won't surprise me by doing anything." She reached over and pulled at the small ear gently, and the little elephant sighed.

"My biggest danger is, I'll probably wind up spoiling you rotten!" Sam muttered as she peeled another piece of the ripe fruit. "Don't they feed you?" she wondered aloud as she watched the baby elephant's rapid movement from trunk to mouth.

These two weren't going to be a problem at all. Sam dusted off her hands on the seat of her jeans and glanced at her watch, then glanced again. It couldn't be seven thirty already! She'd been up with the sun, and down here within half an hour. But the time always did seem to race when she was with animals.

"So long, you little peanut!" she called to the baby, and began to jog back toward the tents. She gave the tiger cage a wide berth.

As she entered the other clearing she was aware of laughter and voices coming from the direction of Helen's trailer. Glancing over, she saw a small makeshift picnic table was set up outside, and the smells of coffee and hot chocolate made her realize how hungry she was. The last thing she had eaten was her lunch in San Juan with Ryan.

She wasn't really sure what to do. She could see Ryan, but his head was turned away from her. Just the sight of his dark hair and broad shoulders made her heartbeat quicken. What could she possibly say to him after what had happened last night?

Helen looked up and saw her, then looked away, pointedly ignoring her presence. She had just about decided to head back to Ryan's tent and wait for him when a strange voice broke through the breakfast chatter.

"My God, it's Eve, straight from the Garden of Eden! What a lovely creature you are, sweetheart!" The slim blond man turned toward the others around the table. "Look at those cheekbones! My God! Honey, you were made for the silver screen!" He talked in explosive sentences, his hands moving constantly as he spoke, and Sam liked him immediately.

"Hi." She walked toward the group, but her eyes held those of the young man who had hailed her. She smiled. "Not Eve. Samantha. Samantha Collins." She extended her hand.

"Don Hayward. Are you another actress? Say that you are," he rushed on dramatically. "I can't wait to get my hands on your face. I'm the resident makeup artist," he added by way of explanation.

"I wouldn't say artist," Helen called from her end of the table. Sam drew in a breath, shocked by the woman's obvious rudeness.

"Honey, I am an artist. But I'd have to be God himself to repair your face after you've had an evening with your bottle." Don tossed off this remark as easily as the others, not noticing the ugly red stain that began to creep up Helen's neck.

Sam laughed. She couldn't stop herself. Ryan didn't seem to be amused.

"Okay, that's enough." He pushed his chair away from the table and stood up. "Sam?" He was offering it to her.

"Thank you." She sat down, suddenly conscious of all eyes on her.

"Come on, Ryan, confess. Who is she, and what does she mean to you?" Don winked at her conspiratorially, and somehow she wasn't offended by his brash manner. He was dressed in tight Calvin Klein jeans and a bright turquoise muscle shirt with the word *heaven* splashed across it in large letters. His thick blond hair was cut close to his head, and his blue eyes twinkled merrily as if life were some great cosmic joke he found endlessly amusing.

"Tell us, dear, how you enslaved the great stone face over there." Don leaned on his elbows and pretended to be hanging on her every upcoming word.

He was just too much. Sam started to laugh again. "I'm not an actress," she confessed. "I'm an animal trainer. Ryan brought me down here to see to the animals." She sat back and waited for the reaction she knew was inevitable.

"Wow." Don was shocked into silence, but not for long. "Do you want a cup of coffee, sweetheart?" At her look of disbelief he explained. "I know it's getting hot, but Puerto Rican coffee is terrific. Normally it's so strong, it's used after siesta, but Ryan makes sure we have it every morning so we can wake up." Before she could answer he poured her a large mug, passed her cream and sugar, and handed her a croissant.

Sam took a bite of the buttery roll. Don continued talking to her. "Maybe bwana here has finally met his match." He inclined his head toward Ryan. Sam looked up, doubtful of his reaction. To her astonishment Ryan was smiling, and the lines around his eyes and mouth were more pronounced than ever.

"Maybe bwana would like to get a little work done," Ryan replied. But he didn't seem angry.

"Well, boss, I'd say she's certainly a sight for sore eyes around this place, but then again, how would I know?" He grinned, and Sam knew she had found a friend. Perhaps things weren't going to be so bad after all.

She was in the middle of a bite of croissant when Ryan's question caught her attention. "What did you think of the animals?" he asked her quietly.

She glanced up at him. "How did you know where I was?"

"I happened to see you cross toward the trail when that blasted elephant started to make noise."

"I thought someone was ravishing the little pachyderm," Don remarked.

She smiled, not at all upset that Ryan had been watching her. "He's a doll," she said enthusiastically, "and so is his mother. They act like they've been around a lot of people. They should be no trouble."

"Is there any way to shut him up in the morning?" Helen asked crossly. There was obviously no love lost there on the animals. "We were trying to sleep." She was talking to Sam, but her brilliant turquoise eyes were on Ryan.

At the plural we Sam dropped her eyes and studied her hand curled around her mug. "I'll try to think of something." Though she had resigned herself to Ryan's and Helen's affair, it hurt to hear her suspicions given credence.

"What about the lion?" Ryan asked.

"He seemed pretty sleepy, a little lazy, but nothing out of the ordinary." Sam thought of something else and quickly asked, "Did any of the other trainers leave notes?"

Ryan thought for a moment. "I think so. I'll see if I can dig them up. Come back to my tent after breakfast."

"Watch him, Sam, Ryan's always had a soft spot for blondes," Don teased her, and Sam decided the time was right to let her feelings be known.

She smiled sweetly, completely contradicting what she felt inside. "Not this blonde," she said softly.

Don whistled. "A challenge, Ryan! You've never been one to give up without a fight."

Sam could feel Ryan's gaze boring into her, and she deliberately took as long as possible with the last few sips of her coffee. She was beginning to enjoy all this in an extremely perverse way. She could tease and fight and stick up for herself along with all the rest. No one was going to do her in emotionally.

Helen was watching the two of them closely, but when Sam made her announcement, she smiled.

"What a charming child you are, Samantha. We may just become friends after all."

Don rolled his eyes comically, and Samantha almost choked on the last of her coffee.

"Is there anything else I should know about the animals?" Ryan's tone was soft, but Sam noticed that his eyes were hard.

"I can't work with the tiger."

At Ryan's look of disbelief she pressed her point. "His responses seem a bit pathological. I don't feel I can trust him to behave predictably. I'd like to call Jake today and send for one of the tigers on the compound. Filming shouldn't be delayed." As the thought suddenly struck her, she turned in her chair and addressed the rest of the people seated at the table. "And for safety's sake, I don't want anyone going near the tiger cage. I think he's potentially dangerous."

Don threw up his hands. "You've got *my* promise. I can't even housebreak my dog!"

Helen was enjoying Sam's confession, and as soon as Helen started to speak, Sam knew her little remark about "being friends" had been for show.

"What kind of a trainer are you," she purred, "if you can't deal with a tiger?" She looked around the table. "Am I correct in saying my big scene takes place with that animal?" She turned to Sam. "Just what are you planning to do?" She directed her next remark to Ryan. "I thought you said this"—her next word held a note of disbelief—"*trainer* knew what she was doing!"

Ryan ran his hands through his thick hair in exasperation. "You're sure you can't work with the animal?" he asked.

"Yes. And it's within my rights as an animal trainer to refuse," she replied evenly, struggling to keep a hold on her temper. If she had disliked Helen before, she despised her now.

"I've got an idea," interjected Don. "Let's put Helen in the cage with Iago. We can improvise the entire scene." He smiled up at the actress sweetly.

"You bastard," she hissed, her face beginning to splotch again with angry patches of red. "You're nothing but a—"

"Uh-uh, Helen, sticks and stones—"

"We'll send for another tiger, then. If you can pick the one you want from the compound, how soon can we start filming?"

"Whenever you want. If Jake will let me take Sultan, I'm sure he'll adapt quickly. I've raised him from a cub." Sam was pleased. Ryan might not care for her as a woman, but she could see he was beginning to respect her judgment as a trainer.

"All right." Ryan put his hands on the back of Sam's chair. "Miss Collins and I are going to have a short discussion, and we'll meet back here in about an hour for script consultation." He pulled out her chair without asking and began to walk toward his tent.

Sam's stomach tightened as she watched him, the line of his back rigid and proud. She had a sudden flash of intuition that told her their little talk was going to have nothing to do with the movie. Squaring her shoulders, she smoothed her hair off her face with a steady hand.

"Good-bye, Samantha. I'll see you in an hour." Don stood up and stretched. "I'd like to work on your face sometime."

"It's a date. Thanks, Don. I enjoyed meeting you." She smiled at him, but she felt her expression fade as she turned toward Ryan's tent.

As she started to walk after him, she almost regretted the smart remark she'd made at breakfast. She could never win a battle with him. Sam felt unnerved by the way Ryan seemed to be able to tell what she was thinking and anticipate many of her emotions. She didn't pursue this train of thought; didn't ask herself why he kept such a close eye on her. It was unsettling enough that he did.

She swallowed against the sudden dryness in her throat as her heart began to beat rapidly. Perhaps this meeting was only a professional matter. Sam wanted to believe that. But even as the thought crossed her mind she visualized Ryan's blazing blue eyes and the way he had scrutinized her at the table. No, it would be more than business. She was sure of that.

She barely noticed her surroundings as she placed one booted foot in front of the other, crushing thick jungle foliage underneath them. There were varied sounds in the rain forest this morning. Though the small coqui were already asleep, birds chattered high in the trees and flashed overhead, bright spots of color against the lush green treetops. Bamboo clicked and rustled in the soft sea-scented breeze.

And suddenly she was there. The tent looked larger in direct sunlight than it had the previous evening. The dark blue material stretched tautly over the tent poles, and Sam noticed that it was worn and stained in some places. It looked as if it were actually Ryan's tent, not merely a prop lent out by the studio. As she studied the structure fleeting thoughts of the previous evening's erotic adventures assailed her senses. She bit her lower lip in vexation.

"Ryan, are you there?" Her question came out more sharply than she had intended.

In answer, she saw the front flaps of the tent open, and Ryan stepped out, bare to the waist. His muscled chest was tanned the color of fine teak, and the sprinkling of curly hair had been bleached by the sun.

Sam looked down quickly at the toe of her right boot. Her nails dug into her palms as she attempted to steady herself. She could remember the feel of his chest under her restless fingers.

"You wanted to see me?" Thank God her voice was steady.

"Yes. Look at me."

She raised her eyes to his face, but Ryan's expression was guarded.

"I think we need to talk about last night." His voice gave no clue as to any feeling on his part. Why was he always so damn controlled, while she was just the opposite?

"About what?" She was deliberately obtuse, stalling for time.

"Stop it, Sam. Quit avoiding the issue." Ryan's expression blazed to life, his eyes cold, his mouth compressed.

"You clearly made your choice last night, so why are you even bothering with me today?"

His eyes narrowed and his lips curved into a smile. "You sound like the jealous wife," he challenged.

"Me? Over you? Not a chance!" Sam crossed her arms and glared across the clearing at him. She almost regretted her hasty words as she saw the tired lines around his eyes and mouth, but then her resolve tightened. He must have had a rough night!

"Do you like Helen?" he asked suddenly.

She paused for a second, then rushed to speak before she felt the need to qualify or soften her feelings. "No, I don't. She's deliberately cruel. And she manipulates everyone to her best advantage."

"Good," Ryan replied. "I don't care for her either."

"But you went to her last night!" Sam exclaimed, her stomach tightening. Was he trying to fool her? He was certainly aware of her response to him. Was he so self-assured that he thought he could use her feelings to disarm and control her? She wouldn't let him! "I don't believe you," she stated flatly.

"Sam," he began, running a hand through his hair in exasperation, "I— Oh, hell!" He grabbed her by the wrist and pulled her up against his body. Bending his head, he gave her a swift kiss. "Come with me for just a second." His expression was more open and vulnerable than she had ever seen.

"What? Ryan, I can't—" She stopped as she saw the vulnerable expression on his face gradually replaced by coolness.

"I didn't think you would understand. I expected you to pretend not to." His voice was filled with contempt as he released her from his embrace. He turned away. "Let's get back to the others."

Sam stood watching the firm, rigid column of his back. What had he meant by that last remark? His swift, uncompromising assessment of her as a woman unable to take emotional chances stung. Part of her deep inside feared that it was true. Had part of her died during the end of her marriage and been silenced forever? Was she capable of taking *any* sort of risk?

Though every rational thought warned her against giving in to his request, she ignored them. Placing a hand on his shoulder, she gently touched the smooth warm skin.

"Ryan?"

He turned back toward her, and Sam saw a hopeful warmth in his eyes. She was amazed that she had this much power over him. They stood together for a moment, as if both realized what a huge step this was for their relationship. Sam took a deep breath, trying to still the fluttering in her stomach.

"Let's go." He took her hand.

She walked with him around the tent, and then the tropical jungle closed over both of them. Ryan followed a small trail that wove through the dense vegetation. Sam stayed close to him, watching the muscles in his bare back ripple as he moved. She had no idea where they were going. It was enough to be with him.

They stepped from the trail into a clearing. A feathery waterfall cascaded over a smooth rock face. Small amounts of sunlight made the treetops a pale, translucent green. In the warm, humid air tropical flowers bloomed like a profusion of soft velvet jewels. She saw clusters of twenty or more delicate orchids on a single stem. Each branch held only one color group, but there were many clusters—pale yellow to brilliant salmon to a pink so delicate, it was almost white, to a vivid deep purple. Though the orchids gave off no fragrance, there were enough colors and smells from the other tropical plant life to provide a feast for the senses.

"Do you like it?" he asked softly.

She nodded, not wanting to disturb the moment with conversation. Not yet. The only sounds were those of water rushing over stone and leaves rustling in the wind. The few birdcalls seemed muted and far away.

Sam was aware of Ryan's fingers tightening, holding her hand more closely. She felt a sudden urge to wrench free, but breathing deeply of the moist, sweet air, she calmed herself.

"How did you ever find this place?"

Ryan smiled. "I always go on long walks after each day of shooting. One afternoon after a particularly bad day I just called a halt to everything and took this walk." He glanced up at the treetops, squinting against the faint light. "It's like a rest for the soul to come here."

Sam shivered. His thumb was circling the inside of her palm with lazy, sensual movements. She felt a sudden, unbidden urge to open herself up to these new sensations, to drown herself in the sensuality of the man beside her. Just as quickly her instinct for self-preservation took over.

Gently disengaging her hand from his, she walked over to the small pool at the bottom of the waterfall. Her back to Ryan, she concentrated on the hidden depths of the water.

After a time she turned to face him. "Why did you bring me here?"

He was standing only a few feet away, his thumbs hooked in the belt loops of his faded jeans. He seemed to be studying her when suddenly he spoke.

"I'm damn tired of being interrupted when we're together. No one knows where we are."

She felt her heart begin to race. Helen had interrupted them last night. But there was no one now. Only the water, the trees, and the tropical flowers. They could have been in paradise.

"I want you, Samantha." He spoke quietly, but his words sounded loud in the silence of the clearing.

She stepped back just a fraction. "And do you always get what you want?"

"Not always. But this time I'm planning on making a special effort." He began to walk toward her.

"No!" She darted to her left and circled the pool, moving to the opposite side of the clearing.

He eyed her, looking as if he were curious about her response. "You're a fascinating woman, Samantha. You're obviously attracted to me and yet you deny your feelings every time." His statement wasn't arrogant, but simply an observation of the facts.

To her horror Sam felt tears stinging her eyes. "Perhaps it's because I don't want to join the ranks of all the women you've left behind!" The words were out before she could help herself.

"Ah, my reputation again, is that it?" His expression hardened, but he made no move to come closer. "You should know how the press exaggerates. All I have to do is have my picture taken with an attractive woman and the next thing I know I'm reading about my latest affair!" His tone was contemptuous.

"Helen isn't a photo!" Sam lashed out, then stopped, horrified at herself.

"Helen!" Ryan's expression was incredulous. "Helen and I?.... You think—" He began to laugh.

"Don't make fun of me!"

He walked over and took her arm, his amusement under control. "Sam, I'm not laughing at you, it's just that I can't believe you're jealous of Helen—there's no comparison between the two of you!"

She was aware of the touch of his hand on her upper arm. Determined not to be a fool and pull away, she met his eyes.

"Then why did you leave me?" she whispered, the

words barely making it past the ache in her throat. She was conscious of that peculiar tension in the air, and it intensified as Ryan pulled her closer, wrapping his muscular arms around her.

"Did you think I wanted to leave?" His voice was low and husky. Sam felt his chin rest on the top of her head. She held herself aloof, but as he continued to talk she felt herself begin to melt against him.

"Helen is a temperamental, manipulative, highly strung woman. Unfortunately, she's the star of this picture." He stroked her hair, and Sam felt strangely comforted. "She also has her good qualities. She has a marvelous sense of humor and can be very thoughtful. At times." As she began to pull away he lowered his hands and linked them around her waist, keeping her close to his body. "She's terrified, because she feels she's getting old. She's thirty-seven. The whole thing seems ridiculous to me. I'm only five years younger. But the movie industry is very cruel to older women." He brushed his lips against hers gently. "And I have to finish this picture and deal with the psyche of a woman who's terrified of growing old. Can you understand that?"

Sam nodded her head slowly. "But she'll never be happy about my being here," she murmured, remembering Helen's abrasive comments about her ability with the animals.

Ryan laughed, deep in his throat. "Honey, she's scared to death of you! You're everything she wishes she still was."

Sam tried to put herself in Helen's place, but was much too aware of the man next to her. His hands were open against her back, along her ribs. She felt him reach around and tilt her chin up for another quick kiss.

"I could stay here with you forever, but duty calls." He smacked her bottom playfully. "We've got a script session and we're already running late, but we have to talk about us. I'll see you at dinner, okay?''

She nodded. As she followed him on to the trail she took a quick glance back to the clearing, but her view was quickly obscured by foliage.

RYAN GLANCED UP from his full plate. He could barely discern the figures sitting at the table in the distance, but as he listened he heard Sam's laugh float toward him in the cool evening air. He smiled to himself.

Samantha and Don were sitting alone, and she seemed to be totally absorbed in the story he was telling her. Ryan could see Don's gestures silhouetted in the dim evening light. The lanterns would have to be lit soon, he thought.

He could see that she didn't notice him as he approached. He watched her facial expressions as she listened to Don's story and could feel the familiar stirrings of desire: the tightness of his muscles, the quickened pulse. His skin felt hot for just an instant in the cool tropical evening air. And even as he felt these stirrings, he was disgusted by the vulnerability of his responses. She was, after all, only a woman. Why did she have this power over him, and why was she steadily beginning to invade his thoughts?

He continued to watch her. Don had lit a lantern on top of the table, and her features were thrown into relief in the soft light. Her classical profile was disturbed just enough by the slight uptilt of her nose and the fullness of her mouth. Her slanted green eyes were half shut, lazy as a cat's.

He smiled slightly as she burst into laughter at the conclusion of Don's story. She lowered her face into her hands for just an instant, then looked up. As she did their glances met and all expressions of amusement left her face.

Ryan felt his chest tighten with anger. Why did she have to get that damn wary look on her face whenever their eyes met? Before he could think any further he placed his plate beside her half-empty one and sat down beside her.

"What was so funny?" he asked, trying to keep his tone of voice soft. He didn't want her running away into the darkness before he'd had a chance to talk to her.

Don began to clear his place of his plate and flatware. "Just a silly story about another film. I don't think you were there." He gave Sam a shuttered look, then Ryan detected a certain amount of amusement in his gaze. It annoyed him.

"I know when I'm not wanted," Don murmured. Ryan noticed Sam's eyes held a brief moment of panic before Don walked away.

He began to eat. He could barely taste his food, he was so conscious of the woman sitting beside him. And for some reason that angered him again. He hadn't felt this vulnerable around a woman since his early twenties. Why now?

But at least she hadn't run away. He watched her out of the corner of his eye. She was picking up her fork, then her knife. She was cutting into what was left of her steak. He decided to break the silence.

"Is the food good?"

"Yes—I'm surprised."

"You shouldn't be. An army travels on its stomach. I brought along a cook I could trust."

"It's delicious."

They ate in silence for a few more minutes, and he noticed that she was almost finished. He couldn't let her walk away, not just yet. He said the first thing that came into his head.

"Have you made your decision yet?"

It was the wrong thing. He was so sharply attuned to

her senses that he felt her tense her muscles, felt her draw ever so slightly away from him. He could have kicked himself.

"Yes." She paused for an agonizing moment. Ryan set his flatware down, his hands clenching into fists. "Well?" His impatience was getting the better of him. He could already taste the sweetness of her mouth, feel the softness of her body beneath his.

"I can't." The words hit him like a physical blow, but he remained perfectly still.

"Can't or won't?"

"Won't, then. I won't have an affair with you. Not on location. I just—"

"Then how do you explain your reaction to me? I can feel it. The body doesn't lie, Samantha."

She was quiet for an instant, and Ryan watched the stark planes of her face as they were emphasized in the lamplight. And he knew that part of the reason he was attracted to this woman was because of a simple beauty that was almost addictive after his long association with glamorous women. He had had his fill of more sophisticated types and was looking at her, feeling a longing he hadn't felt in quite some time. With a start, he realized that he hadn't really wanted anything or anyone in a long time. It had always been so effortless before this.

"It's my own peculiar standard, then. I just won't— I'm choosing not to."

"Because we work together?"

"Yes, partly. And because—"

"Because it looks too much like all my other supposed affairs, is that it? Am I right?"

She nodded.

"And you want to be special?"

She nodded.

"And if I told you that I think you are?"

She shook her head.

"What does it take to convince you?"

"Ryan, you're very charming, and I *am* attracted to you, but I can't—"

"Once we're finished, then? When the film is done?" He hated himself the minute the words were out of his mouth. It sounded too much like begging. But he also knew, as quickly as the thought crossed his mind, that Sam was a woman who would never use any weakness of his to betray him.

She shrugged her shoulders, not looking at him. But he noticed that her hand was trembling.

"What the hell does it take to reach you? I don't believe you're as cool and controlled as you try to appear—not after the way I've seen you." As soon as he saw the hurt in her facial expression he lowered his voice, ashamed of himself for digging at her that way. "Sam." He turned toward her and took her face in his hands. She flinched slightly, but he could feel a small bit of response, and it gave him hope and a fresh burst of desire at the same time. "I don't know what you're scared of, and I try to remember why you're here on location with me, but sometimes I can't control the way I—" He stopped, noticing the puzzled look in her clear green eyes. He knew that she was scared of him, and though it frustrated him, he knew she had reason to be. His hands slipped away from her face and came to rest on top of the table.

"Ryan?" He felt her hand on top of his and he closed his eyes against the way she was assaulting his senses. How could one woman make him feel this way? "I'm sorry," she whispered. "Please give me some time. It's just that—" Her voice trailed off, and he knew that she was uneasy with the subject, that she was venturing into emotional expressions foreign to her.

"I'm not sure that I can." He reached for her hand and, clasping it in his, brought it to his lips and placed a kiss in her soft palm.

She drew her hand away and her voice shook when she spoke. "Please stop." She stood up. "It's work with me on my terms or no way at all."

"As you wish." He stared straight ahead and thought for one crazy instant of telling her he loved her. Telling her he wanted to wake up every morning with her golden head against his on the pillow. That he wanted to talk with her until the small hours of the morning, take her back to his house in Malibu, and have both of them never leave, make love to her until he had his fill of her. But it was all too raw, too new.

He watched as she disappeared into the darkness. When he could no longer hear her moving through the underbrush, he gave a deep sigh and rested his head on his forearms.

Chapter Seven

A week after Sam's and Ryan's encounter in the jungle, they were all deep in filming.

"Quiet on the set. I said *quiet!*"

Samantha stood out of sight of the camera's lens, but her eyes never left the small tableau in front of her.

Helen and Arthur, her leading man, were seated in what was supposedly the ruins of a once-great palace. Sultan, the tiger, was lying at Helen's feet, and tropical birds were situated in perches above.

Sam had been amazed by the skill and dexterity of the set designers. Where there had once been nothing but dense jungle, now there were fake stone columns, parts of an old tile floor, and a low stone wall where the two actors were seated. Early-afternoon sunlight filtered through the tops of the trees to wash the entire scene with a soft, muted light. The cameramen had been delighted with the light. The set looked perfect. Sultan seemed to be in a good mood. But the scene was not going well. Sam held her breath, hoping this would be a final take.

"Take fifteen" she heard someone call, then the snap of the clapboard told her that filming had begun.

"Whenever the two of you are ready," Ryan called.

Helen looked up at Arthur. "I know you thought my father was a vicious warrior. But he never had plans to kill you."

Sam winced at the stilted dialogue. Still, she had to admit Helen did an admirable job of making the whole thing believable.

"My darling," said Arthur, "I never believed any such thing. All I wanted, in this entire paradise, was to have you in my arms." Pulling Helen with him, he got up and stepped closer to her, drawing her into his arms for a passionate kiss.

All was going well until Sam noticed where the actor's foot was landing. He stepped lightly onto Sultan's tail, his boot just touching the animal's flank. All hell broke loose.

Sultan's massive head jerked up. Sam groaned as she realized that to the tiger a touch was synonymous with a signal to play. He rolled over and waved his large furry paws in the air. At the same time a startled Arthur stepped backward rapidly, lost his balance, and began to fall into the foliage, taking Helen with him in his arms. The movement was so quick and unexpected that Sultan swiped playfully with his paw, delighting in this new game and catching the robe of Helen's costume as she fell, screaming, to the ground.

Sam ran onto the set, oblivious to Helen's screams and the crew's laughter. Sultan was pleased to see her and waved his paws again, but she spoke firmly, and he slowly rolled over, then butted his head against her legs in a show of affection.

It was only then that she heard the fighting on the set.

"For God's sake, Helen! That cat has nothing against you. Arthur stepped on his tail with that goddamn boot. Now, the light's leaving fast, and we've got to get this shot!"

"I'll be damned if I'm going to be in one more shot with that stupid animal! I wouldn't be surprised if she trained him to do that! My big scene is next, and I can't work with that cat. I won't, and there's nothing you can do to make me!" Helen was screaming, and the camera crew seemed to be in sympathy with Ryan. No one was laughing now.

"Helen, if we can just get this one shot! I promise you—''

"You promise me nothing! I could have been killed by that animal, or injured in the fall I took! It's easy for you to say, you're behind the camera! I'm the one who has to take all the chances with these damn wild animals! And I'm not doing it anymore! You can fire me if you want to, but if you think I'm getting back up there with that, that—you're out of your mind!'' Helen pushed past Ryan and stormed to her trailer.

Sam watched Ryan rake his hand through his hair and let out a deep sigh. She had come to know that gesture of his well; he used it whenever he was deeply frustrated. And it seemed to her that all his frustrations, one way or another, involved her.

"Oh, Sultan," she whispered. "Why did he have to step on your tail?'' As if in answer, the large cat rumbled deep in his throat, then began to lick his tail.

She heard Arthur apologize to Ryan for the incident. "It was just bad blocking on my part. I did step on the animal's tail. I don't think he meant any harm.'' Sam was glad at least one person on the set besides her seemed to have some idea of what had happened.

"Were you hurt at all?'' Ryan asked him.

"By the tiger, no. But Helen landed on top of me when I fell over.'' Arthur rubbed his elbow ruefully, then smiled. "Did we get it all on film?''

At that Ryan began to laugh softly. "I'll have to ask Ben, but I think we did.''

Sam was amazed as she watched Arthur start to laugh. "I'd like to see that, but you'll have to run it when Helen isn't around. I think her pride was hurt more than anything else.'' When Ryan remained silent, he added, "Come on, Ryan, you've worked with her before. She'll be back on the set in the morning.''

Ryan rubbed his hand over the back of his neck, and

Sam glanced away. Even though she had made it perfectly clear she didn't want to have a brief affair with him, he still exuded a powerfully male appeal, and she wasn't totally immune.

"I know, but we're losing time, not to mention the light." He glanced back at the camera crew. "Everyone take a break, but be back here in half an hour."

Sam was sitting next to Sultan and patting his head when Ryan approached her.

"I'm sorry," she said, not knowing what else to say.

"It wasn't your fault. What happened?"

"Sultan was staked out and lying down, but if anyone touches him, it's an automatic signal to play unless I give him another spoken command. I knew what he was going to do the minute Arthur knocked him with his boot." Almost in answer, Sultan licked her hand.

"It seems like he's a gentle boy," Ryan remarked.

Sam met his eyes, wanting desperately for him to see her point of view. "I've raised him from a cub. He's one of the sweetest animals on the compound. Any trained cat would have reacted that way. I'm sure we could set up another shot in a matter of minutes if only..." She let the sentence trail off. She had been very careful in her attitude toward Helen since that talk with Ryan in the clearing. She didn't want to say anything against the actress.

"She's gone for the day. I guess I have to try and understand her point of view. She's never really worked with animals and she doesn't like them."

"How did she ever become the star of this picture?" Sam asked. The question had been nagging her since filming had started.

"Studio politics. I took over the film a third of the way into production. A friend of mine couldn't finish it. I had nothing to do with the casting."

"Ryan." Don came running up to them but stopped

short of the tiger. "I just came back from Helen's trailer and I tried to calm her down, but she's already taken off her makeup and refuses to return to the set."

"It's all right." But Ryan looked tired as he spoke.

"It just seems a shame to waste the rest of the day," Don mused. As his glance fell on Sam, his face lit up.

"What size do you wear, Sam?"

"A ten. Why?"

"How tall are you?"

"Five seven."

"What are your measurements?"

She blushed. "Don . . ."

He turned to Ryan. "Close your ears." He glanced back at Sam. "Okay, sweetheart, give."

"Thirty-four—twenty-four—thirty-five. What are you getting at?" But she was afraid she already knew.

"Would you object very strongly if I rinsed your hair, say, an auburn shade?"

"Are you telling me that—"

"She'd look beautiful, wouldn't she, Ryan? We could finish this scene shooting her back and Arthur's face. Sam could do all the rest of the scenes with the animals." He rushed on before either of them could say a word. "Think how cooperative Helen will be when you tell her she won't have to work with an animal again!"

Ryan looked as if he were beginning to be convinced. "Think you could do it, Sam? I'd pay you extra."

"But I don't even look like Helen!" she exclaimed.

"You'll be close enough in the long shots, and we can shoot you indirectly a great deal of the time. Believe me, this film isn't great art, and I think the sooner we get the crew off this island, the happier they'll be." Don folded his arms across his chest, obviously pleased with himself and his idea.

"How soon can you have her ready?" Ryan asked.

"An hour. And we'll still have the light. Come on, Sam!"

She shook her head. As crazy as it sounded to her, she couldn't fight both of them. "All right. Just let me put Sultan in his cage."

"QUIET ON THE SET! Take sixteen."

Sam was intensely aware of the cold wall underneath her bare legs and the skimpiness of her costume. But she looked up into Arthur's eyes as Ryan had directed her to do.

"I know you thought my father was a vicious warrior. But he never had plans to kill you." She knew Helen's voice would be dubbed in on top of hers in the final product, but they had to pace the film correctly, so she had to say the words.

Arthur looked down at her, and she noticed the passionate gleam in his eyes. She wondered how much was acting. She had seen the older man's eyes on her as she made her way around the set day after day. But before she had time to think further he was saying his lines.

"My darling, I never believed any such thing. All I wanted, in this entire paradise, was to have you in my arms." He threaded his hands through her now-auburn hair and tilted her face to his.

Sam felt his lips touch hers, and she couldn't help but contrast Ryan's kiss with Arthur's. This kiss left her cold, but she remembered her direction. Slowly, sinuously, she raised her arms up around his neck, twining them together and pulling him closer in what was supposed to seem a passionate embrace.

In the back of her mind it registered that Arthur was drawing out the kiss longer than he had with Helen. She thought quickly to her direction, and realized he was supposed to break the embrace. Sam stiffened involuntarily as she felt his tongue probe her lips, and she clenched her teeth. Arthur tried for a moment longer, then broke the embrace.

"You are everything in the world I desire." With her back to the camera, Sam glared up at him, but he was gazing into her face with adoration. "With you by my side, I have truly found paradise on earth." He drew her against his broad chest.

"Cut!" Ryan strode onto the set. "That was very good," he remarked, but there was no warmth in his expression as he looked at Sam. "I think it's a wrap."

"Ryan," Ben called from behind the camera. Sam turned and glanced at the chief cameraman. Ben was a large man, with a full beard and twinkling blue eyes. He had a penchant for puns and teased Sam unmercifully. She liked him a great deal. Now his expression was concerned. "I think we need one more take. Just to be on the safe side."

"I don't think it's necessary." Ryan's voice was low and strained.

"The tiger yawned during the middle of Arthur's last speech," Ben replied. "The rest of it was terrific, but that may draw a laugh in the theater."

"All right." Ryan glared at Sam, and she stared right back. She'd be damned if he'd make her feel guilty. She hadn't wanted to do this in the first place!

"Quiet down. Take seventeen."

The scene went well until the kiss. Sam felt Arthur pull her up into his embrace. Now that she had some idea as to what was on the man's mind, she was aware of the way he held her tightly against him. It was a very intimate embrace, as he was dressed in a thin leather loincloth and she had on a leather bikini covered only by a sheer colored robe that was more decorative than functional. Arthur managed to sweep the robe aside, and she was angrily aware of their bare stomachs touching, their thighs pressed together. She was relieved when he broke the embrace and finished his lines.

"That's a wrap!" Ben called. The crew burst into applause. Then he looked up from his camera and his twinkling eyes met Sam's. "Honey, you almost fogged up my lens with that last embrace. I was afraid the celluloid was going to go up in flames!"

Sam smiled weakly, then walked off the set to Don, who was waiting for her. He wrapped her in a cotton kimono.

"Put this on, sweetheart." He glared at the older actor. "I noticed Arthur didn't waste any time with you!"

"Was it that obvious?" Sam asked as she wiped off her smeared lipstick with a tissue. She tried to remove the memory of Arthur's mouth on hers.

"Was it obvious? I think Mr. Fitzgerald was almost ready to have a coronary occlusion." Sam closed her eyes as she saw Don take out a large powder brush, then a moment later she felt the soft bristles move gently over her hot, flushed face.

"You look terrific, though. Helen's beginning to gain a little weight, but you fill out this bikini to perfection." Don continued to talk as he applied more blusher and touched up her eye makeup, but Sam was oblivious to it all. Her lips felt bruised and tender from Arthur's attack. She could still feel her sense of revulsion from the way he had treated her. And the worst of it was, there was nothing she could do. She jumped when she heard Ryan's voice, soft and expressionless.

"That was some scene. You have the makings of a terrific actress." His tone was decidedly sarcastic.

"Ryan, leave her alone," Don interjected. "You know Arthur's considered the resident lech." He took a tissue and wiped off a bit of lipstick that had smeared, then applied a little more to Sam's lips with a brush. "Anyway, who can blame the man? She's gorgeous."

Sam closed her eyes. She knew Don was only trying to defend her, but given Ryan's temper, he was only making matters worse.

When Ryan spoke again, his voice was so cool that she shivered. "We have one more shot in the series. You and Arthur leaving the ruins, with Sultan by your side. Let's get it done before the light fades."

"There goes one jealous man," Don murmured as he brushed her hair. "What's with the two of you?"

"Oh, he's attracted to me all right." Sam was surprised by the bitter words that came out of her mouth. "He'd love to have an affair with me. You know, something pleasant to pass the time while we're out here in exile!"

"I think you're wrong."

Sam said nothing, and Don continued. "I've never seen a man watch a woman the way he watches you. He's smitten but good."

"Don—" Sam began.

"I'm not saying he doesn't have a reputation, because he does. But believe me, a man gets to a certain age and that whole thing loses a great deal of its charm. My personal opinion is that you're a welcome change from all the phoniness he usually encounters." He brushed off the excess powder with another fat soft brush. "You look beautiful, darling. Go out there and knock 'em dead."

As shooting progressed Sam grew more and more frustrated. What should have been a simple scene was turning into a nightmare. And Ryan was absolutely no help.

"What the hell is the matter with you, Arthur? This is the seventh take. It's a simple scene. The two of you get up and walk off into the jungle, the tiger by your side. What's so hard about that?"

Sam stared at the ground. She wanted to tell Ryan

that her short career as an actress had convinced her she would never consider it as a profession. Arthur, thrilled to have his arm around her as they walked, kept stumbling over roots and pieces of plant life. She was disgusted with him and only wanted this horrible day to come to a quick end.

At last they had walked down the makeshift path. Arthur hadn't stumbled, and Sam was in a much happier mood. She'd be able to wash off the makeup and go get some supper. Her thoughts were a million miles away from the scene when suddenly Arthur stopped in his tracks and pulled her into his arms for a passionate kiss.

She sagged against him, but he stopped kissing her and whispered against her cheek, "You'd better inject a little life into this or we'll be out here all night." Then his lips returned to hers.

In desperation, because she knew he was telling her the truth, she put her arms around his neck and leaned into him, feigning passion. He pulled her nearly naked body tightly against his, and Sam could feel her breasts being crushed against his chest, feel one of his legs between hers. She shuddered in revulsion, which Arthur mistook for passion as he molded her even closer to his body. Then, to her complete surprise, he picked her up in his arms and carried her off, Sultan walking obediently at his side.

"Cut! That's a print for sure!" Sam heard Ben call. "Let's wrap up!"

Sam struggled out of Arthur's tight embrace and glared up at him. Her voice shook as she started to speak.

"Don't you *ever* touch me that way again. I'm only a stand-in for Helen, not a piece of meat for you to play around with!" She looped her fingers around the chain hidden in Sultan's thick ruff and stood her ground. Arthur began to back away. "Do you understand what I've said to you?"

Arthur's surprised expression seemed genuine. "But everyone knows you're having an affair with Ryan. Why not spread the fun around?" Taking no notice of her horrified expression, he went on, "I can do a lot more for your career than he can." He sniffed delicately. "I know you're supposed to be an animal trainer, but I think you'd have a real career in front of the camera."

Sam felt her legs beginning to shake as white-hot anger licked its way through her body. "For your information, I am *not* having an affair with Mr. Fitzgerald, nor do I have any intention of having one with anyone on this picture! I'm here to see to the animals. Period! And if you don't respect my wishes, I'll walk off this set and call in the proper authorities to take the animals with me. You'll never see this film anywhere but in the trash can!" She turned away from him and walked back in the direction of Sultan's cage.

Once the big cat was safely locked in, Sam headed in the direction of the empty set. With nothing further on her mind than getting out of her ridiculous costume and turning in for the night, she was surprised when she saw Ryan standing outside the makeup area. Not wishing to undress with him anywhere near, she walked into the tent and grabbed her T-shirt, pulling it on over her costume. She could give it to Don in the morning. She unlaced the high leather boots that were also a part of her costume, then pulled on her jeans. Skinning her hair back off her face, she caught it up with a hairband, then reached for the cold cream and began to rub it into her face. She grabbed a tissue and started to take off the heavy makeup with long, angry strokes.

She heard Ryan come into the tent but paid no attention to him as she started to remove her eye makeup. Once her face was clean again, she took down her hair and ran a brush through it. Bending down, she reached for the costume boots and propped them against the large table that held most of Don's supplies. She began to pull on her own boots.

The light was fading fast, and she could hear small rustling sounds outside and an occasional call from a bird. She got up and began to walk toward the door, ignoring the man who stood so near.

She felt his hand grasp his wrist, and she stopped. She was not going to humiliate herself further with any more fighting. "What do you want?" she asked dully.

"Sam, I'm sorry about what happened out there." Ryan paused, and she knew that he was searching for words. "I was jealous at first, because it looked as if you were giving yourself willingly, but on that last take I realized what he was doing to you. I apologize for him, and I'm angry at myself for not putting a stop to it sooner."

Whatever she had expected him to say, it was certainly not this. "It doesn't matter," she whispered. She was tired. It was an effort to talk. "I think I'm going to retire early tonight," she said as she passed a hand over her brow in a weary gesture.

"Go get settled, and I'll bring you some dinner. You have to eat." Before she could protest he had left the tent.

The last thing she wanted was for Ryan to see her in the small confines of her private tent, but it seemed she had no choice. And she *was* hungry, even though she had no desire to be with other people and talk about what had happened that day. Helen would probably hate her even more for this.

She walked back to her tent, which one of the men had pitched for her the day after her arrival, all her muscles stiff and aching from the unreleased tension. Unzipping the flap and stepping inside, she took off her boots and jeans, then crawled underneath a cotton blanket. Laying her head down on the pillow, she tried to think about all that had happened in a single day.

She didn't blame Don for his sudden idea. And although she knew Ryan had to bring the picture in on time, she wished fervently she didn't have to be Helen's stand-in. She didn't want any more abuse from Arthur. She had never had the slightest wish to be in movies, probably from her early exposure to the reality of the business. She knew that behind the premieres and the glamorous life-styles there were the endless takes and waiting, the uncomfortable locations, and the tempers of some of the most monumental stars. While she respected anyone who was a true professional, she had decided long ago if it weren't for the animal involvement, she'd be perfectly happy if she never worked on a movie again.

Another difference between us, she thought wearily. Her thoughts had returned to Ryan and she remembered his face throughout the long shooting day: angry and frustrated when Helen stormed off the set, speculative when he considered Don's idea, furious when he watched the love scene between her and Arthur. And yet he had apologized. That certainly hadn't sounded like a man who used women as objects. He had sounded truly sorry for her ordeal.

She turned over on her side on the soft sleeping bag and closed her eyes. Even though she knew that Ryan would be there soon, the day's events were catching up with her, and as she settled herself more comfortably the urge to sleep was irresistible. She gave in.

WHEN SHE WOKE, it was to find a gentle hand shaking her shoulder.

"Sam, here's your dinner. I want you to eat this before it gets cold. Luis fixed some soup especially for you."

She recognized the soft voice as Ryan's. Warily opening one eye, she sat up. Not even caring what a sight she must look, she tucked the blanket around her waist and reached for the bowl he gave her.

The chicken broth was hot and fragrant and filled with rice, chunks of meat, and vegetables. She sipped it slowly as he watched her, partly because it was hot and partly because she was still half asleep.

"Pepito fed all the animals and got them settled for the night. I told him you weren't feeling too well."

"Thank you." She lifted another spoonful of soup to her lips.

"Sam, why didn't you tell me when Arthur started to take advantage of you on the set?" Ryan's expression was grim, and Sam didn't envy the actor the next few days shooting. Ryan was a difficult man to placate.

"Each time I looked at you, you seemed so angry. I didn't really know what to do; it all happened so fast."

"Couldn't you feel a difference between acting and what he was really trying to do to you?"

"Do you mean, did I know that he was taking advantage of me?"

He nodded.

"Yes, I did. As soon as he dragged out that first kiss, I knew."

"If anything like that happens again, I want you to tell me. I don't care if we have to shut down the entire movie."

"Ryan, it's okay, nothing really—"

"No, it's not okay. You're being paid to do stand-in work, not be a sexual toy."

She finished the soup and set the bowl down. "Actually, I don't think Arthur will be giving me any more trouble. I told him off after that last kiss and I think he got the message."

"You did?" Ryan smiled suddenly, and Sam noticed

how the lines around his eyes crinkled and fanned out, giving more expression to his face. "I'd like to have seen that—you telling off someone besides me."

She laughed suddenly, but when their glances met, there was something else in his gaze. She couldn't pull her eyes away.

"I brought you something else," Ryan said. Sam sensed he was making an effort to make this meeting comfortable for both of them. He gave her a glass of something cool, and she tasted it tentatively. It was sweet and thick.

"It's a fruit juice, but I can't place it."

"Papaya. Luis swears by it. He says you'll be feeling fine by morning."

"I'm not really sick, Ryan—"

"No, just tired and upset and discouraged, and maybe a little homesick."

She nodded her head, touched by his perception. She missed being able to walk over to Jake's and Maria's, missed their evening talks and laughter. There were times here in Puerto Rico when she felt terribly alone. Except when she was with Ryan.

"Drink that, and when you're done, there's something I want to show you."

She downed the juice in one long swallow. The sweet liquid was cool against her throat. When she gave the glass back to Ryan, he stood up, collecting it and the empty bowl.

"Meet me in my tent in fifteen minutes. It's something I think you'll enjoy."

As soon as he left she got to her feet and pulled on her jeans and her boots. She brushed her hair, then twisted and secured it in back of her head with several hairpins. She thought about putting on some makeup, then almost laughed to herself. What a picture she'd made in bed right now.

After zipping the tent shut behind her, she walked over to Ryan's tent and waited outside. He came back a few minutes later and motioned her in.

"What's the surprise?" Her good humor was returning.

"I brought you here to show you my etchings." At the smile his remark brought to her face he seemed pleased. "Actually, I thought you might be a little more secure if you knew precisely where your stand-in work would be going. I'm sure I can work things so you won't be in another close scene with Arthur."

"That would be wonderful!"

"The only thing I'll need you for is a few more long shots and perhaps a couple of stunts we can work out. The storyboards should explain it all."

"I'll see what I can come up with," she promised. "Sultan's done a few stunts, and I think the older elephant—Babe—can do just about anything."

As Ryan pulled out pieces of the storyboard, Sam was impressed by the artistry applied to each sheet. The tiny figures even seemed to resemble Arthur and Helen. She smiled as she recognized the white lion, the chimp, and even the baby elephant.

"They're very good," she said as Ryan flipped through them.

"It helps a lot, because they really spell out where the film is going. When I first took over, they were a godsend."

Sam was surprised by how easy she felt sitting next to Ryan on the floor of his tent and going over the sketches.

"Here's the scene we tried to film today. I think we can get by with what we' shot. I'd hate to put Sultan through it all over again."

"I'm sure he could do it," Sam replied, lost in the sketches. "It was just an unlucky break, Arthur stepping on his tail."

"What I wanted to show you," Ryan said as he lifted the stack of drawings off her lap and flipped to a particular section, "is where I'm going to need your help. We need a spectacular stunt with the animals, and I thought you should plot it out, because I'd hate to see any of them get hurt."

"I see what you mean. It would really pick up the pace of the picture in the middle."

"Exactly. It isn't what the producers envisioned in the beginning, but this film is scheduled for a June release and it'll be competing with all sorts of thrillers and action films. I don't think it will stand a chance unless we get some terrific footage for the trailer."

Sam nodded. "I never realized there was so much to making a film."

"This particular genre isn't my favorite, but I should have taken that into consideration when I signed on." His humor was gently self-deprecating, and Sam was startled to discover another aspect of the many-faceted man.

"Why are you doing this film, Ryan?" she asked.

"As a personal favor for a friend. He had been on location for two weeks when he found out one of his children was seriously ill. He asked me to take over and make sure the film was finished."

As Sam studied the storyboard sketches in front of her, she thought about the other side to Ryan she had learned of tonight. The press would have one believe he was a playboy, a person who couldn't care about children or women. But he had cared in this instance. Could he possibly care about a personal relationship?

She put down the sketches. "I'd like to take a few of these back to my tent and study them. Is it okay?"

"More than okay. You can take them tonight." Ryan smiled down at her, and his lazy grin caused her heartbeat to speed up a fraction.

Sam bit her lip, then blurted out the thought before she lost her nerve. "I like you this way, Ryan." The words sounded immature and childish in her ears, but Ryan didn't give her a chance to become embarrassed.

"I know what you mean. I like us this way, too." She held her breath as he leaned over and kissed her gently on the lips. "Go back to your tent and have a good night's sleep. I'll have someone come and get you as late as possible so you can sleep in."

As she walked back to her tent, the sketches tucked under her arm, Sam realized how tired she still was. Being with Ryan always seemed to have an energizing effect on her, but without him she thought of bed and a good night's sleep.

Bed. The thought made her face grow warm. He had offered to walk her to her tent, but she had refused, claiming she didn't mind the short walk alone. In truth, she was afraid she'd make sure Ryan guessed she wanted him to spend the night with her.

Easy, girl, she thought, unconsciously lapsing into the soothing words she used as a trainer. *If it's meant to be, it'll last.*

Chapter Eight

The next morning Sam slept until ten. She took a quick shower near the mobile home reserved for Helen, then walked over to Luis's food wagon.

When the small dark man saw her, he broke into a smile. "You are feeling better?" he asked politely.

"Mucho," Sam replied, and then, "Much better, Luis. Thank you for the soup and juice you sent me last night."

The little man's smile widened. "That was Se~or Ryan's idea. He came to me and asked for something good for you."

She was touched by this information. *"Muchas gracias,* Luis. Could I get some coffee and toast?"

He shook his head. "Se~or Ryan has told me to take care of you. I think you are too skinny for him." Ignoring Sam's look of astonishment, he said, "I will fix you a proper breakfast."

"But I never eat much this early in the morning," Sam protested, then stopped. She might be talking to a brick wall for all the good it was going to do her. Luis was already cracking two eggs onto the hot grill and pouring her a fresh glass of papaya juice. He motioned for her to sit down at the nearby table.

She fixed herself a cup of coffee, but Luis confiscated it and replaced it with a steaming cup of hot chocolate. Sam wasn't annoyed anymore. The whole thing was rather amusing. She preferred chocolate to coffee anyway.

"How did you meet Ryan?" she asked. There was so much she didn't know about him.

"I was cooking for a hotel in San Juan. Ryan, he come into the kitchen one evening and ask me to come on location." He laughed. "The hotel was real mad, but Ryan helped them find a new cook." He slipped two eggs onto a plate, some toast beside them, and placed the entire meal in front of Sam.

"*Gracias,* Luis. This looks delicious."

He beamed down at her, and she could have sworn he was watching to make sure she ate. She picked up her fork, and Luis turned away.

"What would you like for lunch?" he asked.

Sam almost choked on the food in her mouth. "But I haven't finished breakfast!"

"Ryan told me you are not needed today. You are supposed to rest."

"Oh, for God's sake!" Sam exploded. "I was a little tired last night, that's all!"

Luis puttered around his makeshift kitchen, ignoring her outburst. As Sam looked at him a thought occurred to her.

"I'll help you with lunch, then."

When the cast and crew straggled in for lunch, they were treated to a strange sight. Sam and Luis were busy by the ovens, and the smell of freshly baked dough filled the air. Instead of the usual sandwiches or stews, there were several pizzas on the tables, along with large bowls of salad and pitchers of beer.

"Whose idea was this?" Ryan remarked, and Sam turned around quickly to face him, a satisfied smile on her face.

"I hope you like it. Luis has been teaching me to make pizza a la Puerto Rico."

"And what's that?" he asked.

"Just pizza with fresh shrimp topping. I happen to think it's delicious."

"I think you're delicious. Come here, Sam. You have

flour on your nose.'' Before she could refuse, he had her hand and was leading her out of the kitchen area.

''Where is it?'' She rubbed her face.

''Right here.'' He had led her around in back of the food wagon and now he kissed her nose, then lowered his lips to her mouth. It was a quick kiss, but his lips were firm and insistent. Sam leaned against him for a brief second before breaking contact.

''How are you feeling?''

''Ryan, we've got to get something straight. I was tired and discouraged last night, but I don't need to be treated like an invalid!''

He placed a gentle hand on either side of her face. ''You don't see it at all, do you?''

''See what?'' She didn't know what he was talking about.

''You overwork yourself. Don't you ever consider giving yourself permission to have fun?''

His criticism stung. ''What are you trying to do, make me over? I was having fun with Luis!''

''You were also fixing lunch for over fifty people.''

Sam eyed him with mock suspicion. ''And I suppose you're just the man to teach me!''

''Well, ma'am,'' he drawled wickedly, his thumbs massaging the corners of her mouth, ''you took the words right out of my mouth.''

She laughed then, and he took her hand and led her to the lunch tables. They squeezed in on one of the benches and grabbed some pizza.

''This is perfect,'' Ryan said after he took his first bite. ''Did you make this crust?'' He was looking at her with new respect. ''Your talents never cease to amaze me.''

Don sauntered by, catching the tail end of their conversation. ''I keep telling you, Ryan, the kid's a whiz.'' He affected a mock falsetto. ''When I'm not out in the bush training my new tiger, or running around on a movie set in a leather bikini, why, I just head right for the kitchen and make my man a pizza!''

Sam began to laugh until she caught a glimpse of Helen's facial expression. The actress was clearly not pleased with her.

Ryan noticed the direction her gaze took. He lowered his voice. ''I talked with her this morning. She seemed relieved at the thought of you taking over the animal scenes, so I'm not sure what's bothering her.''

Men could be so dense, Sam thought. Helen was clearly jealous of the attention Ryan was giving her.

Don reached for another piece of pizza. ''Don't let her bother you, Sam. I think she's as happy as anyone else to see production speeded up.'' He took a large bite, then directed his next statement to Ryan. ''And she's losing weight! We may have to take in one of her costumes.'' His eyes twinkled merrily. ''I think it might be the result of late nights with Mr. California over there.''

Sam knew that he was referring to one of the stuntmen, Scott Reynolds. The man did look like an overage surfer, with his light blond hair and pale blue eyes. Sam had spoken less than a dozen words with him since they'd met on location. She didn't care for him.

As she glanced back in Helen's direction she saw that Scott had joined her and was whispering something in her ear. Helen laughed, and the two of them got up and sauntered away.

''Good riddance to bad rubbish,'' Don muttered. He brightened. ''Sam, this pizza is terrific. Ryan, you're a goddamn fool if you let this one get away.'' Don patted Sam on the shoulder and walked over to another table.

Sam hoped her face wasn't as flushed as it felt. She glanced at Ryan quickly, and their eyes locked.

''How's that stunt coming along? Any ideas yet?''

She shook her head. ''I was dead to the world last night. But I'll start working on it.''

"No hurry. We don't need you on the set today, so just take it easy. I'm sure a good idea will come with time." He stood and gave her shoulder a gentle squeeze before he walked off.

As Sam watched him head back toward the set she bent her head and her shoulders slumped. She was more tired than she cared to admit. It rankled her to know that Ryan could see it more easily than she could. Yet she was touched by the trouble he had gone to, taking dinner to her tent and making sure she received special food.

But the question of where their relationship was going was still not clear. If Don thought Ryan cared for her, she had yet to hear it from Ryan.

She straightened suddenly, surprised at the turn her thoughts were taking. Why should she care? Though he was charming and had proved he could be thoughtful as well, nothing changed his basic nature. She was sure nothing ever would.

Sighing, she stood up and started toward her tent.

THE FLAMES DANCED WILDLY, their reflection flickering over the stone columns as the tiger ran along the high wall. When the animal reached the end, it leaped into space, the orange-and-white fur brilliant against the fire. As the tiger fell through the air an elephant trumpeted.

Sam woke with a start, then groped for her flashlight. When she flicked it on, she reached for the storyboards and cursed softly as her sleeping bag twisted around her legs, impeding her movement.

But she finally got the boards and, propping her pillow under the small of her back, she sat up in her bag and scanned the large drawings resting in her lap. As she flipped through them her excitement grew.

It would work! It had to! If the stunt she had just thought of could be pulled off, she'd make sure that

Ryan's film would be the most spectacular summer release.

She set the storyboards down and wriggled out of her bedding. Grabbing a pair of soft faded jeans, she pulled them on and tucked her nightgown inside. The flashlight lit the tent in an unearthly fashion, causing familiar objects to take on elongated, distorted shapes.

She put on her boots and passed a comb through her sleep-ruffled hair, securing it off her face with several pins.

Stepping outside, with storyboards firmly in hand and flashlight in the other, she ran lightly to Ryan's tent, the full moon illuminating her path. Not stopping to think that he might not want to see her in the middle of the night, she unzipped the front of his tent and stepped inside.

She kept her flashlight covered by turning the beam against her nightgown, and it cast a soft red glow over the inside of the tent. Setting down the storyboards, she knelt by his bedroll.

"Ryan?" she whispered.

He mumbled softly and turned over on his back. His covers had fallen away, revealing his smoothly muscled chest. Before she was conscious of what she was doing she touched his chest, her fingers spread against the hard muscle and springy hair. She started to take her hand away, but his fingers moved over her arm, then held her hand against him.

"Am I dreaming?" she heard him ask softly. She met his eyes and recognized desire. He bent his head slightly and brought her fingers to his lips, kissing each one separately. She trembled at the intimate contact and started to pull her hand away.

"No," she answered shortly. But her voice shook.

"I thought not. In my dreams you never pull away." Her head snapped up sharply at his remark, all her senses alert. She studied his face, shaded in the soft glow from the flashlight. Had there been a twinkle of amusement in the depths of his eyes, or had she imagined it?

"What else do I do?" she whispered. The words were out of her mouth before she could help herself.

He touched her face gently, running his fingers over her cheek in a caress. She shivered and tried to pull away again, but he sat up and put an arm around her waist. As he slowly lay back down in his sleeping bag he pulled her with him until she was lying full length on top of him.

"Don't fight me," he whispered an instant before his lips touched hers. She groaned under her breath as she felt his hands press against her lower back, molding her shaking body close against his hard length.

His mouth brought fire wherever it touched her: over her brow, her cheekbones, her eyelids, back to her mouth, then to her throat. She felt his lips curve into a smile as they came to rest on the pulse in her neck. It was beating frantically, erratically.

But before she knew what to do next he claimed her mouth again, and she felt a melting sweetness invade her body, setting her blood aflame and turning her bones to water.

A sigh rose to her lips as he continued to kiss her. She felt his arm move as he reached over the edge of the bedding and snapped off her flashlight, tossing it aside. The tent was dark. She surrendered to her senses.

He reached up and pulled the pins out of her hair one by one, then crushed the silken mass in his hands. He released it to fall sensuously across her back and over his chest. Then he buried his face against her shoulder, inhaling her fragrance as if it were the most desirable scent on earth. Her stomach quivered as she felt his teeth bite the skin on her shoulder gently.

Ryan's hands moved softly underneath her nightgown, and Sam realized in the dark recesses of her mind that he had already pulled it out of the waistband of her jeans. She felt cool air on her skin as the gown slid off only to be replaced by his warm hands.

Her bare breasts were pressed against his chest, and the hair tickled their sensitive tips until they were full and aching. Sam gasped as he slid a hand between their bodies, and she lifted herself slightly so his palm could cup her breast. As his fingers closed around the sensitive flesh he turned slowly so that they were lying side by side. Though she was still on top of the sleeping bag and he was beneath, she was intensely aware of the warm masculinity and power that exuded from his body. It enveloped her and carried her away on waves of sheer sensation.

It was as if she were floating, drifting with desire. She felt his fingers teasing, caressing, loving, while his lips moved hotly over hers. As the last vestiges of common sense left her, she knew she wanted him to make love to her, wanted to feel him become a part of her. All their talks, all her defenses against him, suddenly seemed beside the point. A primal energy had flared between them from the first moment he walked into his office and saw her. And now it was leading to its inevitable conclusion.

He reached back behind her hips and pulled her higher against his chest. Unzipping the top of the large sleeping bag, he eased her inside. Conscious only of her intense need, she molded the softness of her body against the tautness of his.

He wasn't immune to her, of that she was sure. She heard him groan as he dragged his lips away from hers. She laced her fingers through his hair and pulled his head to her tender breasts.

She was hungry for sensation now, a hunger that was suddenly surfacing after too many years held at bay. She drew in her breath sharply as his lips found her breasts. She would have turned away from the too-intense feeling, but he held her still. His mouth began to evoke sensations from her inflamed body that she hadn't known she was capable of feeling.

She was shaking now, and her legs were trembling as she wrapped them around his lean hips. She didn't resist as she felt his hands move to the snap of her jeans. His fingers eased down the zipper, then he pushed the soft material away from her. His hand stroked the bare skin of one hip. She groaned and arched her body upward toward his, giving him freer access to her breasts. His hot mouth moved from peak to peak, the slight stubble on his jaw scratching the deep valley between. She could hear him unzipping the sleeping bag, then felt him kick the heavy material away.

His fingers had an exquisite butterfly touch. If Sam had felt a psychic connection with him, she couldn't have told him how to please her better than he was pleasing her now. He caressed the backs of her legs, then eased them away from his hips. He gently pulled her jeans down and away from her body.

And suddenly there were no barriers. She could feel the warm, hard length of his body all along hers. She twisted toward him as he kissed the hollow between her breasts, then the flatness of her stomach, then lower still. . . .

Her eyes opened in surprise. She tried to sit up as she realized where she was, what he was doing. But he held her firmly. She had never thought any man would want to make love to her that way. Certainly Paul had always made her feel inadequate, even dirty.

But Ryan was making love to her as if that secret, intimate place were as precious as any other part of her body.

She turned her hot cheek against the softness of the sleeping bag, then blindly reached for his pillow and placed it against her mouth, trying to stifle the incoherent cries she realized were her own. Sensations piled against each other, one after another. The pleasure as they were taken by force from her trembling body was too much. She couldn't feel any more; she was afraid she would explode in a million pieces.

And then, suddenly, she forgot everything. Her body strained upward against his lovemaking, instinctively reaching for further sensation. And then she found what she had never shared with any other man. Her lips arched upward. Her hands clenched his thick hair and pulled him closer. She cried out as she hit one peak, then another and another, then floated softly, shudderingly, back to reality.

She felt as if she were suspended within sensation. She could barely feel the sleeping bag against her back, was only vaguely aware of Ryan as he slid up beside her and took her gently in his arms. She saw his blue eyes as if from a great distance, felt his lips touch her damp brow.

She turned her head into his shoulder and buried her face against his neck.

Her heartbeat was deafening, or was it his? They lay quietly for what seemed a long time until she raised her head.

"Samantha?" Ryan's voice was warm and vibrant. "Are you all right?" There was a note of uncertainty in his voice, and she was overwhelmed with a swift rush of joy. So he felt as vulnerable as she did! It was a revelation.

"Yes," she whispered into his ear. "I feel wonderful." She paused, unsure of what his reaction would be. "But..."

"But what?" he urged softly. His arms tightened around her.

She took a deep breath. "I feel so selfish."

He laughed, deep in his throat. The sound was warm

and melodious. He pulled her closer still. "Is that all? Why?"

"Because..." She felt her face grow warm. "You didn't—I mean, we didn't—"

"Because you feel we didn't make love?"

She nodded, feeling miserable. Why did she have to feel as awkward as an adolescent?

"Listen to me." He turned his face against hers. "How was I supposed to know you'd be coming to my tent tonight? Not that I minded, but you did catch me off guard, and there was no way of protecting you."

"Oh." It was a small, strangled sound, and she felt tears of embarrassment fill her eyes. She certainly hadn't been thinking of anything so practical. She swallowed painfully. "But it couldn't have been—I mean, for you—"

"It was exciting as hell for me." He laughed gently, then ran his fingers over her shoulders and drew her tightly against him. She leaned against him and closed her eyes, welcoming his strength.

She felt his breath tickle her ear. "There are many ways of making love, Sam."

She sighed. How naive she must seem to him! And after all the pleasure he had given her, she couldn't just drift off to sleep.

She touched his cheek gently, then she kissed him. Her hand smoothed over his chest with sensual motions, up to his broad shoulders, then lower, down his stomach. The smoothness and heat of his flesh excited her.

He inhaled sharply and reached to touch her breasts. She stilled his hand with her own.

"No," she whispered, and placed his hand firmly up by his dark head. "This is just for you."

Her eyes were used to the darkness now and she could make out his head on the pillow, his arms crossed behind. His eyes were dark and slumberous, watching her.

She smiled at him, then pushed some hair out of her eyes. The backward motion of her arm caused one of her breasts to lift slightly, and she saw his eyes follow its soft movement. And though she had never taken the initiative in lovemaking, she suddenly realized Ryan would find whatever she did exciting.

The inside of the tent was like a warm, dark cocoon. Gently, softly, she eased herself on top of him so that their bodies were molded together. His hands came down and circled her waist. She removed them and, kissing each callused palm, she placed them back up above his head.

"Witch," he murmured, but his voice was slightly hoarse. She knew he was excited by their love play.

Emboldened by this discovery, she kissed him softly, feeling his lips part willingly. She darted her tongue inside his mouth, exploring with silken caresses. Out of the corner of her eye she saw his hands come up, then slowly clench and ease back down.

She moved to his cheek, pressing soft kisses over the side of his face, his eyelids, his temples, down by his ears, and on his neck. She spread one of her hands over his chest and could feel the rapid, powerful beat of his heart. Her other hand touched his hair, delighting in its thickness and texture.

She moved farther down and pressed her lips against his chest. She found the small raised nipple and teased it with her tongue. When she heard his indrawn breath, she smiled against the warmth of his chest.

She teased the other nipple with her mouth, then her hand. Then she moved lower still. She kissed and caressed his strongly muscled stomach, then slid her hands down his taut thighs. She was careful not to go near the evidence of his desire, not yet.

She heard him breathing deeply, felt his muscles tighten, sensed the pounding of his heart. And yet she took her time, remembering how he had built her excitement step by step, and how satisfying it had been.

When she finally closed her hand over him, she heard him groan low in his throat, a pure sensual sound. She handled him gently, almost afraid of hurting him, then grew bold and began to kiss and caress him.

She knew she was pleasing him, knew from the way his body reacted, the way he groaned with pleasure. His hands came down and smoothed her hair away from her face. His fingers were trembling against her skin. Her sensual power over him excited and surprised her.

Later, after she had taken him to fulfillment and beyond, when she lay curled in his arms, she felt a sense of peace and deep happiness well up inside her. No one could ever take away what had passed between them this night.

She watched through half-shut eyes as Ryan opened the front flap of the tent. Early-morning light streaked in, luminous and fresh. Birds were just beginning to sing, and the small coqui were silent.

He laughed softly, then zipped the tent shut. Turning toward her, he lay down and pulled her against his shoulder. His warm mouth tickled her ear. "Get some sleep, or I won't be responsible for my actions."

She smiled, her body too tender yet for laughter. Snuggling deeper against him, she breathed in his musky scent. His arms wrapped around her waist. She felt the hard muscles pull her more closely against him.

She was full of feeling and yet very tired. She turned her lips to his ear, fighting the drowsiness that threatened to overwhelm her. "I love . . ." she whispered, but before the last word was out of her mouth she was asleep.

SAM STIRRED as something tickled her leg. She shifted position on the sleeping bag and sighed. The sensation was annoyingly persistent, so she wrinkled her nose and buried her face in her pillow. When she felt a warm hand curve around her breast, she slowly opened her eyes.

As soon as she sat up she knew where she was. The inside of Ryan's tent was bright, as he had tied back the flap and the sun was high in the vivid blue sky. Sam glanced to where Ryan had levered himself up on one elbow. He was grinning, that lazy smile making her heart beat crazily with an erratic rhythm. He looked for all the world like a cat that had just finished a big bowl of rich, thick cream.

"Come here," he whispered, his hand on her shoulder. She felt a wave of weakness assail her, a longing for the sensuous feeling of his naked body against hers. Her mind, ever concentrated on emotional survival, quenched that thought with the thoroughness of a cold shower.

"Ryan, no!" She struggled upward. If he realized how vulnerable she was, she wouldn't be able to handle their relationship at all, let alone finish the work on his film. Although right now, work was the furthest thing from her mind.

"Don't be shy," he whispered. "There's no one around." He grinned again, but she saw a glimmer of uncertainty in his eyes. "I thought we might take a shower together."

Sam pulled her knees up against her chest, hugging them for support. What had possessed her to come to his tent last night? As she thought this her gaze fell on the storyboards on the floor.

"I wanted to talk to you about the stunt," she murmured.

"What?" Ryan was clearly puzzled.

"The stunt," she repeated. Perhaps she could put him off. Her mind worked furiously. Things were still moving too fast for her. The last thing she had thought when she had run to Ryan's tent was that he might make love to her. Or was it? a small voice inside nagged her. She pushed the thought away. But wasn't it partially her fault as well? She had to have time to think.

"Could you hand me my nightgown?" she said, her voice cool.

He gave it to her without a word, the expression in his eyes clearly puzzled. "Sam, about last night," he began.

"No." Her voice was thick and her throat tight, almost choking her. She couldn't bear it; didn't want to hear the obligatory "Thank you, I had a wonderful time, it's been nice." It had been more than "nice" to her. It had been heaven and hell and ecstasy all wrapped up in a few short, intense hours. She couldn't bear to hear him belittle it.

Ryan got up off the sleeping bag. Unconcerned with his naked masculinity, he casually reached for his jeans and pulled them on. Raking his hands through his dark brown hair, he crossed his legs Indian fashion as he sat down a short distance away from her. "Let's talk." His voice sounded oddly flat.

Sam cleared her throat. "I need the storyboards," she stated quietly. Where was the closeness, the intimacy they had shared last night? A part of her mind reminded her she could have been in his arms right now, but for her fears.

"About the film?" He sounded incredulous.

She nodded, aware of the furious energy that emanated from his strong body.

"After last night! Lady, you must have ice water in your veins if you think I'm going to talk about some stunt after what happened between us last night!" At her disbelieving look he continued, taking a deep breath. "Didn't it mean anything at all to you?"

She looked away. If there ever was a time for putting her heart on the line, this was it. She nodded. "Yes, it did." Her voice came out soft but strong.

"And if I'm thinking correctly, you believe it was nothing but a good time for me." He sounded sarcastic.

She winced at his barbed words. "Am I right?" he demanded.

"Yes," she replied, miserable. She reached for her jeans, wanting to leave.

"You're wrong." His words were so soft, she could hardly believe he'd said them.

She looked up and met his hard, arrogant expression. As her hands clenched the material of her jeans she noticed he was moving toward her. He was sitting down beside her and pulling her into his arms.

"Damn it, Sam, what do I have to do to get it through your head that I'm crazy about you! I've been wanting to get you into bed from the first time I saw you in my office." At his last sentence she started to twist away, but he held her firm. "And I don't think that what we shared last night was particularly casual for either of us." His voice roughened. "I love you, you idiot!"

She stopped struggling. "You what?"

"I said I love you, damn it!"

"Oh."

All of her breath escaped in a sigh. She felt his hand tracing the bone structure of her face, felt the rough palm move intimately up and under her nightgown until he was caressing the tips of her breasts lightly. Without waiting for a reaction, he half pulled her gown up and kissed each rosy peak, then bent her back down into the warm depths of the bag.

She felt his lips meet hers, then part them lazily, gently, as if he had all the time in the world. She put her hands on his shoulders, running her fingers over their hard muscles, then across his back. As the kiss deepened and she wound her arms around his neck, she felt what little control she had maintained beginning to slip. Her blood was humming, her heart pounding, her senses following every move this man made. He loved her! The words sang in her thoughts, burned in her blood, made her love him all the more. With the confidence that his love gave her, she felt her body responding, felt the passionate emotion that only this man seemed to ignite.

"Ryan! Where the hell are you? I thought we were shooting some of Helen's close-ups this morning!" Sam recognized Ben's voice. She could just picture the big man walking into the tent. She pulled her nightgown back down.

Ryan pulled on a T-shirt and stepped outside, shielding her from view.

"Sorry, Ben. I seem to have overslept." He sounded totally serious, and Sam could tell that Ben believed him by his apologetic reply. She quietly struggled into her jeans and ran her fingers through her tangled hair. Quickly straightening the large sleeping bag and pulling on her boots, she gathered the storyboards next to her in a neat pile and waited for Ryan.

He ducked inside a few minutes later. "I'm sorry. It seems like an instant signal to anyone on this damn location—the minute we get together, someone has to come around!" But his smile softened the sting of his words. "Maybe it's best you got dressed. I might have forgotten we aren't exactly prepared for the big time." He claimed her lips in a quick kiss. "I have to get going, but I'll talk to you at lunch."

She looked up at him, and some of her old fears must have clouded her eyes, because he knelt down beside her and took her face in both his hands.

"Sam, listen to me. Forget what you've heard about me, anything you've ever read or any bull that anyone has told you." He kissed her forehead. "I'm just Ryan, and what we have is very special. Can you believe me?" She nodded.

"I'll see you at lunch." And he walked out the front of the tent.

Sam sat still for a moment, stunned at the turn of

events, at all that had happened in a few minutes. Her life had changed. He loved her.

She lay back on top of the sleeping bag after setting the storyboards to the side. She'd get to the animals in a minute, but she wanted to savor this moment, to enjoy what the morning had brought.

She felt the everyday tightness in her chest relax. A feeling of looseness and light seemed to pervade her body. Rolling over on her stomach, she buried her face in the pillow they had shared, breathing deeply of the masculine scent that still clung to it.

She was happy. It had been such a long time since she'd felt this way, she actually had to stop and think about it to realize she was. Happiness was something she took for granted when she was working with the animals, but this feeling was such that it threatened to fill her up completely and bubble over.

Not content to lie still, she sat up, then jumped up and walked out the door, closing the flap carefully behind her. She wanted to skip, to jump, to make noise, to throw coconuts down from the highest palms. She wanted to shake the first person who crossed her path and tell her or him the entire story. She felt her body tingle, felt her blood soar with delight.

As she reached her tent she jumped up and pulled off a leaf from a nearby rubber plant, then ducked inside the canvas door.

Sam spent the morning feeding the animals and working with Sultan on the rudimentary beginnings of his stunt. It was almost two in the afternoon before she reached the lunch table. Ryan was sitting with a few of the men. His expression brightened visibly when he saw her.

"Where've you been?" he asked.

"Where else?" She inclined her head in the direction of the animal compound. She looked down at her plate piled high with crab, rice, beans, and avocado. "I'm going to get fat if Luis keeps putting so much food on my plate."

"Not if I see you every night." His voice was low and intimate, for her ears alone.

She sat down next to him, then picked up her fork and speared a piece of avocado. "Did you get any of this?" she asked. She had felt a rush of hot blood come into her face at his remark.

"You're cute when you blush. And no, I didn't. Luis doesn't favor me the way he does you." He curled his fingers around her wrist and guided the fork to his mouth.

Sam felt pleasurable little flickers of heat move down her arm, and the fork trembled slightly in her hand. But it wasn't the way it had been between them. Where there had once been uncertainty and fear, now there was excitement and desire, and the knowledge that there was more than just the physical between them.

"I was thinking about driving into San Juan tomorrow. Would you like to go with me?" Ryan asked, his voice near her ear.

Sam shivered as his warm breath tickled her cheeks. She glanced up at him. "I'd like to." She gasped as she felt his hand come down on her thigh, and suddenly the food on her plate was tasteless and formless. All that mattered were the sensations this man beside her was evoking.

Ryan moved his hand in light, feathery caresses, from the top of her thigh to the sensitive skin of her inner leg. Sam started as if he had placed a live flame there and dropped her fork. Rice and beans scattered over the red tablecloth.

Ryan laughed and put an arm around her shoulders.

Sam stiffened, noticing how the rest of the crew were watching them. There wasn't any speculation or joking, just quiet, human curiosity. Ryan sensed her discomfort and dropped his arm.

"They won't think you're my latest conquest, if that's what's bothering you," he whispered.

"I'm sorry, it's just that—"

He put a finger over her lips. "There's no need to explain to me."

Sam dug into her lunch. When she had finished most of what was on her plate, Ryan surprised her with another question.

"Have you given any more thought to the stunt?" he asked casually.

"Yes. I know exactly what I'm going to do! I even worked Sultan over some of it today. When you see how I have it pictured, I know you'll love it!"

He smiled at her with his eyes, and Sam's stomach quivered. "Tell me about it, then."

"I can't without the storyboards. They're in your tent."

"How convenient," he drawled. "That's just where I was thinking we might go after lunch."

She felt her heartbeat begin to accelerate at the promise in his words. "I'm finished," she said, indicating her plate.

Ryan picked it up and walked over to the large table by Luis's open cooking counter. He set down the plate and walked back to the bench where she was sitting. "Let's go." He held out his hand for her, palm up.

She placed her hand in his, feeling his fingers curl warmly around hers. They left the table. Sam could feel the curious stares. It didn't bother her as much as it had before.

Once inside Ryan's tent, with storyboards scattered all around them, Sam began to explain.

"This scene, the one where the jungle princess has to escape because the warriors have set fire to the ancient village— Ryan, what are you doing?'' she cried out as she felt his hands move to her waist, then underneath her shirt as he gave her a quick kiss.

"The answer to that should be obvious, even to you," he teased. He swept her on to his lap and pulled her back against the hard wall of his chest. "Now tell me about the stunt," he murmured, his lips brushing the sensitive side of her neck.

"When they set fire to the village— Ryan, I can't concentrate on what I'm saying when you— Oh, you!" She turned to wriggle out of his embrace, but he was too quick for her. He caught her mouth, trapping her lips beneath his.

He kissed her deeply, and she could taste him in her mouth. The pressure of his tongue made her shiver, and she clasped his head with her hands, delighting in the feel of his thick hair beneath her palms. He moved his lips to her neck, then slowly began to unbutton her blouse until the top of her lacy bra was exposed.

"I've been thinking about several stunts I'd like to try with you," he murmured in her ear, a slight note of laughter in his voice. His warm breath against her flushed skin sent shivers of anticipation up her spine.

He finished unbuttoning her blouse, then kissing the deep cleavage that was open to his gaze, he reached behind and unclasped the back of her bra. Sam groaned as he slid his searching hands underneath the wisps of lace that were scant protection. He lay her back on his sleeping bag and began to torment her breasts with his tongue and lips.

"Ryan, you have to go back to work," Sam breathed. Speech was becoming more and more difficult.

"I called a long lunch," he muttered thickly as his lips trailed down her stomach. In another minute he would be unfastening her jeans.

Sam felt as if she were struggling out of deep water,

trying to make it to the surface. She put one of her hands over his and eased it away.

He sat up, his hands on either side of her body so he was over her, effectively pinning her. As his gaze swept her half-naked body she felt as if his eyes were scorching her with desire. His attention stopped at her breasts, which she knew were rising and falling with her rapid breathing.

"I'm glad one of us has some sense," he said before brushing aside her trembling fingers and helping her fasten the back of her bra. He then proceeded to button her blouse. He sat back on his sleeping bag, as if he had to put some space between them.

"Tell me about it, Sam." His voice was gentle, but there was a dangerous twinkle in his eyes.

She got up off the sleeping bag, her body languorous and heavy with unsatisfied desire. As she moved a bit further away from him, she saw an amused smile curve his lips.

"Weren't you the one who wanted to finish this film and get off this godforsaken island?" she asked, mimicking his speech pattern.

Ryan's lips twitched with suppressed laughter. "I don't know about you, but I'm having a great time."

Sam decided to ignore his teasing, though her heart was still fluttering. She started to set out the storyboards. "When the princess escapes after the ancient village is set on fire, I thought we could use the high stone wall with the moat in front of it. You know, part of the ruined fortress?" At Ryan's nod of comprehension she continued. "Since she has such a good rapport with the animals in the jungle, and has grown up with them as her only companions from birth, I thought this might be a good time to use the fact to our advantage." As Ryan looked puzzled, she added, "To *show* her with the animals, doing something exciting, as opposed to always hearing about it in dialogue."

"Go on." He looked interested, and Sam's confidence in her work soared. She could hardly wait to see the expression on his face after she explained the stunt to him. Ryan the lover was partially forgotten, to be replaced with Ryan the director of the film.

"I thought the princess could ride Sultan along the fortress's high wall, then he could leap the moat and land on the elephant's back!" At Ryan's look of incredulity she continued quickly. "Sultan has worked with elephants before, and I found out Babe was in a circus for almost fifteen years, so she's used to anything." She noticed Ryan's blue eyes were beginning to darken ominously and, mistaking his reaction, she hastened to add a few technical facts. "Of course, I'd use some sort of regal covering for the elephant, and there would be a back pad below. Babe would be chained, so there would be no danger of her moving. I'd need two weeks to train the animals, but I started with Sultan this morning, and he's doing just fine."

"And who, pray tell, is going to ride the tiger?" Ryan asked softly.

Sam looked at him, astonished. "I am. Sultan can wear a leather collar hidden in his fur, and I can lean low against him and curl my legs around him. If you're worried about my not looking like Helen, I'll do whatever it takes with makeup and rinses. We can get Babe used to the sudden weight by throwing sacks—"

"No."

She swallowed, not certain she had heard him correctly. "What did you say?"

"I said no, and that's final!"

"Why?"

"I won't have you risking your neck on some dam-fool stunt, that's why!"

"But it's my job! And you asked me for a stunt!" Her anger was beginning to rise, and she clenched her fists in frustration.

"No."

"You can't be serious! We'd have nets around the wall and beyond the elephant. There would be water in back of her—"

"The answer is still no."

"I've ridden that tiger from the time he was big enough to carry me!"

"No."

"Are you saying you don't trust my professional opinion?"

"Samantha—"

"You can call Jake if you don't think I have all the angles covered."

"That's not—"

"I was even going to ask you if I could send for two more trainers for the duration of the stunt, so you see, I *don't* think I can do everything!" She was fighting to hold back her anger. This wasn't at all as she had thought it would be.

"No."

"Then you can just go to hell!" The words were out of her mouth before she could control her inflamed temper. "If this is what love means to you, that you can dictate my every move if it doesn't suit you, then you can take this relationship we have and—"

"That's not what I'm trying to—"

"Isn't it? Would you say the same thing to a man?" At his look of uncertainty she pressed her point. "The stunt will be as safe as I can possibly make it. I've broken a few bones working with animals and I've had a close call now and then. You can't just give up when you get scared—"

"Those are strange words coming out of your mouth." He was angry now, too.

"You bas—" She stopped. This was exactly what she had feared about getting intimately involved with Ryan.

It had put a strain on their working relationship. She knew the stunt was safe if properly executed, and she knew Ryan was scared for her personally. The whole situation was impossible.

She began to gather up the storyboards, her hands shaking. "I'll put these over on the table, and I'm sure that after you study them, you'll see why my idea makes sense. In the meantime, I'm going to start working with Sultan and Babe."

She managed to walk out of the tent with steady legs. But as soon as she was out of sight she felt hot tears beginning to sting her lids. Was this what it meant to be involved with Ryan Fitzgerald? Would he smother her, protect her to the point where she wouldn't be able to do work she loved? She knew the stunt was good. She was even willing to call Jake and talk over the final execution with him. But nothing mattered if Ryan didn't even let her try.

She skirted the lunch area, where the sounds of voices and laughter rang out as if to mock her previous happiness. As soon as she was under cover of foliage and had found the trail to the animal cages, she began to run. The physical activity helped ease some of the tension in her body, and by the time she reached the clearing she was ready to begin work again.

Sultan rubbed up against the bars in his cage and made soft, chuffing noises as soon as he saw her. She angrily wiped the tears off her cheeks with an open palm.

"Come on, Sultan," she crooned, her voice breaking. "We've got a lot of work to do."

Chapter Nine

Two weeks later Sam was stationed at the animal clearing for midnight watch. She took turns with the men, even though they had tried to discourage her at first.

Sighing, she leaned her head back against the pile of blankets on the floor of the tent. They had built a small raised platform in the middle of the animal compound, and the sides of the tent were sheer mesh. A person could see out, but bugs couldn't get in, and the elevated floor discouraged scorpions.

She heard Galahad, the white lion, roaring gently in the distance. The evening breeze carried the sweet song of the tiny coqui, and she smiled to herself as she heard their melodic chant. The bushes rustled, and Iago, the tiger, snarled deep in his throat.

She stiffened. He still hadn't been shipped back to wherever he'd come from. She'd have to talk to Ryan.

Not that they talked much anymore. In the past week and a half he had been curt and abrupt with her, and she had been coolly polite in return. She knew their relationship had put a strain on the rest of the crew, but she was too upset to care.

And yet she missed him. Sam wondered where the loving, gentle, teasing man she had known for a short time had gone. In his place was a dark stranger who worked everyone on the set mercilessly, barked at people before listening to their side of the problem, and looked at her with cool fire in his deep blue eyes.

She got up off the floor and stretched her cramped muscles, then glanced at her watch. Three thirty-five and still the sky was black as midnight. But her shift would be over at six, when Pepito would come and relieve her.

She started again as she heard noise along the trail and turned in the direction of the sound, her heart pounding. Though she was sure anyone could hear her if she called, and the animals would cause a ruckus if anything went wrong, she was jumpy as a cat tonight.

She peered into the darkness and her eyes made out a tall black figure. She squinted her eyes, trying to see more. There was something about the way the figure moved. Her body realized who it was before her mind did and she felt her pulse begin to hammer. She put her hand to her throat, trying to ease the tight feeling.

It was Ryan. He was heading toward the small raised structure. She was sure he had seen her.

Sam smoothed her hair away from her face with damp palms, cursing herself for her nervousness. Why had he chosen this night to come to her? She had been ignoring him as much as possible and had turned all her energy and emotion into training Babe and Sultan into accepting her stunt as part of their learned behavior. Pepito had become invaluable with the elephants, and it had been his patient help that had enabled Sam to try the stunt without the assistance of another trainer.

But all thoughts flew out of her mind as Ryan entered the tent. An acute physical awareness settled over both of them.

"Hello, Samantha."

"Hello, Ryan." If he could be civil, so could she, even though she had no doubts they'd soon be at each other's throats. Was it only possible to love or hate this man, to desire or fear him? She remembered with longing the brief times he had teased her and the gentleness he had displayed.

He looked anything but gentle tonight. Dressed in

tight black jeans and a black shirt rolled up at the sleeves, he looked like some powerful creature of the night. Sam noticed that the lines around his eyes and mouth were cut deeper and he looked tired. Ryan might work his cast and crew mercilessly, but he worked no one harder than himself. The strain was showing in his face and in the tired way he carried his muscular body.

"I brought you some coffee." He set down the backpack he was carrying and took out a large thermos and two mugs.

"Thank you." All the time they were talking formally, Sam searched his expression in vain for some welcoming sign, some warmth. Could this cold stranger be the same man she had made the most gentle love with on a night that seemed so long ago?

He knelt down and set the mugs on the floor, then unscrewed the top of the thermos and poured the fragrant liquid. Closing the thermos again, he set it to the side and waited for her to make a move.

She sat down next to him and picked up one of the mugs. The hot ceramic surface felt soothing against her fingertips, and she blew on the hot coffee to cool it.

"Do you ever get lonely out here?" he asked.

The question was loaded with sexual innuendo, but it was spoken so softly and with such straightforwardness that Sam doubted Ryan meant it that way. *What a hurry we've been in to get as close as possible physically, and yet there's so much we don't know about each other,* she thought sadly.

"No," she answered truthfully. "Especially here, it's so beautiful at night. The dark is like velvet, the air—" She stopped, self-conscious, and took a sip of coffee. It was good, hot, and strong with just a little cream and no sugar. With a small sense of satisfaction she realized he had remembered how she liked her coffee.

"Go on." The sound of his voice was strangely comforting to her. How different he was from the man he had been this afternoon, his voice raised in exasperation.

"It's almost as if. . ." She paused, hoping to find the right words. She wanted this moment with him to last. "As if the island really comes alive only at night. The scents are stronger, everything takes on a more mysterious quality. And yet it seems to open up." She flexed her legs slightly, then drank a bit more coffee. She wasn't sure if he understood.

"I think I know what you mean. I've always loved this island best at night." He finished his coffee, then put the mug down on the floor in front of him, turning to face her. "Like a certain woman I know."

Sam felt the blood begin to pound in her ears. A distinct tight feeling preluding desire began to tingle through her body. She finished her coffee and held out her cup.

"Is there any more of this? It's very good." She hoped the neutral words would lead them back to safer footing.

He poured her a cup, then filled up his own, replacing the thermos cap with deliberate movements. She took a deep breath of the fragrant beverage, then closed her eyes and took another sip. His next words startled her.

"Why the hell is it we're both so stubborn?" he asked quietly.

She smiled. It was true. He had forbidden her to do the stunt, but she had been out every day with Pepito, working with Sultan and Babe until they had their behavior down perfectly. And Ryan had just as steadfastly refused to budge on his decision. He had taken out his anger and frustration on the crew, and she had poured out her energy into intense training sessions. Neither of them had spoken to each other more than what was absolutely necessary.

She cleared her throat, feeling she should be doing more to meet him halfway. After all, he had come to see her, had made the first move.

"I'm glad you came out here."

She saw him smile in the dim light of the lantern, his chiseled features thrown into relief.

"So am I," he admitted. "It was getting harder and harder to stay away from you."

Sam's throat tightened at his words. "I hated being mean to you," she whispered. "But you were so hateful about the stunt." The crux of their argument had to be brought into the open sooner or later.

She felt him move closer, felt his arm come up over her shoulder and pull her close against his hard body. "I talked with Jake today when I went into San Juan," he admitted.

"What about?" She tried to keep her voice calm.

"What do you think? I asked him to explain every single detail of how you would do that stunt." He chuckled, low in his throat. "I must have kept him on the phone for at least an hour. I almost made him figure out the odds of your getting it right."

She felt some of her irritation returning. "What did he say?" she asked coolly.

"Hey, I didn't mean it like that. There's an element of risk in any stunt." He rubbed his hand over his eyes wearily. "That's how I got my start in the business, doing stunts. I have a lot of respect for you, Samantha. But I still get scared."

"I do, too." His arm tightened around her shoulders, and they sat in silence for a while.

"What did he say?" Sam broke the quiet.

"He told me if anyone could get those two damn animals to do something as crazy as that, you could."

She blinked back sudden, unbidden tears. Sam missed Jake more than she realized. She could almost hear him saying those exact words to Ryan.

"So do we do it or not?"

"Is the day after tomorrow too soon for you?"

"Oh, Ryan!" She put her hand on the side of his face, stroking the hard plane of his cheek gently. "I won't make you sorry for this."

He took her hand and kissed each finger, almost absently. "Just don't get hurt, that's all I ask."

She saw the tension in his face, was aware of the sudden roughness in his voice. *He really is afraid for me,* she thought.

"I promise to be careful. If anything seems to be the slightest bit off, I won't do it. I'm always very careful."

Iago snarled in the distance, and Sam was instantly alert. But there was nothing. As usual, the tiger had been spooked by the rustling of leaves overhead. She had observed him carefully from her first day, and his temperament hadn't improved. The word that came to her mind was evil, but she pushed the thought away. It wasn't wise to give animals human emotions. But this animal was dangerous.

"Ryan?"

"Hmm?"

"I want that tiger shipped out as soon as possible."

"I've been calling around, Sam. I'll get to it as quickly as I can. In the meantime let Pepito take care of him. He seems to be able to get closer to the cage than you can." He wasn't belittling her ability, just stating a fact.

Sam snuggled against him, satisfied for now. "I'll need two trainers for the stunt," she reminded him.

He reached into his pants pocket and pulled out a key ring. "Here's the key to the Jaguar. Rebecca and Timothy are coming down from the compound tomorrow. Jake insisted. There's a map in the glove compartment, but the airport's pretty easy to find. You just turn left when you get to the main road and follow the signs.''

"Then you knew at dinner?"

He nodded.

"Why didn't you tell me then?"

"I wasn't sure you'd even speak to me."

In answer, she moved closer against his comforting presence. He tightened his arm around her shoulders. Sam leaned her head against his chest, feeling the warm, smooth muscles under his shirt. She reached out and curled her fingers around his free hand and sighed with contentment.

All the important things had been said.

THE FIRST THING SAM DID on the morning of her stunt was take a look out the front of her tent and check the weather. It was unpredictable in Puerto Rico, but so far they had been lucky. Except for daily, but brief, showers, the climate was sunny and warm. Perhaps the only flaw was excess humidity.

But this morning the sun was already beginning to burn off the moisture over the thick jungle vegetation. She zipped the tent shut and reached over to touch Rebecca on the shoulder.

"Time to get up," she whispered.

"Oh, no! Why are you always so damn cheerful!" Rebecca groaned from deep inside her bedroll. The two women had gone through basic training together, and Sam admired Rebecca's gift for working with elephants. They had never had the time to form an especially close friendship, although they liked and respected each other. Still, Sam had been happy to see a familiar face.

"You won't have time for a shower if you sleep too late," she teased. "Then even Babe won't want to go near you!"

"Give me five more minutes." Sam smiled as she watched Rebecca's dark brown hair disappear further into the depths of her bag.

When she came back from her shower, Rebecca was hastily tucking a T-shirt inside her jeans.

"Shooting begins at eight," Sam informed her. "Ben says the light is best then. Why don't we grab some breakfast, then I'll go get Sultan, and you can get Babe?"

"Sounds good to me," Rebecca replied, smoothing on Chapstick and sunscreen. "Is Ryan going to be there?"

"I don't think he'd miss this," Sam replied. There was no anxiety in her eyes. She was already mentally imaging the stunt in her mind.

"Give me one more minute," Rebecca said through clenched teeth as she struggled with her boots. "You know, he's better looking than in the magazines."

"Who?" Sam asked, momentarily coming out of her fog. "Oh, Ryan. Yes, he is." She grinned, then glanced at her watch. "We'd better get going."

"I'm ready."

The two women sat side by side at breakfast. Tim joined them soon after, and the three of them laughed and joked as they ate. Sam insisted on catching up on all the news at the compound, and Rebecca was only too glad to fill her in on the details.

Sam watched in amazement at the breakfast that Tim managed to put away. Though only five eight, with dark blond hair and hazel eyes, Tim managed to eat his way through a stack of pancakes, two fried eggs, strips of bacon, and several pieces of toast. He had a lean, muscular build and a strong, silent manner. Sam knew that she could count on him to help her this morning.

"You should eat a little more, Sam," he advised her

as he polished off a glass of papaya juice. Luis looked on approvingly.

They were laughing over Rebecca's story about how Jake's newest raccoon had escaped into Maria's kitchen garden and eaten most of the sweet corn when Ryan joined them.

"How do you feel?" He directed his question to Sam. He had met Rebecca and Tim the night before and had helped them settle in.

"Fine." Sam met his gaze. She sensed a part of her deriving fresh strength from the man beside her. "How about you?"

"I'll be glad when the whole thing is over," he muttered, then looked up to encompass the other two people with his eyes. "Hello, Rebecca, Tim."

"Hi," Rebecca said.

Tim waved his fork in acknowledgment, his mouth full of toast.

"Do you think Babe is ready for all this?" Ryan directed his question to Rebecca this time.

She nodded and picked up a large glass of papaya juice. "As ready as she'll ever be. She's a sweet one. It would take a lot to rattle her." Ryan seemed to visibly relax in front of her and, encouraged, she went on. "Sultan's a big baby; he'd do anything for Sam. She's had him since she could hold him in her lap. You don't have anything to worry about."

"I hope not." He rose from his seat. "I'll meet you all on the set at seven thirty. Sharp." And then he walked over to confer with Ben.

"He's gorgeous, Sam. I hope you realize how lucky you are." Rebecca's voice held admiration.

Tim rolled his eyes as if to say *women*. "Yeah. He's a nice guy."

"He's also hard to deal with, stubborn as a zebra, and egocentric. He works too hard, he overprotects me. . . ."

Rebecca grinned. "And you love every minute of it!"

"I suppose so." Sam took another look at her watch. "Let's get going."

When the three of them reached the set, there was such a bustle of activity, it seemed impossible for everything to be ready in half an hour. Sam left Sultan with Tim for the few minutes it took her to change into her leather bikini and boots. Don had rinsed her hair the night before, and now he plaited it into a thick braid down her back so it would be out of her way. He was uncharacteristically silent this morning, and Sam knew that he was apprehensive about the entire endeavor. After the most minimal of makeups, she went back to Tim.

"You'd better keep out of sight with Rebecca by the wall," she advised him. "If the two of you keep talking to Babe, she should have no trouble accepting this."

He nodded and walked quickly away.

Sam ruffled Sultan's head with the palm of her hand. The large animal responded by making his usual chuffing noises and butting his head against her.

She looked up at the stone wall, looming twenty feet into the still morning air. The voices and confusion around her receded. She pictured Sultan racing along the top, then leaping from the highest part, floating over the moat, his large cat's body a perfect jumping machine. She could see Babe waiting below, the bright red covering on her back a perfect target for the tiger. In her visualization Sultan landed effortlessly and Babe was perfectly still. She knew it would go well.

"Come on, boy." She tugged gently on the chain, and Sultan fell into step by her side.

"We'll be ready in about fifteen minutes, Sam, so you might as well get positioned on the wall." Ben's deep voice boomed over the rest of the chatter.

She nodded, looking over in his direction. Ben gave

her a smile and a thumbs-up signal. Ryan was standing next to him, and Sam noticed his anxious expression, before he realized she was watching him. He crossed his fingers and held them over his head.

The look that passed between them was as intimate as a caress. Sam raised her hand to her lips and blew him a quick kiss. Then she looked away.

As she and Sultan climbed the sloping platform that led up to the thick wall Sam set her mind to the task at hand. Jake had always stressed mental attitude, and she had seen trainers who had everything but that essential ability to have faith in themselves fail in various endeavors. Sam knew that she wouldn't.

She didn't look down as she reached the top of the wall. It wasn't because she was afraid of heights, just that all her attention, the focus of her energy, was on the top of the wall and beyond.

This particular section of the ruined palace had a wall almost twice as wide as a sidewalk. Sam had run Sultan over a similar wall, but lower, hundreds of times in the past two weeks. She knew the cat's natural ability and grace would serve them well this morning.

Though she knew the top of the wall had been checked by Joe, the stunt coordinator, and again by Ryan, she knelt down and touched it. It was dry and cool. Satisfied, she walked Sultan to the section she had marked as their starting point and waited for further instruction.

She knew Ryan and Ben had positioned six cameras at every conceivable angle, covering every shot. A couple of them were up high on massive booms, but most of the shots were from below the wall to give the structure an illusion of even greater height.

"Almost ready, Sam. You can get up on his back." Ben's voice seemed to come from far away.

She unsnapped the chain and tossed it in back of

them. Looping her fingers underneath the leather collar hidden in Sultan's fur, she patted the animal. "Steady, boy."

And then she was on his back. She knew the momentary thrill she always experienced at being seated on top of such power. She felt the cat's muscles underneath his velvet coat. Hooking her legs gently underneath his belly, she felt the soft fur on his stomach tickle her legs. Sultan stood perfectly still. Sam could just imagine the picture they presented—the large orange-and-white cat, five hundred pounds of feline grace, and the "jungle princess" with her flaming hair astride him.

She caressed the soft fur between his huge ears. For all his immense size, Sultan was still a kitten to her. He was doubly special because the tiger was the last animal her father had given to her before he died. She had worked with him for weeks, eager to show her father how much the tiny cub had improved, but he had never had a chance to see.

But thoughts of death weren't good on a morning like this. She looked straight ahead, every muscle in her body poised for what was to happen next. She knew the cat was only waiting for her direction.

A silence fell over the jungle, broken only by a few birdcalls. She heard the snap of the clapboard that signaled action.

"Go ahead, Sam," called Ben.

She tightened her legs around the tiger's body and flattened herself against him. Her cheek was close to his fur and she could hear him breathing, deep and slow. She patted his head, then slipped her hand underneath the collar, gripping it tightly.

"All right, Sultan, let's go."

The tiger broke into a trot, then picked up speed as they covered the distance on top of the wall. Sam moved into his rhythm, feeling the muscles contract and relax under her bare legs. The big cat was cantering now. He was doing beautifully.

She saw the last of the marks she had set out on the stone wall so carefully the previous day, and knew they only had a hundred feet left. She made a soft hissing sound, and Sultan responded to the command with a tremendous burst of speed that brought tears to her eyes. She knew that to anyone watching, the tiger had suddenly become a white-and-orange blur. Sam had just enough time to tighten her legs as the cat reached the edge. She felt Sultan's muscles gathering under her, like the taut mechanism of an exquisite catapult.

And then he jumped. There was no hesitation in his movements. She opened her eyes against the rush of air and watched as the bright red of Babe's elegant covering seemed to rush up to meet them. She tightened her legs again on impact. A part of her noted with satisfaction that Sultan had landed perfectly, using his back claws for traction.

As soon as she was sure the tiger was secure on the elephant's back, she slid off him and groped her way to the elephant's head. Sitting astride the large animal, she tightened her knees.

"Babe, down!"

The large elephant slowly went down on her knees. Sultan was squatting on the red covering. He didn't seem at all perturbed by what had just happened.

As she slid from Babe's head to the elephant's bent knee to the ground, she became aware of the smell of smoke. Looking up, she saw several members of the crew with fire extinguishers, putting out the row of torches that had run alongside the bottom of the wall. She hadn't been aware of them at all.

"I'll take Sultan back to his cage, Sam," Tim offered.

"Thank you." She was elated. As she looked back at

the top of the wall she felt an arm go around her shoulders.

"That was one hell of a stunt." Ryan's breath tickled her ear.

"Thank you." She couldn't resist. "Now do you believe me?"

He smiled, but his eyes were serious. "You did a beautiful job. I couldn't have done it better myself." He laughed and hugged her tighter against him. "I couldn't have done it, period."

She took his hand and pulled it tighter against her shoulders. They turned together and watched Rebecca unchain Babe with the ease of a professional.

"Thanks, Rebecca, you did a great job," Sam called.

"You weren't so bad yourself. Wait till I get back and tell Jake!"

Ryan pivoted away, taking her with him. "Ready for lunch?" he asked.

"But I just ate breakfast!"

"I meant lunch in San Juan."

She stopped and tried to read his expression, but it was inscrutable and impossible. Remembering the last lunch they had shared in San Juan, she felt her heartbeat quicken.

"Right now?"

"After you pack a few things." At her puzzled expression he continued. "I thought you might be up to a small holiday after what you did this morning. Ben was so pleased with the shots he got, I talked him into working with Helen for the next few days. Tim and Rebecca have already agreed to stay and look after the animals."

"You really have this all figured out." Sam wanted to go, but she didn't want to make it too easy for him.

"We aim to please." There were humorous glints in

his dark blue eyes. "I think you need a rest, and since I'm in charge—"

"A rest? With you around? Not a chance!" She laughed out loud. He pulled her against his body, his lips pausing near hers just a fraction of a second before he kissed her.

Since Sam's evening on night watch Ryan hadn't made any type of move toward reestablishing the intimacy of their relationship. But she had no doubts he still wanted her.

His mouth was smooth and hot as it parted her lips, his hands firm as they clasped her to his hard length. She put her palms against his chest and levered herself away from his tormenting mouth.

"Is this a proposition?" she asked shakily.

"Only if you want it to be." He was serious now.

She studied his face, noticing the tired lines around his eyes, the slight circles. It would do both of them good to get away from location. And they might be able to sort out their feelings for each other once they were away from all the confusion of making a movie.

"Yes."

His hold tightened on her arm, then he released her. "I'll meet you at my car in half an hour." His tone was low and conspiratorial. "Try to make it fast so we can get out of here before any problems come up."

Sam made it to Ryan's car in twenty minutes. She hadn't packed many dressy clothes in her original suitcase; she had been prepared for work, not traveling to San Juan. But she had managed to salvage her blue shirtwaist and packed it, along with her sandals. She had dressed sensibly for traveling in a pair of designer jeans and a striped pullover top. Her hair was still the rich, deep auburn it had been for the stunt, but she had brushed it out and it fell over her shoulders in fiery waves from the tight braid.

She was leaning against the Jaguar and swinging her bag in restless agitation when she heard Ryan open the trunk.

"Toss your bag in," he ordered briefly.

She was almost annoyed by his curt command until she realized he was attempting to get away before anyone stopped them. She walked around to the back of the car and set her bag in the trunk next to his. He shut the lid.

"Any regrets?" he asked.

"None so far. Should I be worried?"

He merely smiled and proceeded to open the passenger door for her.

Chapter Ten

The hotel Ryan selected was right on the ocean, a tall high rise with a large circular driveway. Sam had the fleetest impression of steel and glass surrounded by brilliant tropical foliage before he pulled the Jaguar to a stop. A man in a bright red uniform began to walk toward them. Ryan gave him the car keys, then walked around to help Sam out of the car.

She tightened her grip on his arm when she noticed the elegantly dressed men and women going in and out the large glass front door. He sensed her distress.

"What's wrong?"

"I can't go in like this!" Her jeans suddenly made her feel underdressed.

"Yes, you can. See those people over there?" He indicated an older couple coming up the sidewalk. The man was in his fifties and dressed in Bermuda walking shorts with a loud shirt. A camera hung around his neck, while his arms were loaded down with packages. His wife, still slim and rather pretty, wore a sundress and casual floppy sandals.

"It gets dressy at night, but we can eat somewhere else if you prefer," he whispered.

She nodded. Another man in uniform had their bags, and Sam was aware of how small hers looked. It was practically shouting to the world that she was about to begin an illicit weekend with a man she sometimes thought she hardly knew.

Ryan reached the main desk, but Sam hung back, reluctant to approach him and acknowledge they were together. How did one go about this exactly? She felt awkward and almost regretted having agreed to a weekend away so quickly. Was he assuming they would share a room? Perhaps a suite? *You shared a tent, dummy,* she scolded herself.

Trying to distract her thoughts, she turned toward a large stand of magazines and paperback books, pretending interest in the glossy display. As she leafed through one of the magazines her attention was distracted by the cover of another.

Almost immediately the photograph transported her memory back to the afternoon on the compound. But when had the photojournalist taken this picture? She put back the magazine in her hands and reached for the other. As she turned to the article and quickly scanned the vivid color pictures, she remembered that the interview had taken place the same day she had learned about Ryan and his movie. She flipped through the rest of the magazine, when suddenly a full-page photo of Ryan, his arm linked with that of a young woman, screamed out at her.

Shutting the magazine, she let it fall to a pile at the bottom of the shelf. Before her mind had time to start thinking the obvious she cast a glance toward the main desk.

A porter in a dark blue uniform was taking both their bags, and Ryan was walking toward her. She went to meet him, not wanting him to see the magazine. She was sure if he saw it spread out over the others, he would know she had been looking through it.

"We're on the seventh floor," he said as he took her arm. "I don't know about you, but I'd like to go upstairs and get cleaned up."

She nodded, not trusting her voice. Suddenly her impulsive decision to come with him seemed utterly wrong. She was almost to the point of telling him she'd prefer to take a taxi back when she felt his strong hands on the small of her back steering her toward the elevators.

She got inside, part of her wanting to tell him then, part of her wanting nothing more than to lie down on a regular bed and sleep for the next day. As they got off on the seventh floor and her feet sank into thick carpeting, she was intensely aware of how much she had missed simple comforts like carpeting, air conditioning, a bathtub, a soft bed.

She lifted her chin, a little of her spirit returning. She had money with her; she could always rent a room of her own for the night and return by taxi in the morning.

He stopped in front of a set of doors. "Here we are." As he turned to her she steeled herself, prepared for an assault on her tired senses. She was surprised when he pressed a hotel key into her hand.

"This is your room. Mine is next door." He inclined his head to the left. The rooms were next door to each other, but there was a great deal of space between the doors.

"What do you want to do for the rest of the day?" he asked.

She swallowed, then blurted out her feelings before she had time to think. "I'd like nothing better than a hot bath and a long nap." At his amused silence she asked, "Do you mind?"

He shook his head. "I was going to suggest we get some rest." He leaned over and kissed her on the forehead, as if she were his little sister instead of a woman he had claimed at one time to love. "I'll give you a call later in the evening; maybe we can go out to eat."

She nodded and watched as he walked along the carpeted hallway, the lush covering muffling any sounds he made. He reached his door, and she watched as he slid his key into the lock.

He looked over at her, as if aware she hadn't moved

the entire time. "Good night, Samantha," he called, with a trace of humor in his voice.

It snapped her out of her tiredness in a flash. With trembling hands, she found the lock and pushed her key into it, swinging open the door with more force than was necessary. Shutting it behind her, she took in the room.

After nearly a month in the interior of the Puerto Rican jungle, the sight that greeted her was a welcome relief. Deep blue carpeting covered the entire floor, matched by walls of a lighter shade. The effect was peaceful and soothing. A queen-size bed dominated one entire wall, covered with a crisp striped bedspread. The same cool cotton material was repeated in the curtains.

But it was the balcony that drew her attention. One entire side of the suite faced out over the ocean, and a sliding glass door opened onto a sturdy balcony. There was a wooden rocking chair, a hammock, a small table, and several chairs.

Sam stepped across the carpet, stopping to kick off her tennis shoes and wiggle her toes in the lush pile. Then she started for the balcony.

As soon as she opened the glass door a rush of fresh sea air hit her in the face, a strong stimulant to counter the uncertainty she had felt before. She walked to the edge and rested her hand on the smooth iron rail.

The view of the ocean was incredible. The beach was dotted with palm trees, but they were far below. At this height there was nothing to distract her from the magnificent view.

It was the water that had the most hypnotic effect. Bright white foam curled up along the sand, while deeper out the colors reflected and shimmered like many precious jewels. She could see a bit of coral reef in the distance, where the ocean crashed over the natural barrier and foamed white against the almost navy depths.

She stretched her arms over her head and leaned on the railing. The water crashed relentlessly against the sand below and the sound was soothing, calming her. She had almost forgotten another world existed except for their small camp in the middle of the island. The weeks she had been there seemed to have blotted out her past life and made her future uncertain. And a large part of that feeling was because of Ryan.

She turned her head in the direction of his room and was startled to see, though their rooms were some distance apart, that their balconies were quite close. Flustered by the thought that he might come out and see her, she went inside and shut the glass door.

Now what? The bed beckoned seductively, and she almost gave in to the temptation to sleep, but as she became aware of her aching muscles she decided to take a quick shower.

She hadn't inspected the bathroom before, and the sight that greeted her almost took her breath away. The entire room seemed to be made of marble: the deep shower, the double sinks, and a large tub big enough for two. There were small packets of bubble bath in a glass bowl by the sink, and the bathtub had tiny bottles of shampoo and rinse on the side shelf.

Sam didn't need any further prompting. After weeks of hastily caught showers during the early-morning hours before filming, she decided to take advantage of this temporary luxury. Turning on the taps, she poured in a packet of bubble bath and watched as the force of the water caused the bubbles to foam and dissipate their fragrant scent throughout the large bathroom.

There was no need for a heater, but Sam noticed a towel warmer that operated with a simple flick of a switch. She decided against it and went outside to the main room to retrieve her bag.

Back inside the bathroom, she took out her brush and

began to untangle her hair. The deep auburn color was flattering, but she doubted if she ever wanted to be a redhead again. She bent over and brushed her hair from the base of her scalp to the ends, enjoying the satisfying stretch of her calf muscles.

Flinging her head back, her hair settling around her shoulders like a lion's mane, she caught sight of her reflection in the large mirror. Though she always wore a strong sunscreen because of her fair complexion, the intense Caribbean sun had given her skin a golden coloring. There were slight shadows under her green eyes, and she had to admit to herself that Ryan had been right. She was due for a vacation. The sun had also lightened her hair, and even Don's rinse hadn't been able to hide the gold threaded through her auburn hair.

Turning off the taps, she stripped off her top and jeans, then her underwear. Before she stepped into the steamy tub she looked at the mirror again, this time with a very critical eye.

Sam had never been embarrassed by her body. The constant outdoor activity and sunshine while training animals had precluded her having any real problems with her figure or skin. She stared dispassionately at the woman in front of her and noted the firm body, well-proportioned if a bit too slight. Her muscles were firm and rounded without being masculine, her stomach flat, her breasts high and firm. She touched her neck gently, and her thoughts flew to the evening in Ryan's tent, when he had made her very aware of her body as an instrument of intense pleasure. She ran her fingers lightly over her breasts, down her stomach, and over her hips. Had he thought she was lovely? Had he received as much pleasure as she? Her emotions had been so intense, she almost hadn't been aware of him until she had decided to pleasure him in return.

She smoothed the fine auburn hair back from her face

and studied it critically. Her nose was a bit too sun-burned and her skin was peeling slightly. Pulling her hair in front of her shoulders, she noticed that some of the ends were split and raggedy. She wore her hair off her face most of the time when she was working with the animals, but seeing it loose this way, she wondered if perhaps there were a more attractive way of wearing it.

And then she wondered quickly for whom she was trying to make herself more attractive. Turning away from the mirror, she stepped into the bubbles. The water slipped smoothly around her body as she im-mersed herself to her chin. Lying back against the edge of the tub, she stretched full length and wiggled her toes. It was heaven. She fiddled with the tap with her foot, adding a little more hot water, then settled back for a good, long soak.

She could feel the tension leaving her shoulders and neck, slowly, as if it were slipping into the scented water. She flexed her muscles; first her arms, then her legs. She stretched her back. Taking the soap from the dish on the side, she began to work the scented bar be-tween her fingers. Its lather was rich and luxurious, and she soaped her shoulders, enjoying the feel of her fingers as they kneaded out any kinks left.

Once she had finished with her body, she ducked her head underneath the water and wet her hair. Reaching for the shampoo with her eyes closed, she poured out a generous amount and shampooed her hair twice, until she was satisfied most of the auburn tint had been rinsed out. She lay back in the now cooler water and pulled the plug with her toes.

Finishing up with a stinging shower to rinse away any last traces of soap, she wrapped herself in a thick towel and walked back into the main room of her suite.

The tropical sun was still high in the sky, so she shut the heavy curtains, making the room dark and cool. She locked the door and took her travel alarm out of her bag. Setting it for five in the evening, she placed it on the small night table next to the huge bed.

The white percale sheets were cool and crisp as she pulled back the light bedspread and slid between the covers. She rolled over onto her stomach, pulling a pillow under her head and closing her eyes. Within minutes she was fast asleep.

THE TINY SHRILL OF THE ALARM finally pierced her consciousness. She reached over to the nightstand and attempted to shut it off, but only succeeded in knocking it to the carpeted floor.

Sam groaned and turned over in bed, pulling the covers up over her head. She'd sleep for just a little longer. Until she had actually gotten into bed, she'd had no idea how tired she really was. The bath had relaxed all her muscles, making her feel almost weightless on top of the firm mattress.

The travel alarm began to ring again, and she pulled a pillow over her damp hair. It kept ringing at odd intervals, and she couldn't quite manage to shut the noise out of her mind. With a sigh of exasperation she flung the covers back and reached for the clock, pressing in the back button with more force than was necessary. But the ringing continued.

She sat back in bed, raking her fingers through her heavy hair. As the noise continued she realized it was the small blue phone by the side of the bed. She groped for it and picked up the receiver in midring.

"Hello?" Her voice was breathless. There was only one person who knew she was here.

"Did I wake you up?"

"No, not really...the alarm went off about two seconds before you called."

"What would you like to have for dinner?"

Sam rubbed her eyes with her free hand, trying to orient herself to the world of the living. "I don't know. Let me think a minute."

"Are you hungry?"

"Yes." She hadn't realized how much until he had called.

"Why don't I meet you downstairs in the bar, and we can eat here at the hotel?" He wasn't pressuring her, merely offering a suggestion.

"Oh, no." She stopped, not wanting him to think she didn't care to eat with him. She did want to see more of Ryan, but as she glanced at her blue silk blend shirtwaist peeking out of her traveling bag, she realized she had forgotten to hang it up. "What I mean is, I don't really have anything to wear."

"Then I'll call room service and have something delivered to my room. I'll make it for seven, all right? Does that give you enough time? You could even go back to sleep."

Her mind raced feverishly. Dinner in a private room with Ryan seemed to be the utmost folly. If she accepted, would he take it as a signal she wanted everything else such a complex invitation might also entail? But she remembered what he had said on the set, about the entire trip being a proposition only if she so desired.

"Yes, that sounds fine." She made up her mind with a suddenness that surprised her. "I'll be on time." And then she hung up the phone.

She lay back down in bed in the darkened room and pulled the sheets over her body with a childishly vulnerable gesture. Staring at the dark ceiling, Samantha realized she wouldn't be fighting Ryan tonight, but herself. She could remember every detail of their night in his tent, and now that she didn't have constant work and responsibility to keep her feelings and desires at bay, she realized he affected her as no other man had.

She rolled over in bed, not wanting to feel this way. Her thoughts turned to leaving before dinner, going back to the safety of the jungle. But then she sat up in bed, a better idea forming in her mind.

Within minutes she had pulled on jeans and a shirt, had grabbed her purse, and was on her way downstairs to the lobby. She glanced around furtively, making sure Ryan wasn't anywhere to be seen before she went to the newsstand and bought the magazine she had been looking at earlier. If anything could cool her feelings for Ryan, seeing him with other women could. Hiding it in a brown paper bag, she decided to go and get a cup of coffee to wake up completely.

The hotel was one of the newer ones, obviously one of the first built on this particular stretch of beach. Dark wooden paneling and soft lighting made a welcome alternative to the bright sun outside. Sam glanced around for any clue as to which way a coffee shop might be, but there were no signs to give her any indication.

She noticed a tiny woman sitting behind a counter inside what looked like a small clothing store. Walking to the doorway, Sam spoke to her.

"Could you tell me if there's a coffee shop nearby? Just somewhere I can get a cup of coffee?"

The woman looked up, pins in her mouth. She took them out and jabbed them into a pincushion, then slid off her high stool and walked up to Sam. She was quite short and barely made it to Sam's shoulders.

"Go to the left as you leave and down the hall. There's coffee in the bar, or you can take it with you to your room." She was studying Sam, looking at her with the eye of someone used to estimating sizes, coloring, styles. Sam was almost out the door when she heard the woman call to her.

"Señorita, come here."

Sam stopped, more in astonishment than anything

else. The woman beckoned her with a quick gesture of her hand. Not wanting to be rude—and suddenly curious—she followed her.

The woman led her to a small storage area in back of the shop. Sam could see piles of boxes, some spilling over on top of a large table. The woman led her straight to one particular box.

"This arrived today. I think it would look very pretty on you." She held up an evening dress, different shades of blue that seemed to swirl into each other, each shade changing with the subtlety of fine marble. Sam reached out and touched the material. It was cool and smooth beneath her fingers. Where had she ever seen colors as stunning as these? She thought immediately of the changing hues of the Caribbean Sea.

"It is one hundred percent silk, and you have to hand wash, but it will last forever. The softness only improves with time. Try it on," she urged.

As Sam took the dress from the woman she thought quickly to the dinner ahead. If she had something to wear, they could go out after all. She nodded her head and went inside one of the dressing rooms.

She obviously has an artist's eye, Sam thought later as she walked out into the small store. The silk against her skin felt like the bathwater had earlier. It flowed around her, and even barefoot with slightly damp hair, she felt special in it. It was sleeveless, almost backless, and it clung in a way that made the material look as if it were barely wrapped around her body. The small fastening was on the side, and the neckline was deep and veed over her breasts. It was a wonderful dress, made for magical nights and dancing until dawn.

"I'll take it," she decided.

The woman was obviously pleased. "Do you have shoes to go with it?" she asked.

Almost an hour later Sam emerged from the tiny

shop, her coffee totally forgotten. Though she had never given much thought to shopping for clothes before, preferring function over design, the last half hour had been a revelation to her. Sophia, the proprietress, had chosen most of the clothes, some of the loveliest, sexiest things Sam had ever worn. As she stepped into the elevator and balanced her packages she thought about the tiny turquoise bikini, the graceful sandals to match the dress, the silk shawl with intricate lacework, the two other dresses, several pairs of casual pants, and some shorts and skimpy tops. Regular clothes, but the cuts and colors had brought her body to life in a way her faded jeans and work shirts never had. She had laughingly agreed to stop by again before she left in case something else came in.

As she shifted her packages to search for her key she heard someone unlock a door close to her own. Sam looked up over her parcels to see an old man in a dark dress suit and his wife in a burgundy evening dress. They were obviously on their way to dinner.

"Oh, Harry, help the poor thing," she heard the woman say.

And Harry promptly did. Taking Sam's key from her hand and inserting it into the lock, he opened the door and helped her carry her packages inside, depositing them at the foot of the bed. After mumbling a reply to Sam's expression of gratitude, he and his wife continued down the hall.

Sam looked at her travel alarm. Six thirty, and she had agreed to meet Ryan at seven. She ripped open the bag that had the dress inside, then took out the sandals and hose. Running into the bathroom, she picked up her hairbrush and passed it through her now-dry hair. It fell around her shoulders and down her back, shiny and light blond, the golden highlights near her face making her look healthy and outdoorsy. She reached for her makeup.

Twenty minutes later she stood in front of the full-length mirror, studying her appearance with a critical eye. The dress looked spectacular on her, even if she did say so herself. She had styled her hair up on top of her head in a loose knot. The barest makeup accented her tanned face, just lipstick and blush. She had accented her eyes with a pencil the way Don had showed her, and she had to admit that it looked good. The eye makeup gave an unexpected drama to her appearance, emphasizing the slight tilt to her eyes and their deep, pure color.

She felt nearly naked in the dress. It was cut so that wearing a bra was impossible, and the silk whispered over her body as gently as a lover's touch. Sophia had even talked her into a bottle of cologne, and Sam had sprayed it on her throat, her wrists, the back of her knees, and between her breasts.

She picked up her small evening bag and gave her reflection one more look. No, she wouldn't feel ashamed going anywhere with Ryan tonight. She walked back into the bedroom and gathered up her shawl. A quick look at the clock confirmed the time: five minutes to seven. She didn't want to give Ryan the impression she was too eager for this evening, so she sat down and began to page through the magazine she had bought.

She turned directly to the large picture of him with another woman. Her heart began to pound heavily. They were walking down what looked like a typical California beach, the girl in a tiny red bikini, Ryan in faded jeans. She had her arm around his waist, and Ryan had his hand on her shoulder. Sam narrowed her eyes and read the caption.

"Director Ryan Fitzgerald and his constant companion, actress Beverly Easton, walk along the beach by his house in Malibu. Beverly is slated to star in Ryan's next film, a romantic comedy."

She turned the page and was shocked to find a picture

of herself and Ryan, his arm around her shoulders. When had this picture been taken? She recognized the location and surmised it had been taken fairly early during filming. The print looked grainy, as if the photo had been taken from a distance and blown up. Her eyes dropped to the caption.

"Director Fitzgerald gives some instruction in the art of being a jungle princess to his current girl friend. Samantha Collins, daughter of the late John Collins, appears to be the latest in a long series of affairs he has had with the fair sex."

She put the magazine down, a choking sensation in her throat. Trying to breathe calmly and still the dull thudding of her heart, she crossed the room and opened the curtains. She pressed her forehead against the cool glass, staring outside into the twilight.

Why had she ever thought her relationship with Ryan would be any different? Obviously he was attracted to pretty girls and hadn't had to worry about any lack of company. And it seemed, from the photos of his various girl friends, both past and present, that most of the women had been involved with whatever he had been working on at that time.

He had asked her to believe in him, to disregard the press. And yet this national magazine had spelled out his life in various eras, using whatever woman he was with at the time to give some definition to the years. The glossy photos had told her more than any article could.

Suddenly Sam was glad she had bought the dress, glad she had no intention of staying with Ryan and eating dinner in his room. She had a peculiar feeling of sympathy for the other women who had fallen prey to his charms. Where were all his former girl friends now? Aside from Beverly, she thought, who was expected to be in his next film and in his bed as well. Were they married, with children, trying to forget a wild affair and attribute it to youthful experimentation? Or had they remained single, comparing each man they met to Ryan, remembering the way he smiled, the way he had made their bodies feel with the skilled caresses of his hands and mouth.

She wasn't going to join the ranks. Picking up her shawl from where it had fallen on the floor, she put it around her shoulders, then tucked her key into her evening bag.

Squaring her shoulders, she left the room.

Chapter Eleven

As she knocked on Ryan's door she prepared her mind, steeling herself against his potent charm. She would be polite and cool, insist they dine downstairs, then leave him afterward without a word, only to wonder where he had gone wrong.

She knocked again, more impatient this time.

"Just a minute," she heard him call out.

She smiled, her feelings a small, bitter ball in the pit of her stomach. Mr. Fitzgerald was certainly in for a surprise.

And then he opened the door. His hair was still damp, as if he had showered recently, and she could smell the elusive scent of his after-shave. Dressed in a dark suit, he smiled easily as he caught sight of her, but the smile died as he opened the door wider and took in her appearance. He looked at her as if he were oddly shaken.

"My God," he whispered. "You're beautiful."

She knew it was an honest compliment, knew she had taken him off guard. This moment would have delighted her earlier, but now it brought her nothing, not even the smallest sparking of desire. She smiled up at him, but her lips felt frozen.

"I thought it might be better if we ate downstairs." She remained where she stood in the hallway.

He looked puzzled for a moment, then put his hand on her arm. "I've already ordered the food. Come in."

She hesitated and saw the strange, questioning look come into his eyes again. Pride made her stiffen her spine. She'd show him she wasn't weak. She had herself so convinced she was impervious to his influence that she walked inside, casting him another frozen smile.

"Sam, are you still tired? If you'd like to lie down while I wait for our food—"

"Oh, but I'm not tired at all."

"You seemed—" He stopped, confused, then walked over and put his hands on her shoulders. "You're absolutely beautiful, but you know that, don't you? Where on earth did you get the dress?"

She shrugged her shoulders, disturbed by his touch. "At a little store downstairs."

"I guess I've gotten too used to seeing you either in jeans or close to nothing at all." The pressure on her shoulders increased as he drew her toward him. He kissed her lips lightly, and she held herself aloof from the sensation only by the utmost exertion of her will.

He stepped away, his face oddly expressionless. "Go on out to the balcony. Our meal should be here shortly. I'll join you in a minute."

His suite was almost identical to hers, though reversed, and Sam approached the balcony on rigid legs. It would be hard to do, she thought, but tonight she had no intention of becoming Ryan's latest conquest. After this evening, she would go back to location, vacation or not. She wanted to get out of his life, finish his movie, and try to forget him completely.

The sight awaiting her was like something out of an elegant magazine. A small circular table was set with white linen. The silver gleamed in the light of a single candle set in a hurricane lamp to protect it from the gentle breezes coming in constantly from the ocean. There was a large floral centerpiece, and she recognized the flowers: orchids. Her throat tightened as she remembered the secret clearing Ryan had taken her to. The centerpiece was all white, and the orchids ranged in size from delicate miniatures to blooms she could barely have contained in her hand. There were small lanterns at the four corners of the balcony, and the lighting was soothing, setting a seductive atmosphere. In spite of her earlier resolve she was enchanted.

She heard a knock at the door, then a waiter who looked like a small penguin wheeled a cart out to the balcony and began to set dish after dish on the snowy linen. Sam could smell tantalizing odors; none of them was immediately recognizable to her. The covered dishes were silver and lent their sparkle to the intimate scene.

Reaching underneath the cart to a lower shelf, the waiter brought out a bottle of wine and stood expectantly, waiting. Ryan walked out onto the balcony and came around to where Sam was standing. He pulled out her chair, and she slid into it, glad for the support, as her knees were suddenly shaky.

The waiter uncorked the wine bottle with ease and poured a small amount into Ryan's glass. He took a sip, considered it for just a moment, then nodded his head, and the waiter filled Sam's glass, then Ryan's. He set the linen-wrapped bottle on the table and proceeded to wheel the cart off the balcony and out the door, shutting it behind him.

They were alone.

Sam could feel the familiar fluttering in her stomach, uncomfortable and wonderful at the same time. This was going to be harder than she thought.

Ryan lifted his glass. "To us," he said simply.

She lifted her glass and took a small sip, remembering the last time she had eaten formally with Ryan in San Juan. She'd have to get some food in her stomach before she drank any more. But she wasn't sure if she'd be able to eat a single bite with this man sitting across from her.

There were so many sides to his personality. He could be brutal and abrupt, nasty and sarcastic, when something wasn't going right. She had seen that side of him on the set, even directed at her. He could also be the most tender and gentle of lovers, and she had experienced that side as well. He could be playful, compassionate, thoughtful, sensual— She stopped her train of thought with some effort. He also had the emotional capacity to love intensely and then leave as if nothing had ever transpired. She couldn't bear the thought of that happening to her again. Paul hadn't even loved her and his betrayal had caused her almost unbearable pain. It had taken her months to build her shaky self-confidence back to the point where she could even date again.

But this would be so much worse, because there wasn't a man alive who made her feel as intensely as Ryan did within the space of a few seconds in his arms.

"Pass me your bowl, Sam." She came out of her thoughts long enough to realize Ryan was addressing her.

She picked up the delicate china bowl and gave it to him. Ryan took the lid off the tureen of soup, and the most delicious fragrance filled the air, spicy and warm.

"Black bean soup," he said, as if reading her mind. He served her a generous portion and, garnishing it with raw chopped onion, handed it back to her.

Sam set the bowl down and waited until he had served himself before she picked up her spoon. The soup was delicious, the bland beans transformed into a spicy, rich dish with the addition of wine, garlic, and numerous spices. She was relieved that the task of eating made talking impossible. She needed time to think.

The candle gave off a warm glow, making the silver and linen setting appear almost dreamlike. She took another sip of wine and felt the unfamiliar fluid softness in her blood. She set the glass down, a little away from her place setting. But was it the wine or the dark man across the table affecting her?

The various courses were served in an orderly fashion. After the soup, a small salad, then langosta—small native lobsters—served in butter and garlic and several other spices she couldn't quite place. Sam tried to pick apart the shellfish with her fork and knife until she noticed Ryan was using his hands. There seemed to be something terribly erotic in that simple gesture. She watched as he dipped the seafood in melted butter and proceeded to eat it, licking the excess off his fingers. Eating could be as erotic an art as anything else. Sam vaguely remembered a scene in the movie *Tom Jones*. She looked back down at her plate.

After cleaning their hands in finger bowls and with linen napkins, Ryan cleared away a few of the larger dishes, setting them to the side of the table carefully.

"Would you like dessert now?" he asked softly. He looked as if he were trying to uncover the hidden mechanisms of her mind.

She nodded her head. Though she was almost full, anything would be better than talking. She didn't want to draw out this dinner any more than was necessary.

Ryan was looking at her wineglass as he spoke. "You didn't like the wine, did you?"

"Oh, no. It's fine." She took a small sip.

"Why are you nervous?"

She stiffened her shoulders, calling on the last of her reserves of strength. "I wasn't aware I was." She took a deep breath. "Is this dinner in exchange for something else?" She phrased the question in a blunt manner deliberately, hoping that if he became disgusted with her, she'd be able to leave quickly.

"Not in exchange. But perhaps something else would grow out of the mutual desires of two mature people after a relaxing evening together. I thought women enjoyed being romanced. I know I enjoy romancing you."

She averted her eyes from his gaze. "I *have* enjoyed

this, Ryan. Please believe me. It's just—'' But how could she tell him? How could she say, *I read another journalistic report about your sexual adventures and I don't want any part of it.* This wasn't going to be easy.

''Your father died when you were only seventeen, is that right?'' His question caught her completely off guard, and she looked at him in amazement.

''Yes, but what—''

''You were married to Paul Hartnell, that actor, when you were eighteen.''

''Ryan, I don't want—''

''No, you never want to talk about anything even remotely uncomfortable, do you?''

She felt her face flush and her hands start to tremble. She clenched them into fists in her lap. ''That's not true!''

''Good. Then we'll continue our discussion.'' His voice told her he would have his way in this matter. ''You were divorced when you were nineteen, when you found him in bed with another woman. Isn't that right?''

She felt tears starting in her eyes. The food she had eaten could have been mud for the enjoyment she was getting out of this dinner. ''I don't see that this is any of your business!''

''But it is. It's not that I enjoy taking on charity cases. But I can't stand to see a woman like you shut herself away from all life has to offer.''

She was deeply hurt now; he had bruised several sore spots. ''Don't you mean what *you* have to offer me? And isn't that a quick little affair until you go on to your next picture, your next public performance for the press? I don't give a damn what you do to other women. Maybe they can put up with it. But don't try anything with me!'' She took a deep breath, preparing to heap another string of insults on his head. His next words shook her to the core.

"Samantha, I'm not going to leave you. Ever."

Her insults were caught in her throat. She couldn't say a word. She just looked at him, then quickly down at the linen in front of her.

"Please," she whispered. "I don't know what you're trying to do, or why you're doing this, but—"

"I love you." She looked up and saw Ryan leaning forward in his seat, an anxious, vulnerable look in his dark eyes. Gone was the supremely masculine, arrogant self-confidence that had characterized his every action since the first time she had met him.

She took a deep breath. He was good enough to go in front of his own cameras. Either he was telling her the truth, or he was a consummate actor.

"I'm not lying to you, Samantha." When she didn't answer him, he reached over and touched her cheek lightly. "I saw the same magazine in the lobby this afternoon when I went down to lunch. There was quite a lot written about you, too."

Sam reached up to brush a wisp of hair away from her hot forehead, and Ryan captured her fingers in his hand, then brought them against his mouth for a gentle kiss. "As soon as I finished reading it I understood what you were up against emotionally." She tried to pull her hand away, but he held firm. "You lost your father, and I don't care what you say, it's not an easy thing to lose a parent at that age. Your mother had died before that, so you were left alone."

She could feel her tears overflowing and bent her head so he couldn't see them streaking down her face. Why was he bringing up the most painful memories in her life? What was he trying to prove? Though his words were highly emotional, his tone was low and soothing.

"I'm sure you jumped into marriage with the idea of replacing your father." This time she pulled her hand away, and he let her go. But she remained sitting at the table, her head bent. "Sam, I've done some pretty self-destructive things in my life, but I was able to forgive myself. Hartnell is a real bastard. I worked with him on a film several years ago. He'd do anything to advance his career. Believe me, it has nothing to do with you or your desirability."

She heard his chair scrape back, then felt his hands on her shoulders, massaging the tension away. His voice continued, soft and low against her ear. "At first I thought you were pulling the oldest trick in the world on me, teasing and then turning off. It made me madder than hell at you, even though I wanted you so much." His fingers stopped their movements on her shoulders and just rested against her bare skin with the lightest touch. "I was a fool. You couldn't manipulate a person emotionally if you tried. When I realized that, I began to fall in love with you."

She twisted in her chair and looked up at him, her eyes full. "I thought you were using me. Everything I read or had ever heard about you gave me the feeling that you could walk away any time, from anybody."

His hands moved lower, circling her waist and pulling her up out of her chair to stand beside him. She rested her cheek against the smooth material of his dinner jacket as he stroked her hair.

"Don't you think it would be painful for me if you left?" he whispered. He held her close, as if now that he finally had her in his arms, had finally told her the truth, he couldn't bear to let her go.

Her hands were moving against his chest, but now she slid them upward, loving the feel of his crisp, dark hair where it met his shirt collar. "I never thought about leaving you, only about your leaving me," she whispered.

In answer, he tilted her face up and grazed her lips

with his, seeking, caressing, until she felt herself beginning to respond. His warm hands moved along the skin of her bare back, and she shivered in response, stepping closer to him, trying to get as close as possible to this man.

It seemed unbelievable that he should love her so deeply, want her so badly. Sam felt herself almost tingling with happiness, the rush of joy singing through her veins leaving her limp. She leaned against him, letting him support them both.

"Would you like any dessert?" he asked, his breath brushing her hair.

"No," she answered truthfully.

He leaned over the table and blew out the candle, then pulled her back against his body. Sam relaxed in his embrace, letting the sound of the ocean pounding against the shore below soothe her. She could smell the smokiness of the candle, the remaining odors of the spicy food that still lingered, the warm masculine scent of the man beside her. The cool sea air felt wonderful against her bare skin, and she felt alternate patterns of warm and cool on her back as Ryan's hands continued to stroke her spine.

He stepped away from her and took her hand, leading her into his suite. Closing the glass door behind him, he let her go and began to remove his jacket. As he unknotted his tie Sam walked over and sat down on the large bed. The intimacy between them seemed utterly right. It was strange, because less than an hour before, the tension had been very strong, a force separating them. Now a different sort of tension was in the air. It was almost magnetic, making their bodies yearn toward each other, then away, yet the outcome would always be the same.

Dressed in his black dinner pants, Ryan came over and knelt by the bed. Sam grasped his shoulder with surprise as she felt his hand on her ankle, then he lifted up her foot and began to remove the sandal with gentle tugs. Once it was off, he massaged her sole gently, then placed it on the carpet and picked up the other foot. Soon that sandal was also on the floor.

He stood up, and she was almost awed by the sheer masculine power apparent in his stance. Though he had been vulnerable in declaring his love, now that he was about to express it physically there was no hesitation, no awkwardness about him.

He leaned over and took her lips in a gentle kiss, at the same time moving her toward the center of the bed. She felt the firm mattress yield under his weight as he lay down beside her.

He deepened the kiss, making her open her mouth to his and intimately exploring its softer recesses. She was so excited, she could hardly breathe. Her heart was pounding so loudly that it deafened her to every other sound.

The silk of her dress was so sheer against his hands that she felt she had nothing on. She was aware that Ryan could feel every curve of her softness and she wound her body tighter against him in blind, instinctive need.

He broke the kiss and his lips made a trail of erotic fire down the sensitive cords of her neck, to rest in the deep cleavage between her breasts. She ran her hands through his dark hair and pulled his head tightly against her breasts, her pulse racing wildly.

She felt his hands slide underneath the thin skirt of her dress and his fingers move underneath her hose, gently tugging them down her legs in a way that made her bite her lip to keep from crying out loud. His hands shifted slowly down her legs, making his undressing of her body into a sensual moment. With her legs bare, he inched his hand upward, underneath her dress, until it rested against her stomach.

She arched her body against his hand, eager for him to explore any part of her he desired, but he kept it there as he kissed the deep vee between her breasts, then moved up to bite her shoulder gently. His other hand was in her hair, his fingers tangled in the blond strands that had come loose. He pulled her head gently, making first her neck vulnerable, then part of her shoulder, then bringing her mouth back up to his to receive the full measure of his passion.

Sam let instinct lead her. Aware of the heat spreading through her limbs, turning her body to pliant fire, making her skin desire his touch, she moved closer. Her body wanted more intimate contact with this exciting, erotic male animal. Their evening together in his tent could not be compared to this moment except as a prelude to what had to follow. This time there would be no interruptions, no one to prevent them from sharing an intimacy as old as time.

She needed him in a way she had never needed any man. Prompted by her body's wild urging, she trailed her hands down the front of his chest to the waist of his slacks. Her fingers fumbled a bit in her anxiety to remove what little remained between them, but she found first the fastening, then the zipper, and finally her hands moved underneath the dark material, underneath the soft cotton of his briefs. She slid the confining clothing over his hips. Moving her hands down his legs as he had done to her, she prolonged the moment, touching him intimately. He broke his hold on her, let her sit up and remove his clothing from around his legs and drop it to the floor.

Ryan rolled over and got up off the bed. Sam couldn't help but react to his magnificent body. She heard her breath in her ears become deeper and quicker as she watched him move to the glass sliding door and shut the curtains. Then she lay back against the pillows as he went to the door and she heard him turn the lock.

He came back to the bed then and turned the light to its lowest setting. He looked at her with half-shut eyes, passion smoldering in the dark depths. His intense gaze made Sam aware of how she must look to him—up against the pillow, her hair spilled over her shoulders in disarray, the silk of her dress molding to her body.

He leaned over her on the bed, his hands on either side of her, and Sam was able to see every hard muscle. His body was taut with desire, energy in check, only waiting to give it all to her.

He lifted her up away from the bedlinen, then pulled the bedspread back. Grabbing the pillows, he tumbled them to the floor. He motioned her to move to a space of white sheet he had just uncovered, then he stripped the bed of its bedspread and top sheet, leaving just the snowy bottom sheet.

And then he turned toward her and took her in his arms, lying full length beside her. She could feel the hard contours of his flesh through the thin silk of her dress, could feel her breasts aching against the hard wall of his chest.

His fingers were searching now, making a sensitive exploration of her dress. Though the fastening was cleverly hidden, he found it within seconds and began to untie it. Sam groaned as he pushed the silken material aside, leaving her breasts and all of her body not covered by tiny silk bikini panties open to his gaze.

He removed the dress from her body with gentle hands, sliding the material over her heated flesh in a distinctly provocative manner. Then he slipped his hands behind her hips and pulled her on top of him.

Sam reached out a hand to steady herself, but she fell slightly forward and Ryan caught her. Twining his hands through her hair, he pulled her close for a quick kiss, then shifted her forward until his lips closed around the sensitive peak of one of her breasts.

She gasped as he tormented the sensitive flesh, pulling and licking it to erect attention. While one of his hands held her upper body against his lips the other hand was cupped against her bottom, massaging the soft skin to a tingling awareness.

She groaned as he took the other nipple in his mouth and repeated the procedure. She could feel the hardness of his desire underneath her and she shifted her hips, her female instincts crying out for fulfillment. But he reached for her hips with both hands and held her still, his mouth continuing the teasing of her now-swollen breasts.

She stiffened for just an instant, then relaxed as his hand moved lower, to her most sensitive, intimate part. His fingers moved underneath the thin elastic of her bikini. She lowered her head, and her hair swept over her flushed cheeks as she moved her hips to give him better access. An almost animal sound of pure pleasure came from deep in her throat at the sensations he was invoking. Her breathing began to come faster and her body tingled as if it was made of molten lava. His lips and tongue continued to make love to her breasts as his fingers caressed her deeply and intimately.

And then she felt that peculiar, hot, almost burning sensation begin to build where he was touching her until somewhere her mind shut off and all there was in the world was sensation: the feel of Ryan's hands and lips and tongue; the pulsating awareness that grew until her entire body shook with wild response and pleasure.

She fell against his chest, her legs feeling soft and liquid against the hard muscles of his thighs. Ryan turned over and laid her against the soft white sheet. He kissed her gently on her trembling lips. She could feel his lazy grin against her mouth.

"What a passionate, wonderful lover you are," he whispered. She moved closer to him, not wanting to break contact after such an intimate sharing. He held her close to him until the shaking subsided, then reached over and turned off the light.

The room was plunged into darkness, but Sam kept her hands on Ryan's broad shoulders. In the darkness it was almost as if her sense of touch were more sensitive, and she traced her fingers over each muscle in his chest, delighting in the rough feel of his hair under her exploring hands. He ran his palms over the silken cloth still covering her most intimate part. Hooking a finger in the elastic waistband, he slid the material down her legs and off her body.

She was attuned to the depth and intensity of his desire, and her hand moved lower over his flat stomach. She smiled in the dark as she heard him groan. Her hands closed over his taut masculinity and she touched him gently.

He put his hand over hers and taught her to excite him further, but not to test his control too severely. He caught her hair with his other hand and, twisting her head up toward his, kissed her with an intensity that surprised her.

She knew when his control had been strained to its utmost, and she shifted her body against his in a way that let him know she wanted him. Ryan kissed her again, then turned away for just an instant. She heard the drawer in the bedside table open, then shut. She kept her hand on Ryan's shoulder as he sat turned away from her, but it was only for an instant. Then he was back against her, pushing her into the mattress with his hot, insistent body.

She felt his mouth move over her lips, her cheeks, her eyelids, then back again to her mouth. She ran her hands over the tensely bunched muscles in his lower back and buttocks, urging him closer. Extending her legs, she felt his hot flesh and she arched her hips, impatient for their joining. And then she felt him enter her.

She sighed deep in her throat at the exquisite pleasure it gave her. It seemed strange, but perfectly right, after all the passion and desire that had raged between them that this final culmination should be so tender, so exquisite.

He pressed her back against the mattress slowly, ever so slowly, until they were as close as a man and woman could possibly be. She eased his head to the side of her neck, and he buried his face against her shoulder. He gave a deep sigh, and Sam felt tears fill her eyes. Where had she ever gotten the idea that this man was invulnerable? It seemed as if the two of them had fought so hard, resisted each other so much, when subconsciously they had both wanted nothing more than to discover this special pleasure in each other's arms.

And then he began to move, and she forgot all thoughts as sensual feelings she had believed were exhausted began to claim her once again. He lifted his head and kissed her deeply, his tongue darting into her mouth.

Totally unselfconscious in the darkened room, she wrapped her legs around him and matched her movements to his. She tried to concentrate on giving him pleasure, but her body burned with excitement. He seemed to know exactly how to touch her in the most intimate ways, and his consummate skill as a lover caused her passion to erupt a second time.

He kissed her forehead and, not waiting for her to recover, continued to disturb her senses with his body. "Wrap your legs around me," she heard him whisper, and she tightened her shaky legs around his lean torso. She arched against him, meeting his rhythm, but soon her head fell back and she felt sensation claim her, again and again. Her response excited him, and she felt his rhythm shift from the deliberate movements that gave her so much pleasure to a sudden burst of uncontrollable passion. She sensed his ardor was seeking a resting place and she opened her heart and her body. She felt the deepest satisfaction when he shuddered and was still.

She relaxed into the mattress, loving the feel of his body, hard and warm, above hers. Running her hands over his back, she felt the muscles, now relaxed. It was several minutes before he rolled over on his back, taking her with him in his arms.

His lips brushed her cheek gently, and she turned her head into his shoulder. She could hear the beat of his heart; it had returned to normal as had her own. They were silent for several minutes, and Sam was almost sure he had fallen asleep. But this time she wanted to make sure he heard her.

"Ryan?" she whispered.

He didn't make a sound, but his arm tightened around her.

She shifted herself on one elbow until her lips were against his ear. The last reserves of the cold, brittle shell she had wrapped around her deepest emotions for many years fell away.

"I love you," she whispered, blinking away quick tears.

He inclined his head toward hers and kissed her, then shifted his body until his mouth was level with hers. "I love you, too. Very much." He sat up, then reached down and retrieved the covers, tucking them around her carefully as if he were nestling a precious jewel in rich velvet. She felt him slide a pillow under both their heads, then his arm was around her.

"Sleep now, my love." And she did, her dreams filled with images of a dark-haired man.

Chapter Twelve

"If you don't hurry up and get out of that tub, I'm going to lift you out!" Ryan teased her as he stood at the sink, half of his jawline covered with shaving cream.

"You're not even finished shaving. Why should I hurry?" Sam replied impudently. She stuck out her tongue at his back, but he saw her in the mirror and laughed.

"What you need," Ryan growled with mock threat, "is a good spanking—"

"And you're just the man to give it to me!" She finished the sentence playfully, then shrieked as Ryan wiped the last of the lather from his face and advanced menacingly toward the tub.

"Ryan, no!" But before the last word was out of her mouth he had stepped into the tub and was lowering himself inside the water.

"We have to be at the airport in little over an hour if we're going to make the flight to Culebra." But his eyes were on her breasts, half hidden in the bath bubbles.

"I'll hurry, I promise," she breathed, but his closeness disturbed her in a very exciting way.

"You've been dawdling in this bath for half an hour," he accused, and she started to laugh again.

"I love this tub. I'm not coming back to location with you. You'll have to force me to return to the jungle and subsist on one cool shower a day!"

He plucked the bar of scented soap from her hands and began to rub it between his fingers. "Stand up. I'll finish your bath for you."

She rose to her knees, noting with excitement the desire that had sprung up between them, thick and fast. She wondered if it would always be this way, for she had no doubts now about Ryan ever leaving her.

She bit her lip against a groan of pleasure as he began soaping her breasts. She noticed an amused gleam in his eyes as he picked up a washcloth and wet it, then ran the bar of soap over its soft, terry surface.

"Now lean toward me so I can get the back of your neck." She did, obedient to his wishes. He glided the warm washcloth, a rough extension of his own hand, over her stomach, her thighs, her hips, his ministrations becoming less objective and more erotic. Sam felt the now-familiar and welcome rush of heat and passion start in the pit of her stomach.

"I'd better wash you, or we'll never get there on time." Grabbing another washcloth, she lathered it up and began to run it over the smooth muscles on his shoulders and chest.

He grabbed her arm and held it still. "You're playing with fire," he whispered, his dark blue gaze holding hers.

She wet her lips and was satisfied to see the simple gesture didn't go unnoticed. "Show me."

He took the washcloth out of her hand, then eased her on top of his body, his arms slippery and wet around her.

The bath water was cold long before either of them noticed.

"WE'RE COMING IN FOR A LANDING," the pilot informed them as the small twin engine plane began to swoop over a series of low green hills. "Fasten your seat belts."

The tiny plane had only twenty seats. It had flown low enough over the Caribbean Sea so Sam could get a closer look at the magnificent variations in color the large body of water had to offer. The shadings of blue had been incredible, sparkling and iridescent like mother-of-pearl.

Now the tiny plane was landing, and Sam reached for Ryan's hand as they bumped along the runway. Their pilot seemed cheerfully unconcerned, and she wondered how long he'd been flying this route. Nothing seemed to faze him.

When the engines shut off and the plane was still, he turned in his seat, a grin on his face. "It's a beautiful flight, isn't it?"

Once on the ground, their pilot led them to a Jeep. "There aren't many roads on Culebra. Actually, there's only about two and a half miles of paved road and just a few cars. But I'll get you to Flamenco Bay."

They climbed into the Jeep, and after twenty minutes that seemed like endless torture, bumping over rutted trails, he pulled into a small clearing.

"Just cut straight through for about fifty feet, and you can't miss the beach." He lit a cigarette. "I have to get back to the airstrip, but I'll come for you before sundown." He swung up into the open seat and started the motor.

Sam felt Ryan take her hand and then he was leading the way through the thickest, densest tropical jungle she had ever tried to walk through. She shut her eyes and followed him, using her free hand to swipe at the small bugs that seemed intent on eating her alive.

At least I'll never be bored with him, she thought. His hand tightened around hers, and she picked up her pace.

She felt, rather than saw, the lack of plant life around her. Opening her eyes, she saw a beach that stretched for miles in either direction, as unspoiled as in the days when native Indians walked the sands.

Ryan was watching her, a pleased expression on his dark face. His teeth flashed in a smile. "Do you like it?"

"Oh, yes! Where do we swim?"

"Anywhere. We can spread our pack under that tree, and I'll get the snorkeling gear. You might as well take off your clothes."

She pulled her T-shirt over her head and stepped out of her jeans. The turquoise bikini she had bought the previous afternoon clung to her every curve, and once again she wondered if she should have worn her sensible maillot.

She wasn't disappointed at the look on Ryan's face as he turned around and caught sight of her.

"Come here." The desire in his eyes was an open invitation.

She stepped away from his grasp. "But you said we were going to snorkel."

He stripped off his shirt, then unsnapped his jeans, discarding his clothing as if it irritated him. "Come on, then, let's go." But once she was within his reach she felt his hands come around her waist and pull her body against his muscular thighs.

"See what you do to me?" he murmured, tickling her neck with soft kisses.

She wriggled in his embrace, then decided not to fight such an irresistible sensation. Her hands slipped around his neck, and she caressed his dark head, pulling his face closer to hers, intensifying the kiss.

He broke off, a wicked gleam in his blue eyes. "We'd better get in to the water, or I may decide never to show you how to do this." He reached into the large pack he had set down on the beach and produced two masks, snorkels, and fins. "Let's go."

She followed him waist high into the warm seawater, where he showed her how to keep her mask from fogging by wetting it, then spitting in it, then wetting it again. Then they slipped their masks over their heads and put on their fins. Holding their snorkels high in their hands, they waded still farther out, until they were almost over their heads, then Ryan showed her how to use the mouthpiece, and Sam lowered her head into the turquoise water.

At first it was strange, and she was tempted to lift her face above the surface when she wanted to breathe, but in a very short time she became used to the sensation of keeping her head below water. Ryan stayed beside her and linked his hand in hers as they floated on top of the warm Caribbean, drifting aimlessly.

After a short time, Ryan touched her, and she surfaced to face him, careful not to push her mask to her forehead so it wouldn't fog up.

"Do you feel comfortable?" he asked, indicating the equipment.

She nodded.

"Then let's swim out by a reef. But keep hold of my hand. If you have any problems, just tap me."

She nodded again, anxious to see more of the strange underwater world all around her.

Sam wasn't disappointed. The sea was calm and she could easily see twenty feet down. In the lukewarm water she felt as if she were swimming in a giant bathtub. Her body floated effortlessly in the salt sea, and all she had to do was enjoy the view nature afforded her.

Schools of brilliant blue tangs and green parrot fish swam beneath her, their movements as synchronized as a ballet. They would dart one way, then all turn in the other direction in the same instant. She squeezed Ryan's hand in delight. The colors were vivid, brighter than anything she had seen on the shore. She began to suspect Puerto Rico's true beauty was in her ocean.

Gorgonian coral branches and swaying sea fans gave the underwater scene a strange otherworldly quality. She almost wished she had taken the time to learn to scuba dive when her darting eyes located a coral grotto.

Her glance was held by a slight movement near the ocean floor. Her eyes widened as she saw a manta ray shake off its concealing coat of sand and glide upward through the water, a graceful sort of creature despite his strange looks.

She felt Ryan nudge her and turned her head in his direction in time to see a huge coral garden, with every color of the spectrum, from palest white to vivid red. It stretched as far as the eye could see.

They drifted on top of the sea for a long time, hands entwined, sometimes with their arms around each other. Sam felt completely safe by Ryan's side. The only sound she could hear was her own breathing, magnified underwater. Her back was warm from the sun's rays filtering through the water, but the rest of her body felt cool from the water around it.

When Ryan finally tapped her and she came up out of the water, it was almost as if some magical spell had been broken.

"We'd better head back. I don't want you to go too far out on your first time. I'm afraid your back and legs might get burned."

"It's wonderful! I want to learn to scuba dive, **then** we can come back and—"

He laughed and kissed the tip of her nose. "I love your enthusiasm."

She smiled at him, and he gently nudged her toward the shore like a playful dolphin. They swam in slowly, taking their time. Much as she hated to admit it, Sam knew Ryan was using good judgment. Her ankles were beginning to hurt from the unaccustomed weight of the swim fins.

Ryan made her laugh by taking a deep breath and diving to the bottom, then surfacing and blowing a huge jet of water from his snorkel.

"You look like a whale!" She laughed at him.

By the time they reached shore Sam was surprised to find she felt a bit winded.

"Lie down on this blanket while I get our lunch." She did as Ryan suggested, her body relaxed after the sea air and hot sun.

When she awoke, it was to find Ryan stretched out beside her, watching her carefully. She sat up and felt cloth sliding off her back and legs. Looking beside her, she saw his T-shirt and jacket.

"You would have burned alive before long. I had to cover you with something."

"Thank you." She rubbed the sleep out of her eyes. "Did you eat yet?"

"No. I thought I'd wait for you."

"What have you been doing?"

"Thinking."

"About what?"

He didn't seem hesitant about sharing his thoughts with her. "Sam, would you be happy living in a place like this?" When he saw the expression on her face, he amended, "I know we both have our work to consider. But I'd like to do the main part of my living away from the rest of the world."

She thought quickly. She had never realized what a strain Ryan was continually under. Before she'd met him, his private life had been continually plastered over the tabloids and cheap movie magazines. She could understand his desire to be alone.

She slowly nodded her head.

Ryan seemed pleased, but then his face registered an expression Sam couldn't quite fathom. She felt a sudden fluttering in her stomach.

"The only person I'd like to share my entire life with is you," he said softly.

Was this what she thought it was? Her voice was almost a whisper as she answered.

"I feel the same way."

He reached behind him into the backpack and pulled out a small dark box. When he opened it, she saw the bright flash of a diamond as he lifted the ring.

Without a word, he slid it onto her left ring finger. It fit perfectly. He tilted her face up to his.

"I've been carrying that damn thing around ever since we arrived in San Juan. I picked it up the last time I drove in to get supplies. Will you marry me, Sam?"

She threw herself into his arms, feeling as light as air, happiness bubbling up through her body. He lowered her to the blanket and kissed her softly.

"I take it the answer is yes?"

"Oh, yes! Ryan, I can't believe—"

"What did you think I meant when I said I was never going to leave you?" he asked, amusement evident in his voice.

"I thought—" She stopped, embarrassed.

"You thought a long-range affair. Am I right?" She couldn't look up at him. He sighed and cupped her face in his hands. "You've got to learn to have a little faith, you know."

They lay back down on the blanket, and Ryan unpacked the lunch he had asked room service to make up that morning. Sam realized she was terrifically hungry after all their exercise. She managed to eat two pieces of fried chicken, a banana, and a large piece of chocolate cake. She was reaching for a fingerful of frosting when Ryan took her hand.

"I won't love you if you get fat," he teased.

"Yes, you will," she replied smugly and smeared the frosting on his cheek. She burst out laughing at the astonished look he wore. Sam wondered what the tabloids would think of the distinguished Mr. Fitzgerald frosted like a cake.

"Take that off right now," he said, his voice low with mock threat.

"Yes, sir," she replied and, leaning forward, she began to carefully lick off the frosting.

She was barely finished when he grasped her shoulders and pushed her gently down on the blanket. As she felt his hands on the string fastenings of her bikini, she glanced hurriedly up and down the wide expanse of beach.

"Ryan, wait a minute!" But he had already divested her of her damp top and was running his hands over her skin in a most disturbing way.

"Our friend won't be back until nearly sunset," he whispered into her ear, then he bit it gently. "You'll have to get used to doing this if you intend to marry me."

She started to laugh, but it turned into a sigh, then all conscious thought was chased out of her mind as pleasure and pleasing the man beside her became of utmost importance.

THE NEXT FEW DAYS were a revelation to Samantha. She had seen the man Ryan was at work, driving everyone relentlessly, always insisting on each person's best effort. What she didn't know was, he played just as hard.

They walked all over Old San Juan, taking in the old-world charm of the city. They went on a tour of El Morro, a fort erected on the island's eastern edge, guarding its richest port from foreign attack in earlier times. Ryan took her everywhere—to the Plaza de Colon, with its statue of Christopher Columbus; and to Fort San Christóbal, with its moats, ramps, and tunnels. They walked along the city wall, built by seventeenth-century Spanish engineers. Sam was impressed by the way they had taken advantage of the island's steep, rocky shoreline, adding intricate twists and angles to increase visibility for its inhabitants and to overlap the fields of fire. The island had certainly been well protected in case of attack.

Sam especially loved Casa Blanca, a sprawling Spanish-style house with tiny gardens. It was filled with relics and pieces of furniture from the early Spanish colonial era. The steep streets reminded her of streets in San Francisco, but the tropical foliage and intricate iron balconies added a charm all their own.

They browsed in and out of stores, ate at different stands, and bought silly souvenirs for members of the crew. Sam found the cheapest, tackiest ashtray possible for Don. It was a study in lurid colors: A huge green island with a large palm tree was painted in the center, and the words *"Puerto Rico me encanta"*—"Puerto Rico enchants me"—were emblazoned around the rim. She laughed the entire time the proprietor was wrapping it, finally having to wait outside in order not to be rude. Ryan bought some ridiculous postcards to send to his family in Boston, and Sam sent off a few to Jake and Maria. They even bought Helen a small lace handkerchief.

Ryan bought a hammock big enough for two, and embarrassed her terribly by making sure to ask the salesman if the seemingly delicate woven cotton could withstand more vigorous activity than an afternoon nap. The salesman had glanced at her admiringly and had assured him it could.

They toured the Don Quixote Rum Distillery, and Ryan tried to get her tipsy, but in a teasing way. San Juan beckoned to both of them until the early hours of the morning. They ate out at many of the best restaurants, danced cheek to cheek far into several nights.

But it was their nights together that were sheer magic. Ryan was the most tender and passionate of lovers, and Sam bloomed under his expert tutelage. She was intensely excited by the contrast of raw sexual power held in check. It seemed her life had never been this full, and she wondered how she had ever existed before knowing this man.

Since he had declared his affection and intentions openly, and she was wearing an engagement ring, she noticed he was decidedly jealous if any man paid her more than passing interest. But she was glowing with happiness, her energy and high spirits alone causing her to attract masculine attention.

Above and beyond anything they did together while on their small vacation from the rest of the world, it was Ryan who filled her senses, made her laugh, urged her to eat more and worry less, and encouraged her to forget about what anyone thought and just have fun.

She wanted this time with him to never end, and was almost depressed on their last day. They spent it quietly walking through their favorite parts of the city. Sam had come to love the gracious Spanish architecture, the welcoming smiles on dark faces, the smells of exotic cooking. She loved to wake up to the sound of the sea, to the feel of Ryan's warm arms securely around her. Colors seemed more vivid, smells sharper, days brighter. She was deeply, irrevocably in love, and it made her days and nights seem like paradise.

She pushed the thought of their leaving from her mind, held it at bay, but the hours sped by relentlessly, and soon they were in his Jaguar, heading back to location and the real world.

Sam had been staring out the window, playing absently with the ring on her finger, when she felt Ryan's hand on her thigh.

"Any regrets?" She knew he meant her acceptance of his proposal.

"Not a single one." She flexed her hand, and the diamond sparkled fiercely in the bright sunlight.

Closing her eyes, she leaned back, and it wasn't until the car came to a stop that she opened them.

"Darn it, Ryan, why did you let me fall asleep? I was supposed to help you drive!"

"It wasn't bad," he replied, and she noticed he was looking at her with open amusement.

She started to get out of the car, then stopped as she realized they weren't where they were supposed to be. He had parked beside a large stucco house with a wrought iron fence in front that spilled over with floral color. Bright bougainvillaea wound around the black metal, and Sam noticed the side of the house facing the sea had a long porch running its entire length.

"Where are we?" she asked.

"Our new location for the next two weeks. Ben called me after two days to say he'd finished all of the interior jungle shots. Helen's close-ups went like a dream, so I decided spirits would pick up if we moved the entire crew to a coastal location."

"But the animals—" she began.

"Tim and Rebecca handled the move just fine. They didn't have any trouble at all. I thought you deserved a rest, and the two of us deserved a chance to get to know each other better."

"But where are they? I can't see them anywhere."

Ryan grinned. "The reason I chose this location was that originally this was a private residence. Whoever owned it had a tremendous desire for privacy." He took her arm. "See how the land drops away to the ocean?" She nodded, impressed by the way the stucco house was built on an outcropping of rock. "Down below, by the beach, it's completely fenced off. Pepito placed the cages underneath some thick foliage so the animals would stay cool, but the compound opens out on to the ocean. You could walk the elephants along the beach if you wanted to, or even Sultan. There's a twenty-foot fence that runs along the entire property, and all we had to do was reinforce it in places.''

"Steel mesh?" she questioned.

"Only the best for this guy, whoever he was. Rebecca checked it out before we brought the animals down, and she was satisfied. The fence runs out into the ocean for about fifty feet, until the water gets deep enough to act as a natural barrier. As usual, there's one door, and we've put a lock on it. Ben will give you your key."

When she didn't say anything, he got out of the car and went around to her side, helping her out. "There's no shooting going on today, so we can unpack and settle in." The tone of his voice told her he assumed they would be sharing a room. Sam walked around to the back of the Jaguar to help Ryan retrieve their bags.

The front of the large house was cool and airy, with bright hammocks swinging gently in the breeze. There were several outdoor tables and chairs, and an area that looked like it was meant for a barbecuing.

"Ryan, is this a hotel?" she asked as they walked up the front stairs and through the door.

"It's called a *parador*. Some of the people in Puerto Rico have opened up their homes to tourists, and they try to make the atmosphere less formal. I found out about this place from Luis. His cousin operates it."

He picked up their key at the front desk, and she followed him down the narrow hall. They hadn't run into anyone, and Sam assumed they were all taking advantage of the day off by spending it at the beach.

She almost bumped into Ryan as he stopped by a doorway, then she set her suitcase down as he inserted his key and opened the door. Picking up her bag, she started inside, but he stopped her.

"Put that bag down. I'm going to do this properly for once." Before she had a chance to protest he had lifted her into his arms and carried her over the doorway into their room.

He gave her a quick kiss, then set her down and flicked on the overhead light. A small green lizard darted into a corner. He flicked another switch, and an overhead fan began to circulate the air.

Sam quickly looked over the room, but her gaze stopped when she noticed the lump in the double bed. Moving closer, she noticed it was a woman, her platinum-blond hair spread out over the pillow. It was obvious she didn't have anything on underneath the sheet. Sam's head began to throb as she tried to place this stranger's face in her mind. The answer came to her with a terrible finality. Beverly, the girl in the magazine, the actress scheduled to star in Ryan's next picture. She felt cold suddenly, as if an icy hand was climbing her spine. She swallowed, trying to ease the sick feeling in her stomach. Was this what their life together was to be like?

The nightmare was starting all over again.

Without looking at Ryan she turned and left the room. She was halfway down the hall when he caught up with her.

"Where do you think you're going?" he asked, grabbing her arm.

"It should be obvious. Threesomes aren't my scene."

"Damn it, Sam, she's nothing to me. I don't know what she's doing here." There was a faint thread of desperation in his voice.

"Don't you read the trades? She's scheduled to star in your next film. You can play with her on location."

Dark anger blazed in his eyes and he took a step closer to her. "You don't know what you're saying and you'd better stop before you say something you'll regret."

Sam opened her mouth to continue their argument, but then she noticed Beverly leaning in the doorway down the hall, listening to them. She stared at the woman until Ryan turned around and saw her.

"Ryan, I'll be waiting inside for you when this is over." Her eyes hardened as she glanced at Samantha, but she smiled a lazy, bedroom smile when she looked back at him. Dressed in a pearl-colored satin slip, her voluptuous body was clearly visible underneath the form-fitting garment.

"Go inside, Beverly. This has nothing to do with you." Ryan turned back to Samantha and saw she was taking off her ring.

"Take it. I don't want it."

He tried to give it back to her, but she put it in his hand and turned away from him, running for the door.

He caught up with her in the doorway, his fingers digging into her shoulders. "Damn it! You can't be serious about this!"

She turned to face him, her green eyes icy. The only way she would ever be able to get away from him without totally breaking down was if she kept her most emotional part frozen, completely out of his reach.

"You're the one who doesn't understand. You may think you want to marry me, and I can see how it would be an excellent arrangement for you, but it would kill me. I can't take it, Ryan. I don't belong to this world and I never will. I'd always worry about you not coming back to me. I'm sorry."

His shoulders slumped suddenly, as if all the energy had been drained from his body. "But that won't happen!"

"It would always be in my mind."

His eyes hardened. "What you're saying is that you can't trust me. Is that it?"

She shrugged her shoulders, trying to feign indifference even though her heart was breaking. "It doesn't really matter now, does it?"

He glanced at the ring, then back at her, and a cold fury filled his face. He grabbed her hand and pressed the diamond ring into it, closing her fingers around it. "Consider it payment, then, for a job well done. I thought I was wrong about you. But the bottom line is, you're nothing but an emotional coward." He stalked off in the direction of his bedroom, and Sam saw him walk in and slam the door. The force of the reverberation shook the hallway.

She stood there dumbly, then looked down at the ring in her hand. The diamond was sparkling softly in the shaded light. She tightened her palm around the gem until it hurt, then walked out the door and down the steps.

"I THINK YOU'RE BEING A FOOL, SAM." Don picked up a shell as they walked along the beach, inspected it casually, then tossed it back into the surf.

"It would never work, Don. Maybe I'm more jealous than I even realize, but I just saw red when I saw that woman in his bed."

"They aren't sleeping together," he murmured.

Sam tried to ignore the sudden thumping of her heart. "How do you know?"

"I asked him." At her look of amazement he went on. "I care about you, Sam, and I wanted to know if he was as big a louse as you thought he was. He didn't even know she was coming down to see him. And all she really wants is to make sure she has a part in his next picture."

"But the trades said—"

"Forget the papers. How many times have you seen them print something and then the exact opposite happens? Ninety percent of this business is illusion anyway."

She kicked up some sand as they kept walking. "What would you do if you were me?"

Don didn't hesitate. "I think the two of you came home from an emotionally charged weekend. It took courage for both of you; you made yourself vulnerable, and he proposed. And that was definitely a first on his part. So the two of you tear up the town and come back to the real world, and the real world is that the ladies are never going to leave Ryan alone. And you're going to have to learn to deal with it or else."

"Or else what?" she whispered.

"Or else the relationship isn't going to work."

"It's not working now." It had been almost two weeks since their argument in the hallway. Sam had tried to put all her energy into getting the film done and working with the animals. Only this time, for the first time in her life, she couldn't.

"It's not working because he's probably scared to death of approaching you."

"I can't believe that."

"Didn't liberation teach you a thing? If nothing else came of all that upheaval, the myth of the strong, silent man went out the window. We're all still scared children underneath."

"Don, what should I do?" Sam's voice was tight and strained.

He took her hand and squeezed it. "Do you miss him?"

To her disgust two big tears slipped down her cheek. "Oh, Don, I've been such a fool. But I was so scared, and the whole thing—"

"Reminded you of the entire mess with your first husband. I know, darling." He patted her shoulder. "But Ryan isn't the same man your husband was. I think he's ready for a commitment. I think he was the moment he really took a look at you."

"Do you think if I talked to him..." Her voice trailed off. The prospect was frightening after the shouting match they had had in the hall; the bitter words they had thrown at each other.

"I think"—Don smiled as if amused by some private joke—"I think we should go to the wrap party this weekend. You should look spectacular and make a play for him. Then once you've enchanted him all over again, it shouldn't be hard to talk."

"What if he won't talk to me?"

"Darling, he *proposed* to you! That should tell you something right there."

She felt the tightness slowly leaving her chest. "I'll think about it. I will—"

"Don't think about it, do it. We all get ourselves into trouble by thinking too much. I'll go to the party with you and protect you until we spot Mr. Fitzgerald."

"Thank you, Don."

"Thank *you*, Samantha. Watching Ryan fall for you gave me hope that maybe there's justice in the world. I can't think of two people who would be better for each other. He needs you as much as you need him. Don't you ever forget that."

Chapter Thirteen

Samantha glanced covertly toward the main entrance of the large hall. The man framed in the stucco archway wasn't Ryan. She looked away, but not before Don saw her.

"Not yet, Sam." He handed her a glass of rum punch. "I'm sure he'll arrive eventually."

She closed her eyes for a brief second. She knew, logically, that Don was right, that Ryan would probably want to talk and make up. But that didn't stop her stomach from fluttering and her hands from shaking. Steeling herself, she opened her eyes and flashed him a brilliant smile. But the worried look didn't leave her eyes.

"That's my girl. At least you're trying." Don studied he face with the critical expertise that had made his career as a makeup artist brilliant. "You should wear makeup more often; you're an attractive woman."

Sam lifted the glass of punch to her lips, shrugging her slim shoulders. She knew she looked good tonight. That had been the entire point, hadn't it? The electric blue of her strapless silk evening dress brought out the cool tones in her blond hair, and made her green eyes more vivid. Don had helped her with her makeup, and she knew, despite what she felt inside, she looked the picture of sophistication. Her shimmering hair was done up in a classic twist, and her height was emphasized by high-heeled sandals. Don had applied most of the make-up to her eyes, emphasizing their delicate slant. The slight golden tan she had acquired on the island was flattering, and her high cheekbones looked more prominent after a skillful blending of several blushers. Don was quite an artist. Impulsively she put her hand on his arm. "Thank you."

"For what?" He seemed embarrassed.

"For helping me."

"What are friends for?" He cleared his throat. "Seriously, Sam, if you're ever in Manhattan, drop by my apartment. I'd love for you to meet Jim. We could show you a great time." He changed the subject, his voice rising slightly. "I'll freshen up your drink. Let's go over by the bar."

Some sixth sense made her aware of what Don was trying to do. She looked up toward the door, but nothing could have prepared her for the shock in store.

Ryan had just entered the room. He appeared forbiddingly masculine in a dark dress suit. The whiteness of his shirt emphasized his dark tan. He looked tired, but it only served to make him more attractive, as if that were possible. The small lines around his mouth and eyes were etched deeper, but his dark blue eyes flashed as brilliantly and sardonically as before. He was talking with one of the crew, his smile lazy, his stance assured.

Sam put her drink down on the nearest tray and, involuntarily, began to walk toward him. She felt some-one catch her arm and turned back, annoyed. It was Don, trying to restrain her.

"Let me go. It's Ryan!" Her eyes were dark and strained.

"Sam." Don's warm blue eyes were sad as he looked at her. "He's not alone." He watched as she looked back toward Ryan and he groaned as he saw her face go white.

Ryan was with Beverly. The starlet had been behind him, but now she was all over him. Her petite, voluptuous figure was encased in a tight red sheath, and diamonds flashed at her ears and throat. Her hair, an unnatural mass of white-blond curls, tumbled riotously over her shoulders. Scarlet-tipped hands gripped Ryan's arm tightly, and her small, narrow eyes never left his chiseled face. She leaned toward him, rubbing her body against his. Laughter bubbled out from her perfectly glossed lips. Ryan smiled down at her.

Samantha turned her back on them. She touched her forehead gently; it was ice cold. She closed her eyes, trying to obliterate the scene from her memory, but hot tears pressed against her lids.

"I'm leaving, Don." She couldn't break down in front of Ryan.

"All right. I'll walk you back to the *parador*."

"No. I'm leaving Puerto Rico. Tonight." She kissed him on the cheek. "I'll miss you, but—" She studied his troubled face. "It's for the best. Good-bye." Her voice broke and she began to walk rapidly to the front entrance. Ryan and Beverly were already down among the main assemblage, and she managed to get her shawl and leave without them noticing.

Once outside, Sam breathed deeply. Hot tears coursed down her face, and the tropical wind began to play havoc with her hair. She wiped her eyes, smearing Don's artistic efforts across the back of her hand. Strands of hair whipped across her cheeks, and she was glad to sense the stinging; at least she could still feel something.

She realized she loved Ryan as she loved no other man on earth, but she had taken their love and shattered it. He had been right to be angry with her; she had been incapable of trusting him. Yet she had thought she could make things right again. But Beverly had moved in before she'd ever had a chance.

Fight for him, a small voice inside whispered, but she bent her head against the wind and kept walking. Maybe Ryan was right: She was a coward.

She caught her breath shakily as she ran up the steps of the *parador,* then leaned against the railing. She had to leave tonight no matter what the cost. She couldn't face Ryan again. He had clearly chosen Beverly.

She ran into her room and let herself in. Opening her suitcase, she stuffed the last of her clothes inside and snapped it shut. Then, outside in the lobby, in rather shaky Spanish, she asked for the phone and rang for a taxi. The driver was unconvinced she would pay the amount to San Juan International Airport, but once she persuaded him she was one of the crazy movie people from California, he agreed to be there within half an hour.

Sam hung up the phone wearily. Leaving her suitcase in the lobby with the night receptionist, she walked out on the front porch. The wind was stronger now, and the ocean below looked gray and uninviting. Wild curves of foaming water crashed against the smooth sand beaches. Palm trees were beginning to sway sharply against the gale. Sam clutched her shawl against her bare shoulders and shivered as she felt the wind tangle the smooth fabric of her evening dress around her legs. The weather mirrored her feelings and she welcomed it, turning toward the cleansing storm and inhaling deeply of the plant smell. Closing her eyes, she leaned into it, welcoming devastation.

Her eyes flew open as she heard shrill trumpeting from the direction of the animal compound below. Peanut! The small elephant had to be frightened by the beginning of the storm.

All thoughts of Ryan left her as she ran back down the front steps of the *parador* and descended the hill toward the compound, ignoring the main road. Her heels sunk into the soft earth and she cursed herself silently for not having the foresight to change clothes first.

By the time she reached the compound entrance her stockings were snagged and torn. Reaching into her evening bag for the key, she unlocked the heavy gate and moved inside, locking it carefully behind her.

She ran toward the elephant barn, where Peanut's squeals still rang out, loud and terrified. Sam unbolted the barn door and went inside. She could see Peanut in the corner of the large stall. The baby elephant was shifting his weight nervously. The squeals stopped when he saw Sam, and he followed her movements with large eyes. She walked to his side and reached up, pulling his ear soothingly.

"Calm down, Peanut." She scratched his head absently, talking to him in a melodious, singsong voice. The elephant leaned his weight against her gently, and his small trunk snaked out and encircled her arm.

"Good boy, that's good," she crooned. She'd miss the little elephant. She was glad to have this chance to say good-bye. Tim and Rebecca had already left with Sultan, and she had made all the arrangements for the elephants, the chimps, Galahad the lion, and Iago the tiger. There was nothing to stay for.

Peanut seemed less frightened now, and she disengaged his trunk. She'd have to get back to the *parador* to catch her taxi. She started in the direction of the door when she heard the little elephant trumpet again.

"No, Peanut! Quiet!" But as soon as the words were out of her mouth she knew the reason for the animal's distress. Fire! Why hadn't she noticed it earlier? The smell of smoke was pungent against the cool fragrance of the island before a storm.

Samantha rushed outside. Scanning the area around the enclosed compound, she saw smoke rising near Iago's cage.

Without consideration for her dress or sandals, she ran through the underbrush, ignoring the neat pathways. She stumbled out into the clearing by the tiger's cage, then stopped, confused. Several dark figures surrounded by four torches were squatted around the base of the cage, their backs to her. Peanut squealed shrilly in the distance, terribly frightened. Sam was furious as she approached the group.

"Get away from that tiger cage! Who gave you the authority to light those torches around the animals—" She stopped abruptly as one of the men turned to face her, a small gun cocked in his hand. She recognized Bob, one of the stuntmen. Her eyes widened in surprise as she recognized the others: Helen, Scott, and Miguel, who was supposed to have been on watch.

"What are you doing here?" Helen demanded. Sam stayed very still, conscious of the gun Bob was pointing at her. She was fairly certain he wouldn't shoot her, but she didn't want to give him any provocation.

She swallowed, her throat suddenly dry. "I was on my way to the airport when I heard Peanut crying. I came down to see if anything was wrong. He was frightened by the smoke." Her eyes flicked over the small cluster of torches, then lower. Plastic bags full of white powder lay neatly stacked on the tarpaulin.

"Well, it was unfortunate you came this way," Helen murmured. "Bob, watch her!" She turned to Scott and twined her arm through his. "Let's get everything loaded."

Sam watched in sick fascination as Scott pulled up one of the torches. He waved it past Iago's face through the bars. If Sam had thought the animal was pathological in its behavior before, it had been nothing compared to what she saw now. Iago seemed to be going out of his mind. The tiger snarled in fear and pressed itself into the far corner of its cage.

As if on cue, heavy steel bars came down the center of the small traveling cage. Sam looked up and saw Miguel on top of the enclosure. The animal had been effectively trapped in back, his cage cut in half.

Scott moved quickly, Helen behind him. He walked into the front of the cage, and Sam watched as he slid open a partition in the floorboards. Helen handed him package after package until the small pile on the ground disappeared.

While Scott was loading the tarpaulin into the truck, Helen walked over to Sam. "So you were leaving tonight?" she asked. Sam met her eyes but didn't answer. "Whatever happened to Ryan?" she taunted, and Sam bit her lip. She wasn't exactly sure what Helen was up to. "You're not even going to say good-bye to him?" Her face hardened abruptly. "Perhaps because you saw him with Beverly? He was always out of your league."

Sam didn't know why she had to ask, especially in the face of this woman's bitterness and anger. But she forced the words out. "Helen, did Ryan— Does he know about any of this?"

The actress gave her an incredulous look, her eyes filled with amused hatred. "You don't know him at all, do you?" She laughed, an abrasive sound that made Sam want to cover her ears. "Of course Ryan doesn't know. He doesn't even use cocaine—he has to make sure he's *in control* at all times, if you know what I mean." As Sam continued to look at her Helen's manner became slightly defensive. "It isn't as if we sell it or anything. It's just for us."

Scott came up behind Helen and put his arms around her waist. "Let's go," he whispered in her ear. He turned toward the darkness. "Miguel, fix the cage!"

"No, wait, Miguel!" Helen called sharply. "What about her?" She glared at Sam.

"What about her?" Scott seemed unconcerned. "She's leaving tonight."

"I don't trust her."

"Helen, what can go wrong? Who'd believe her?"

"But if she did open her mouth..." Scott looked doubtful, and Helen pressed her point. "We could get thirty years for possession. They'd be hard on us because we're movie people."

"What do you think?" He was listening to her now.

"We could arrange a small accident." She leaned on his shoulder, on tiptoe, and whispered into his ear.

Sam watched Scott's face as it registered various emotions in the firelight: horror, doubt, admiration, and finally acceptance. She started to move toward the main gate, but Bob clapped a restraining arm on her shoulder.

"Sam, be a dear and give me your key," Helen commanded softly, with the assurance born of knowing she had the upper hand. When Sam didn't respond, Helen grabbed her bag and dumped it open on the soft earth. She knelt down and pawed through Sam's compact: lipstick, perfume atomizer, Kleenex. She stood up triumphantly, the master key to the compound in her hand. "Bob, get in the truck and keep the gun on her." She gave Miguel directions in rapid Spanish. Sam couldn't decipher them. She stood alone by a torch, conscious of Bob's gun.

Bob was backing the truck up against the cage so Miguel could climb down, but before he did, Helen looked at Scott. "Go ahead, do it now. But be careful, you're blond as well."

Sam tried to think quickly. None of this made any sense. What did being blond have to do with anything? Before she could think further Scott had twisted her hands painfully behind her back and was pushing her along toward the side of the tiger cage.

He pushed her up so she was almost against the small mesh, and Sam froze. Iago went out of control, throwing himself against the side of the cage, growling and trying to attack both of them. Scott used Sam as a shield between himself and the tiger, and Sam closed her eyes. She thanked God the mesh was small, too small to allow the tiger access to get a claw through. She had seen the damage a big cat could do. The summer she turned twenty-one, one of the tigers had pushed open an improperly locked gate at feeding time and gone for a young man standing between him and the meat. Sam remembered going to the hospital with Jake and the poor young man's endless sessions with a plastic surgeon.

She opened her eyes and forced herself to look at the tiger, and a part of her mind realized this time she would be fighting for her life. If her training had taught her anything, it was to be calm in the face of disaster. And yet she didn't totally believe that Helen was capable of violence. She didn't want to.

The animal was irrational. She couldn't be sure what had upset him, all she knew was every time Scott pushed her against the cage, Iago went for her. And he was out for blood. There didn't seem to be any rational explanation she could think of. Her mind worked desperately, but time was running out.

"That's enough." Helen seemed pleased. "I think you've got him fired up. Get in the car."

Scott dragged a suddenly limp Sam back in front of the entrance to the tiger cage. "I think she fainted," he called to Helen.

Sam thought feverishly as Scott struggled to move her body. She had gone limp deliberately, stalling for time. A small part of her mind hoped one of the men might think she was ill. But Helen had them well trained.

"Dump her. Let's go."

Sam crumpled to the ground as Scott dropped her. She lay on the sand with her eyes slitted open, watching.

"Helen, I don't know about this." Scott was beginning to weaken. "She's fainted. She won't even come to before we're long gone."

"Get in the truck before Miguel raises the bars, or he'll go for you, too." She laughed, and Sam heard Scott run toward the truck.

She heard the truck door slam, and Helen called to Miguel again. She could also hear a peculiar buzzing sound in her head, as if this entire scene wasn't real and was being played out in front of one of Ryan's cameras, another endless take.

Her senses sharpened and came back into focus as she heard the steel bars grinding slowly upward. She opened her eyes and saw Iago was trying to squeeze himself underneath.

And then Sam knew. There could no longer be any illusions.

She had thought they were merely trying to frighten her. Or perhaps they were going to leave her locked in the other side of Iago's cage. But her legs began to tremble as she realized the front of the cage was still open. Helen meant to kill her.

"Scott, get down and cover your head! I'm not taking any chances!" Sam looked wildly in the direction of the truck. The entire scene came into sharp focus; the pieces clicked into place effortlessly. Helen's auburn hair, Bob and Miguel's dark heads. She and Scott were the only blonds, and the tiger's cage was ringed with fire from the four torches. She also remembered Jake reading her an article about a circus tiger that had been forced to do a trick with fire until he had turned around and killed the man who had been training him. A blond man. And tigers remembered.

The animal was thoroughly panicked and enraged. The fire and the tight enclosure coming together had compounded his fear. He sprang furiously around the small area, roaring, his muscles rippling underneath his sleek fur. As the bars continued to grind up, Sam tensed. She knew he would run down and attack the first thing in his path. She could only hope that he was afraid of water. She had to reach the sea.

She jumped up and ran.

There was a dull explosion behind her, and she felt a sudden pain shoot through her right arm. She clasped it tightly, but kept on running, crashing through spongy underbrush. The adrenaline racing through her bloodstream made her heart pound as if it were going to burst. She fell once but was on her feet so quickly, she barely touched ground.

As she broke out of the jungle onto the beach she stopped, catching her breath, which was now coming in long, shuddering sobs. Perhaps she could make it over the mesh fence before the tiger got to the beach. She ran to the mesh, eerily outlined by the moonlight, and reached for the first links.

Pain shot through her right arm, and she cried out. Looking down, she noticed that the blood looked black in the moonlight—she had been shot.

She heard Iago roar and made her next move instinctively, without conscious thought. She backed into the ocean.

Her sandals filled with water and sand, and she kicked them off. Reaching under her dress with her good arm, she tore off what was left of her pantyhose. Then she grabbed her slip and, gritting her teeth against the pain, used both her arms to tear it up to make an improvised bandage for her injured arm. The wound was bleeding badly, and she couldn't afford to let blood get in the water. There was always the danger of attracting sharks or barracuda.

She wrapped the makeshift bandage around her arm clumsily with one hand. The coolness of the water felt good, but right afterward she felt the saltwater sting her open wound, and she cried out in pain. Tears filled her eyes, but she blinked them back and forced herself to look at the shore.

Iago was on the beach, only a few hundred feet away, but he was coming closer. Sam watched as he approached the waves, then shied. Even animals used to water were sometimes scared of the movement and noise of the ocean.

She glanced at her bandage again. The material was still white, and seemed to be stemming the flow of blood. The wind was becoming more violent, and salt spray crashed over her shoulders and face. Her hair had fallen, and hung limp and wet.

The sand shifted beneath her feet, and she shivered. She held her arm up above the water, trying to keep the sodden bandage from falling off. Sam remembered Ryan telling her the sharks came in closer to the shore at night; the thought made her tremble convulsively. She couldn't stay out here much longer. How different it was during the day, when you could see the bottom and count individual pebbles. At night, seeing nothing but the silvery-black surface of the water, she was terrified.

Sam glanced up through the high mesh fence and saw the huge hall against the cliff, ablaze with lights. She swallowed painfully against the sudden tightness in her throat. Where was Ryan now? Dancing with Beverly? Back in his room—with Beverly? Tears misted her eyes, and she wiped them away with her good hand. Would he even notice she was missing?

She returned her attention to the tiger. He was closer now. She backed into the water a little deeper. The sands shifted again, and Sam almost fell. Something brushed against her leg, and she choked down a scream before her rational mind took over; it was only seaweed.

She gritted her teeth against the pain and kept her eyes on Iago. As she watched the large animal on the beach her body began to tremble convulsively. It didn't seem possible to escape him. Unbidden, images of Jake's face flashed into her mind. Would he be able to bear the pain if he lost her this way as well? Tears welled up in her eyes as she remembered the look on his face when he told her of her father's death. She had been numb for over a month. The newspapers and television had played up the accident for days, until she had finally left the house and fled to the hills. She had stayed away for a week, trying to come to terms with the loss of her father. But she had never forgotten him, and even in the midst of danger the image of his face still had the power to move her to tears.

She shifted her feet in the tropical water. Six months after her father's death she had tried to read the coroner's report, but Jake had refused to let her see it. Two years later he had given it to her. Sam had locked herself in his study and opened the document with trembling fingers. As horrifying as the accident had been, she had had to know. Disjointed phrases echoed through her memory. Massive lacerations on face and neck. Broken vertebrae. Crushed chest. He had died instantly when the big cat had gone for his throat. Animals killed by instinct. To a tiger, killing a human being would be similar to a cat snaring a mouse. One quick shake and the victim would be left as lifeless as a rag doll.

Sam glanced at her arm. The bandage was beginning to stain. The wound was worse than she had thought. She touched it gently, then winced in pain.

What had her father thought the instant before he died? Had he even known? Jake had assured her that his death was quick and painless. But Sam had refused any attempt to alleviate pain. Her pain had been the only thing that kept her alive.

Iago moved again, closer. Her attention was riveted

on the big cat and she backed deeper into the water, almost losing her footing again.

But her mind was working more clearly. Damn Helen and Scott! She wasn't going to die. She remembered following behind her father, from cage to cage. He would squat down and explain each animal and how to handle it. She had adored the big man. Her father could make animals do anything. He had also taught her everything he knew. She could almost hear his soft, resonant voice, patiently answering her endless questions. The memories triggered a deep reserve of strength. Sam clenched her fists.

She wasn't going to die. She was John Collins's daughter, wasn't she? What would he have done? Her mind began to work swiftly.

She couldn't continue to stay in the water and she couldn't go in deep enough to get around the mesh fence. She had to try and distract the tiger and make it to the compound. If she'd left Peanut's barn unlocked, she could shut herself inside with him. Or perhaps signal for help. But she couldn't stay in the water.

She could feel the wind blowing steadily and thanked the stars she was downwind from Iago. What she had to do would excite and enrage him more, but it was a calculated risk at this point. It was all she had left.

Sam ripped off her bandage and wadded it tightly into a ball. Though her right arm was already stiff, she steeled herself against the pain and, using all her strength, threw the bandage down the beach past Iago. It was a clumsy throw, and she was tossing the bundle into the wind, but it landed in the general area she'd wanted it to.

Iago turned away from her. The smell of fresh blood attracted him. He approached the bundle, sniffed it, then went down on his massive haunches and began to shred the material.

Sam made her way out of the water and up the beach as silently as possible. Once under the protection of the dense foliage, she ran toward the elephant barn. The full moon turned the green undergrowth to silver, and she felt slightly unreal as she ran along. She could smell the crushed plants under her feet, feel their slippery texture as she tested her footing. Sam didn't panic; all her years of training made her cool, almost calm, even in this emergency.

She reached Peanut's barn and tried the door. Her heart sank. She had locked it.

Sam ran back to the tiger cage, but either Helen or the storm had slammed the heavy door shut, locking it automatically. She looked around quickly, her ears picking up the sound of noise in the underbrush. The bloody cloth hadn't detained the animal long.

Her anxious glance fell on the torches. Two of them had been blown out by the wind, but the other two still smoldered. She grabbed one of them in both hands, fear making her oblivious to pain. She wrenched it from the earth.

The crashing sounds were coming closer now, and she thought quickly. Dragging it clumsily back toward the elephant barn, she touched the end of the torch to a pile of hay bales in a clearing. The hay wasn't close enough to any structure to endanger the animals, but, once ablaze, Sam hoped someone would spot a fire in the compound and bring help.

It took several seconds to ignite. Sam feared the tiger would appear before the fire started. But suddenly the flames bloomed white-hot and leaped into the night sky. The torch she held was burning brightly. Peanut trumpeted in fear.

Sam anchored her torch into the ground by the stack of blazing hay bales. She picked up a handful of small stones and threw them toward the chimpanzee cages.

They began to scream and call, adding their noise to that of the small elephant. Thick black smoke studded with sparks billowed up from the pile of burning hay. Sam pulled up the torch and turned, her back to the blazing fire.

Though she had been chilled before, now she was uncomfortably aware of the heat emanating from the burning hay. But she stayed close to the flames; she saw the tiger circling by the other cages. He shied away from the fire, but she knew he had seen her and smelled blood. She glanced up quickly toward the *parador* as she heard shouts. Someone had spotted the fire!

Some of the tension eased out of her body as she sensed her ordeal was almost over. Her legs began to tremble with relief. She kept a careful eye on the tiger, and was concentrating on him so intently, she started when something hit her head.

Huge raindrops began to fall slowly as the tropical storm finally broke. Sam felt her heart jump into her throat as she watched the fires beginning to flicker and hiss.

All noise ceased from the animals as the rain started to pelt their cages. The only sound was water spattering against the earth.

Sam's torch died. She moved closer against the fire, but it offered feeble protection. She faced Iago.

The tiger was angered by the rain. Its black-and-orange fur was plastered against its body; the gold eyes burned with fury. Iago looked like some hideous apparition from hell, his ears back against his head. He snarled, showing his teeth, then crouched. Sam saw his muscles bunch as he prepared to spring. She closed her eyes, her body suddenly calm.

She heard a dull thud, then the tiger started to cough. She opened her eyes, and it was moving toward her, but slower, almost as if drunk. It snarled again, and Sam watched, horrified, as dark blood trickled out the side of its mouth. There was another thud. The tiger jerked and fell.

As if waiting for some preordained signal, the skies opened up and rain poured down in torrents, flattening the motionless animal's body against the muddy earth. She barely heard the shouts and movements behind her as she walked unsteadily toward the tiger. She only knew if she didn't face him now, Iago would weave in and out of her dreams for the rest of her life, haunting her.

Sam crouched down and touched the massive head gently, smoothing back fur that was now a tangle of mud and blood. Her fingers shook, but not from the cold. The animal's body was still warm despite the cool tropical rainfall. She stared at it for what seemed like a long time until warm hands touched her shoulders. She began to tremble violently as she was wrapped in a scratchy wool blanket and picked up in strong arms.

She stared into Ryan's strained face. She tasted salt against her lips and realized she was crying. Sam tried to breathe, tried to relax the tight knot of fear in her chest. It broke, suddenly, and violent, uncontrollable sobs shook her entire body.

Ryan cradled her tightly against his heart as he carried her up the hill.

Chapter Fourteen

Ryan Fitzgerald sat stiffly on one of the chairs in the hospital waiting room. He stared at the white tile floor. Though his clothes were still wet, he was past the point of feeling anything. All his emotions were tied up with the woman who was now about to wake up after her operation.

He looked up from the floor as voices echoed down the narrow hall.

"Then you tell me how in God's name this was allowed to happen!"

"Mr. Weston, I know you're upset. We all are, but..." Ryan recognized Don's voice, strained yet placating. And, of course, Mr. Weston had to be Jake.

As the two men rounded the corner Ryan stood up. He didn't expect an expression of friendship from Jake, but he was surprised when the older man verbally attacked him.

"You!" In that instant Ryan saw the Jake Weston millions had seen on screen in the forties. The older man pulled himself up to his full height and faced Ryan, his eyes snapping angrily under bushy gray brows. "You and your damn picture! If it weren't for you, my little girl wouldn't be here!" He started to say something else, then his craggy face began to crumple. He turned away. "She was always just like her mother," he whispered to no one in particular. "She never hurt anyone in her life." He covered his eyes with his hand.

Ryan felt absolutely helpless. The tension in the air

was a living thing. He looked at Don and noticed that his eyes were moist.

"How is she?" Don asked softly.

"She was in shock when I brought her here." Out of the corner of his eye he could see Weston watching, listening. "They took the bullet out about an hour ago, as soon as they were sure she could stand the operation. She lost a lot of blood." The words hurt him physically as they were forced past his tight chest. Ryan stopped talking as Beverly walked in, looking out of place and slightly garish in her red sheath against the pristine whiteness of the hospital.

"God, Ryan, I heard! It's too exciting! What happened to that girl?"

Ryan didn't even spare her a glance. He noticed Jake staring at the two of them, the wisdom of forty-odd years in his face. Ryan was sure those glacial blue eyes didn't miss much.

"I'd like a word with you." Jake motioned Ryan toward an empty lounge. "Alone."

Ryan followed him, suddenly feeling about twelve years old. As soon as Jake shut the door he came straight to the point.

"I'm an old man, and I don't have time for formalities. What's going on with you and Sam?" When Ryan didn't answer, he shook his head in disgust. "You think you have such a wonderful life, traveling around the world and making films, fooling around with women like that?" His glance included Beverly, outside the glass door. She was lighting a cigarette and talking animatedly with a quiet Don. "You have nothing."

Ryan stared out the window to the quiet beach below. He concentrated on the endless rhythm of the waves as they crashed against the shore. If he looked at them hard enough, maybe he'd stop thinking about Samantha. But memories of her face haunted him: intense as she worked with a stubborn animal, delighted at the end of a particularly good take, at peace in the aftermath of their lovemaking. He was remembering a thousand tiny things that had seemed so inconsequential at the time: the way she wrinkled her nose when she laughed, the feverish brightness in her green eyes as he kissed her, the soft way she had of melting in his arms. And he knew then, with astonishing certainty, if he lost her, he would lose the world and more.

"Mr. Weston, I'd like to—"

"No. I'm telling you now. You get out of her life, and I mean for good. When I take her back to my compound, I don't want you to ever see her or talk to her again." Ryan started to protest, but Jake held firm. "She's the genuine thing, Samantha. Her first husband treated her like dirt, and she came back home to rebuild her life. I was the one who talked her into going on this assignment, and if you think I won't have to live with that knowledge for the rest of my life, you're crazy."

"Mr. Weston, please—"

"Jake. Call me Jake. I can't stand Mr. Weston. It sounds like I have one foot in the grave. I'm going to tell you one more thing, and then I'm going to go in and see that little girl." His light blue eyes seemed to pierce right through Ryan. "I grew up with her father, so I think I have a pretty good handle on her family. Before her father died I remember we used to joke, and he'd say, 'Jake, if anything ever happens to me, take care of Sam.' 'Course, we never thought anything would. And then I got the telegram from India. It was doubly hard for Sam, because she never knew her mother. She died of cancer when Sam was only seven." He cleared his throat, and Ryan sensed the memories were hard for the old man to deal with.

"I guess you're thinking. What the hell is this fool talking about? But what I'm trying to say is, you don't get that many chances. In anything. I led a pretty wild life until I fell in love for the first time. The crazy thing about it all was that she was my best friend's wife.'' He cleared his throat again while Ryan stared.

"You mean Sam's mother?"

He nodded. "Your generation probably wouldn't see the problem, but in my day we respected marriage. And I loved John like my own brother. When Sam was born, it was as if she were a gift to all three of us."

Jake stopped talking and dug into his pockets. He handed Ryan a cigarette, then pulled one out for himself and lit them both.

"I want the best for her. She deserves it, and I'm going to see she gets it. I want some man to love her the way her father and mother loved each other. And quite frankly, I think all you've ever known how to do to a woman is hurt her. I don't want her hurt."

Ryan stubbed out his cigarette, angry now. "Listen, Jake, you don't know what's between—"

"I know Sam, and I know every time she called home and I mentioned your name, she didn't say much of anything. I know that girl, and I know she loves you. And I don't want her hurt."

The two men glared at each other. Ryan was about to speak when a doctor entered the room.

"She's waking up, Mr. Weston, and she's asking for you." The doctor smiled as she reached out to take Jake's arm. "I'll take you to her. I think she's going to be fine."

Ryan watched as the two of them disappeared around a corner of the hallway. He stepped out of the lounge and began walking toward the exit. There was nothing for him here.

"Ryan, wait!" Beverly jumped up, hugging her evening bag to her chest as she ran awkwardly after him in her high heels.

He kept on walking. It didn't surprise him that Beverly could think about a part in a picture while another human being was seriously injured. He jammed his hands in his suit pockets and turned the corner. The automatic doors opened, and the cool ocean air hit him in the face, refreshing after the antiseptic smell of the hospital.

"Ryan!" Beverly's voice was fainter now.

He bent his dark head against the wind and didn't look back.

SAM STARED OUT at the cool aqua water in the pool. The bright sun reflected off the surface, and she closed her eyes. She always seemed to be tired, and today was no exception.

She stirred slightly and opened one eye as she heard a noise by the sliding glass door. Maria was coming outside, a small tray balanced in one hand as she shut the screen with the other. She approached the chaise longue that Sam was lying on and put the tray down on a nearby table.

Sam sat up. "Thank you, Maria, but I'm not that hungry."

The older woman pulled up a chair and sat down, her figure small and petite in jeans and a plaid shirt. She had been cleaning out the kitchen cupboards that day, and the sleeves of her shirt were rolled up past her elbows. Her thick black hair was caught back from her head in a severe twist, but it suited the angular lines of her face. Only her eyes were soft and brown, and her expression was distressed as she looked at Sam.

"You have to eat. You must keep up your strength. Come, this is your favorite. Chicken salad." She motioned toward the tray with her hands.

"Maybe a little later."

"How is your shoulder? Does the swimming help the stiffness?"

Sam stretched her arms gingerly. "I think so. I've got almost all the natural movement back, but Jake still doesn't want me to do anything with the animals for a while."

Maria looked uneasy. She leaned forward and touched Sam's arm gently. "Do you still miss Ryan?" It wasn't in her personality to do anything but come straight to the point.

Sam closed her eyes and nodded. "The thing I don't understand," she said, trying to keep her voice steady, "is why he never tried to contact me that last night." She shifted in her seat and tried to relax, but it was impossible now that his name had been brought into the conversation.

"He sent you those flowers," Maria reminded her.

"I know. But he never even called." The thought still hurt.

"Maybe he felt guilty," Maria suggested. "Jake still thinks the tiger almost attacking you was his fault."

"I don't feel that way at all. None of it would have happened if Helen hadn't been involved in smuggling."

She kept her eyes closed, not really wanting to talk, but Maria stayed where she was. Finally Sam opened her eyes and looked up at the older woman. "I'll eat it all in a little bit. Honest." She tried to smile.

"Sam, I think there is something you should know."

She sat up, swinging her legs around in front of her. "What are you talking about?" With some sixth sense she knew the "something" had to do with Ryan. Her body tensed.

"I would have told you sooner, but Jake only told me the other evening." She took a deep breath, then let out her confession. "When you were in the hospital, Jake told Ryan never to come near you again."

"What?" She couldn't believe what Maria was saying.

"He thought the man would only hurt you, and I think

he is wrong, because you are hurting when you are away from this man.'' At Sam's stricken expression she touched her arm gently, then took her hand. "Don't be mad at Jake. He only wanted what was best for you, but this time I think he is wrong.''

Sam knew it took Maria a tremendous amount of effort to admit this, because she usually thought Jake was right about everything he did.

"Is that why Ryan's stayed away?'' she asked, still not quite believing the whole story.

Maria nodded. "I'm sure he thinks he is doing the best for you by leaving you alone. But I think it is wrong to keep the two of you apart when you are only truly happy together.''

Maria watched as Sam dropped her head into her hands. She thought for an instant the girl was depressed, but a moment later Sam straightened her back.

"I'm going to Malibu.''

"To see this man?''

"Yes!'' She jumped up and hugged Maria. "Thank you! I'll phone you when I get there!''

"You're leaving right now?''

"As soon as I take a shower and put gas in my car.''

She was gone before Maria could say another word. With a sigh of relief, she gathered up the tray and walked back inside the house.

THE SUN WAS SETTING over the Pacific as Sam wound her way up Pacific Coast Highway. Bloodred, the large ball of fire was sinking into the ocean, casting its vivid coloration over the shimmering water.

She was casting quick looks at the house numbers as she crawled along in the late-afternoon traffic. There was still quite a way to go. Thank God Jake had had Ryan's address in his file. She remembered the beach house he'd told her about, and she was hoping he'd be there when she arrived.

The sky turned a deeper blue, then stars began to peek through the twilight. She could see a faint moon over the horizon, full and pale.

As she drove she tried to rehearse what she was going to say. She practiced the words out loud, making sure her windows were rolled up, and avoiding looking at any of her fellow drivers.

The traffic seemed to ease the farther north she drove, and soon her green Volkswagen was skimming over the road. Before she had time to be afraid she was pulling across the highway and into the driveway of his house.

It looked like a place Ryan would live in, all rough redwood and huge glass windows. There were a few flowers blooming by the mailbox, and the door had a small stained-glass window in its upper half.

She opened her car door. Her heart started to pound as she noticed there was a car in the driveway. Someone was there. Slamming the VW door behind her, she walked up to the house, trying to still the trembling in her legs. Suppose he told her to go away? Before her courage could fail her she grabbed the brass door knocker and rapped it quickly against the wood three times.

What if another woman was with him? Her throat began to constrict as she heard someone coming toward the door. And then it opened, and Ryan was looking down at her.

He looked awful. His face was unshaven and he had deep circles under his eyes. Wearing nothing but a pair of old, faded blue jeans, he looked as if he had lost weight. But more than that, he didn't seem to be *there*. The tremendous life force that characterized the man was no longer a part of him.

"Sam?" His manner seemed uncertain. "What are you doing here?"

All her carefully rehearsed speeches flew out of her head. She stepped closer to him. "Maria told me this afternoon that Jake ordered you never to come near me again. Is it true?"

He nodded his head, looking as if he still didn't believe she was standing on his doorstep.

And then, once and for all, Sam knew she had to put everything on the line for this man. Seeing the way he looked, knowing he had been going through as much pain as she had, she blurted out the truth.

"I missed you so much. I had to come see you."

Before all the words were out of her mouth she was in his arms and he was kissing her—her face, her eyes, her throat, and finally her lips. She luxuriated in the feel of his hands on her shoulders, then her waist, pulling her tightly against his body as if he couldn't ever let her go.

When she finally managed to catch her breath, she realized she was crying. He picked her up in his arms and kicked the door shut with a resounding slam, then carried her down the stairs and into his living room.

She didn't even have time to take in her surroundings as he sat down in a large comfortable chair, keeping her in his lap. Even the roughness of his unshaven face didn't bother her as he held her tightly against his chest.

His voice was so low, she barely heard the words. "I love you, Samantha. Don't ever leave me again without at least giving me a chance to explain."

"Never," she promised, touching his face, thrilling to the sound of his voice, the feel of his skin under her fingers. She was here, in his arms, and he loved her enough to never want her to go.

"As if I didn't go through enough hell seeing you all torn and bloody after the accident! When Jake blamed me for what happened to you, I almost went out of my mind. I didn't want to finish the film, didn't ever want to work on anything again. And as time went on and I didn't hear from you, I tried to convince myself... maybe you *were* better off without me.''

''Stop.'' She put her fingers to his lips, and he pulled her closer.

''I never had an affair with Beverly. It was only a publicity shot you saw in the damn magazine. I don't know what she was trying to pull the afternoon you found her in my bed, but after I was through fighting to keep you, I went back and told her in no-uncertain terms I'd never use her in any picture I directed. She wouldn't give up and go away until after the wrap party.''

''Why did you come in with her?''

''She was waiting for me in the lobby and pestered me all the way to the party about the part in my film. I ignored her. I wanted to talk to you that same evening.'' He took a deep breath, then continued, as if in the telling of all this, he would somehow be cleansed of the bitterness he felt. ''I looked for you. And I thought I saw you standing by Don, but by the time I got down into the crowd you were gone.''

She leaned her head against his chest and felt his arms tighten around her. ''I saw Beverly on your arm and couldn't bear to watch the two of you together anymore. I went back to the *parador* and called a taxi, but before it arrived I heard Peanut, and...'' She let the rest of her sentence trail off. Neither of them wanted to remember.

They sat in silence, content to be close. The spacious living room was illuminated by a small lamp on a large oak desk. Sam knew she had made the right decision when she felt his chin come to rest on top of her head, heard his deep sigh reverberate through his chest. She had come home.

They stayed in the chair for a long time, rediscovering the feel of each other, sharing a precious moment all the more valuable for almost having been lost forever.

She was almost asleep against his chest when his voice roused her.

"Do you still have the ring?"

She nodded her head. "If you'd been absolutely horrified at seeing me and told me to leave, I would have given it back to you."

"Give it to me."

She reached into the pocket of her sweater and pulled out a small tissue-wrapped packet.

He unwrapped it slowly, then took her left hand in both of his. The metal of the ring felt cool as he slipped it on her finger, then kissed her hand.

"It's never to come off again."

She nodded, her happiness complete.

"We'll get our blood tests in the morning."

She kissed his neck and felt his muscles tense.

"I think there's a three-day wait, but that's as long as I can stand."

She laughed, deep in her throat, and tipped her head up to give him a soft kiss. She stretched in his arms, lazily, deliberately, provocatively. The diamond on her finger flashed in the lamplight.

"I feel married to you right now."

She saw the blue in his eyes deepen and felt a small flare of that familiar magic start up again.

She kissed the corner of his mouth, then moved her lips to his ear. "I don't want to leave this house for the next few days unless it's absolutely necessary."

She felt his arms tighten around her, and when he stood up, he lifted her easily. He mounted the stairs quickly, then carried her down the hall to his bedroom.

Chapter Fifteen

As the light came up in the small screening room people began to clap and stamp their feet. Sam leaned back against Ryan's arm, happy for his success. The picture was going to be good, and it had come in on time and under budget.

She felt his lips graze her hair and she turned in her seat.

"I thought your stunt looked pretty hot," Ryan teased.

"But not half as good as the direction."

They looked at each other for a moment, oblivious to the people moving up the aisles and into the lobby.

"Wonderful job, Ryan. But then I knew you'd pull the picture through." A dark-haired man came up and clasped Ryan on the shoulder. "This must be Samantha. It's a pleasure to finally meet you—I can see why Ryan keeps you hidden away at his house. I'm Michael Stone. I've known Ryan since we both went to school at USC."

"I've heard about you," Sam replied, holding out her hand and getting up out of her seat.

"I think one of the producers wants to talk to you, Ryan. Why don't I take Sam into the other room, and we can both get something to drink while you discuss business."

Sam allowed Michael to steer her into the lobby. The motif was all plastic jungle, with large displays of tropical plants and huge floral bouquets on the tables.

He disappeared for a minute and returned with two glasses of champagne.

"To a terrific picture. I hope Ryan makes a million." His dark eyes twinkled.

"I'm just glad the whole thing is finally over," Sam admitted sheepishly.

"I heard there were some rough times down there," Michael remarked, not unkindly. "There was tremendous coverage in the news about the night after the wrap party."

"It wasn't fun." There were evenings when she still woke up with nightmares, but time was making the entire incident fade into the deeper recesses of her consciousness.

"I'm glad the two of you met each other. Ryan's been needing—" But Michael was interrupted as a small blond woman in a blue suit came up to Sam.

"Mrs. Fitzgerald, could I get a few words from you on the making of your husband's film?" Her manner wasn't rude, just businesslike and abrupt.

"Of course." Sam set her glass down on a nearby table, then turned back toward the woman.

"How long have you been married?"

"Almost eight months."

"We didn't hear about it in the papers; it must have been a rather small ceremony."

"It was. We eloped."

"Where did the two of you go on your honeymoon?"

"We went to Ireland. Ryan still has some family there, and he wanted me to meet them." They had stayed for almost two months in a cottage with no central heating and an outdoor bathroom. Samantha had loved every minute of it, though she had teased Ryan and told him he'd have to install a bathtub for her.

"Your husband is a very handsome man. Do you ever

worry about his becoming involved with another woman?''

''No.''

''Would you care to elaborate on that answer?''

''No.'' Sam softened her answer with a smile.

She sensed Ryan behind her before he slid his arm around her waist. His touch was firm, comfortable, almost sensual. She reached behind him and placed her hand on his back, her fingers caressing him softly. Ryan met her eyes and kissed her on the nose, then turned to the reporter.

''Hello, Peggy. I hope Sam has given you something valuable for your column.''

The woman's face was expressionless, her mind obviously on her next question.

''Do you intend to continue your career as an exotic animal trainer, even after that almost fatal accident in Puerto Rico?''

''Yes, I do. And that wasn't an accident, it was something very deliberately planned.''

''Would you care to comment on the sentences Helen and the others received?''

''Not really.''

''Ryan, what's your opinion on this matter?''

He deliberately answered the former question. ''I think that the only thing I want is for Sam to be happy. And if it means we have tigers in the basement and an elephant in the backyard, that's fine with me.'' He was clearly amused by this interview.

''You've been married for only eight months. The divorce rate in Hollywood is extremely high because of the pressures inherent in this business. Do you think your marriage is going to last?''

''Definitely,'' they said at the same time. Sam felt Ryan pull her gently against him, then he bent his dark head and kissed her tenderly. She closed her eyes, happiness welling up inside her, and she wasn't even aware of the cameras as they snapped and flashed.

The only thing that mattered was the man in her arms.

A Harlequin

ROBERTA LEIGH

Collector's Edition

A specially designed collection of six exciting love stories by one of the world's favorite romance writers—Roberta Leigh, author of more than 60 bestselling novels!

1 **Love in Store**   4 **The Savage Aristocrat**
2 **Night of Love**   5 **The Facts of Love**
3 **Flower of the Desert**   6 **Too Young to Love**

Available in August wherever paperback books are sold, or available through Harlequin Reader Service. Simply complete and mail the coupon below.

Harlequin Reader Service

In the U.S.   In Canada
P.O. Box 52040   649 Ontario Street
Phoenix, AZ 85072-9988   Stratford, Ontario N5A 6W2

Please send me the following editions of the Harlequin Roberta Leigh Collector's Editions. I am enclosing my check or money order for $1.95 for each copy ordered, plus 75¢ to cover postage and handling.

☐ 1   ☐ 2   ☐ 3   ☐ 4   ☐ 5   ☐ 6

Number of books checked_____ @ $1.95 each = $_____

N.Y. state and Ariz. residents add appropriate sales tax $_____

Postage and handling $___.75____

                                                TOTAL $_____

I enclose_____

(Please send check or money order. We cannot be responsible for cash sent through the mail.) Price subject to change without notice.

NAME_____
                    (Please Print)
ADDRESS_____ APT. NO._____

CITY_____

STATE/PROV._____ ZIP/POSTAL CODE_____

Offer expires December 31, 1983

30656000000

Readers rave about Harlequin American Romance!

" ...the best series of modern romances
I have read...great, exciting, stupendous,
wonderful."
—S.E.,* Coweta, Oklahoma

" ...they are absolutely fantastic...going to be
a smash hit and hard to keep on the
bookshelves."
—P.D., Easton, Pennsylvania

"The American line is great. I've enjoyed
every one I've read so far."
—W.M.K., Lansing, Illinois

" ...the best stories I have read in a long
time."
—R.H., Northport, New York

*Names available on request.

Enter a uniquely exciting new world with

Harlequin American Romance ™.

Harlequin American Romances are the first romances to explore today's love relationships. These compelling novels reach into the hearts and minds of women across America... probing the most intimate moments of romance, love and desire.

You'll follow romantic heroines and irresistible men as they boldly face confusing choices. Career first, love later? Love without marriage? Long-distance relationships? All the experiences that make love real are captured in the tender, loving pages of **Harlequin American Romances.**

What makes American women so different when it comes to love? Find out with **Harlequin American Romance!**

Send for your introductory FREE book now!

Get this book FREE!

Mail to:

Harlequin Reader Service

In the U.S.
1440 South Priest Drive
Tempe, AZ 85281

In Canada
649 Ontario Street
Stratford, Ontario N5A 6W2

YES! I want to be one of the first to discover the new **Harlequin American Romances**. Send me FREE and without obligation *Twice in a Lifetime*. If you do not hear from me after I have examined my FREE book, please send me the 4 new **Harlequin American Romances** each month as soon as they come off the presses. I understand that I will be billed only $2.25 for each book (total $9.00). There are no shipping or handling charges. There is no minimum number of books that I have to purchase. In fact, I may cancel this arrangement at any time. *Twice in a Lifetime* is mine to keep as a FREE gift, even if I do not buy any additional books.

Name _____ (please print)

Address _____ Apt. no. _____

City _____ State/Prov. _____ Zip/Postal Code _____

Signature (If under 18, parent or guardian must sign.)

This offer is limited to one order per household and not valid to current American Romance subscribers. We reserve the right to exercise discretion in granting membership. If price changes are necessary, you will be notified.
Offer expires December 31, 1983

154-BPA-NACT